ALUMNI

Patrick Laughy

DEDICATION

This book is dedicated to Law Enforcement Officers, who never know what their next shift will bring

ACKNOWLEDGEMENTS

Special thanks to Suzy and Linette
for their editing skills and support
in the creation of this book and to
David, for another great cover

CHAPTER ONE

Finished with the hacksaw, he placed it onto the plastic-covered workbench and reached for the machete resting beside it. The well-honed blade had a residue of flesh and congealed blood clinging to it from his earlier labors.

The single bulb hanging from the ceiling left shadows in the tiny windowless workshop and he shifted slightly so he wasn't standing in his own light as he arranged the severed leg along the length of the bench. Humming softly, he raised the machete and brought it down sharply. The blade entered the open wound, slipped cleanly through the fibula and tibia and easily severed the bottom part of the leg just below the knee.

Except for clean up and disposal, he was finished with this one and already looking forward to the next. This was his third and he was definitely getting better with practice. He'd been caught after the first two and spent eight years of his life behind bars but that was behind him. He'd learned his lesson and he was much more careful how he dealt with the remains of his pretty little girls now.

* * * * *

The tone-alert beep from the in-unit laptop broke through the repetitive sound of the laboring windshield wipers of the marked patrol car.

Rookie Vancouver Police Constable Wayne Denver shifted slightly in the passenger seat of the white Crown Victoria, and with a brief glance at his Training Officer Bill Grant, punched the button to accept the 'Sudden Death' file that waited.

He watched the screen come to life and then repeated the content of the call to his partner.

"Sudden Death... see the manager at 3128 Fraser, suite number 2."

The cop behind the wheel responded instantly.

"Shit. Nice start to a day shift. Not even our area, just gave it to us because we are two-man and she didn't want to tie up two cars. Haven't even had coffee yet."

Wayne knew the older cop well enough by now to avoid making a comment, which he had learned would only fuel the fire and serve to heighten his partner's verbal assault on the nature of the call.

Instead, he tuned the older man out, and diligently studied the 'smack, smack' of the wipers as they fought to keep the windshield clear of the hammering raindrops.

Yes, he knew better than to interject when Bill started on one of his tirades. Experience had taught him that his partner, if left to his own devices, would run down soon enough and that it was simply the older Constable's standard way of dealing with unpopular dispatch assignments.

For himself, Wayne felt a small ripple of exhilaration at the prospect of investigating his first Sudden Death.

As if reading his trainee partner's thoughts, Bill Grant broke off mid sentence and allowed himself a small grin.

"On the other hand, it isn't every day that you get to investigate your first Sudden Death, and please note the sarcasm. Based on where this call originates, it should be a nice clean one."

Curious, Wayne glanced across at his partner in the hope of some form of clarification. He didn't get it; instead Grant wheeled the cruiser sharply right into a MacDonald's and headed for the drive-through.

"I'm bloody well going to have my coffee before we deal with this, even if I have to drink it on the way!"

Wayne waited impatiently while the hot brews were

passed through the minimal opening allowed by his partner in the patrol car driver's window, as a defense against the pounding rain. He managed a beaming, if short-lived, smile of thanks for the benefit of the matronly clerk as the marked unit pulled away while he struggled to guide his cup to the cup holder.

Stopping for coffee instead of proceeding to the call directly wasn't something he would have done on his own, but after eight weeks with Bill, his initial 'Gung Ho' attitude was beginning to soften and his frustration level was learning to adjust to what Grant referred to as dealing with 'the real world of a cop'.

Wayne receded into his own thoughts as they moved through traffic toward the call. He wanted to ask Bill to expand on his earlier comments about the significance of the location of the Sudden Death, but he knew better than to interrupt his partner's first coffee of the shift.

Instead he let his mind drift back over the months spent at the Police Academy with regard to Sudden Death investigation techniques.

* * * * *

Vancouver Police Inspector Chris Chambers glanced up from the paper he was reading at the kitchen table as his wife Janet bent to freshen the cup of coffee in front of him in preparation for clearing away the morning breakfast dishes.

After thirty years of marriage, their morning ritual of enjoying a quiet breakfast together had become an important part of the day for each of them. These serene breakfasts had started once the kids had grown up and moved on, shortly before he was promoted from Staff Sergeant VPF Homicide and given the overall supervision as Inspector of the new In-targeted Homicide Investigation Team.

IHIT was the multi-force group formed from the best

Homicide investigators drawn from all the Lower Mainland Police Departments and included the surrounding R.C.M.P. Detachments.

Janet returned to the table from the dishwasher and took her seat across from him, sipping coffee from her cup as she picked up a section of the paper and began to read.

Chris shifted his gaze to the clock over the stove and was pleased to note that he still had a half hour before he needed to leave for the office. He really did enjoy these quiet mornings together with Janet. He moved into a more comfortable spot in the chair as he turned his attention back to the sports page.

A few moments later Janet spoke.

"My God, another one; must be the third one this week!"

Chris waited for her to continue and when she didn't, he put down his paper and leaned forward quizzically.

"Another what?"

Janet lowered the paper to reply.

"Delta Police are warning the public about a convicted serial rapist who has been released from jail and has moved into their area. They say here that he has a good chance of re-offending.

Three days ago it was a repeat child molester in Surrey and on Monday it was that maniac from Toronto who raped and killed that little boy fifteen years ago and has been released and is now living here... and each time the Police are advising that they are likely to re-offend. I just don't understand it! What is this world coming to? Why can't you lock these animals up and throw away the key?"

During the past few months, they had discussed their feelings on this topic a couple of times and although Chris more than shared her concern over the situation, he realized that Janet, just like the majority of the public, did not have his 'inside' understanding of the problem. Now, sensing her growing frustration, he attempted to explain it to her more clearly. "We do what we can, investigate and arrest them and bring them before the courts, which treat them liberally and even when they finally convict them, send them off to prison for short sentences, which of course are shortened by Corrections for 'good behavior'. The offenders know that if they don't ask for or accept parole, but serve their full terms and thereby 'pay their debt to society', they are free to do whatever, and live wherever they please once they are released. We try to watch them around the clock when we know they are going to re-offend, but it's a hit and miss solution that costs a fortune in manpower and resources, and the demand just keeps growing as they keep letting them out. So we try to warn the public by giving them as much information as we are allowed, which isn't anywhere near enough. It's like trying to fight with one hand tied behind your back and believe me, it's far more frustrating and demoralizing for the cops that know the full story on these creeps and try to keep them under wraps, than it is for 'Joe Public'."

Janet took a moment to consider his words then put the paper down and smiled across at him.

"Yes, I can understand that, and it really isn't your concern in 'IHIT' I suppose."

Chris laughed and shook his head.

"Not until they kill someone…"

* * * * *

The two men, dressed in casual clothing and wearing light raincoats, paused inside the entrance doorway of the rundown New Westminster rooming house and removed and shook the rain from their ball caps before starting up the ancient stairway to their destination.

Jim Simmons, the shorter of the two men, carried a bulging black plastic garbage bag in his left hand. His partner was a large, powerful man, six foot three and 200 pounds of taut muscle. Although almost fifty-six years old, Mike Stanovich had never given himself the slightest chance to grow soft. He had worked out rigorously three times a week throughout his police career and even more often during his first year of retirement.

They had climbed three flights when Jim reached out his hand and placed it on the other man's forearm. His lungs were giving him hell and not for the first time did he wonder why he hadn't given up smoking. He was feeling every one of his 63 years and sucking deeply for air between his words as he spoke.

"Why do these bastards always have to live in walkups…give me a second to catch my breath."

Mike Stanovich had been watching Jim with concern as the older man had tackled the last few stairs. He had taken note of Jim's increasingly heavy breathing and nodded understandingly before checking his upward progress and leaning against the wall on the fourth floor landing.

He had known Jim for over thirty years and both respected and admired the retired Vancouver IDENT Squad Staff Sergeant, a man who had repeatedly amazed the entire Force with his crime scene finds long before CSI became a television hit and the world found out how it was done.

"Sure, we're in no hurry."

* * * * *

Bill Grant knew his rookie partner was biting his tongue and waiting impatiently for him to finish his coffee before asking him what he meant by the sarcastic 'a nice clean one' based on the origin of the call. He savored the last swallow of coffee then tossed the empty cup between the bucket seats onto the back floor of the patrol car before he spoke.

"It's a dump, lots of ex-cons. Corrections recommends

it for new releases. I've been on calls there before, overdoses mainly...usually not found for a couple of weeks, not until the smell permeates the whole building and can't be ignored any longer."

Wayne felt his stomach knot but put on a brave face, nodded, and released his seatbelt as they pulled into the curb. He waited for Bill to shut the cruiser down, then opened his door and stepped out onto the sidewalk where he waited for his partner to lock the car and join him in front of the rundown building.

Bill led the way through the double, paint-shedding, doors and into the dingy hallway. He turned to Wayne with a grimace.

"Smell it? That's death warmed over."

Wayne had been immediately hit with the sweet sickening odor as he entered the building. He sincerely hoped he wasn't going to make a fool out of himself and upchuck breakfast. His first Sudden Death wasn't so appealing all of a sudden and he wanted nothing more than to get back into the car and drive away. He tried breathing through his mouth and, for the moment at least, it was enough to keep his stomach in check.

"Yes. Christ, how can people not notice that before it gets this bad?"

Bill, seemingly undeterred by the smell, grinned and shrugged before turning to move down the hall.

The older cop found the door to suite number two a few paces into the gloom and let his meaty fist bounce off it a couple of times. They heard the sound of heavy coughing from within and then movement as someone shuffled toward the door. There was a grinding of rusted bolts and the door opened to reveal a disheveled gnome of a man who had definitely seen better days. Bill nodded curtly and as he took out his notebook.

"You called."

"Ya, not sure but I think maybe number fourteen. Haven't seen him for a couple of days. Stinks pretty bad up there, dunno, but..."

Bill cut him off.

"Let's have a look, shall we?"

* * * * *

Chris Chambers had no more than sat down at his desk with a coffee and begun to work his way through his usual pile of E-mails when his office door opened and his second-in-charge, R.C.M.P. Staff sergeant Don LaRue stuck his head inside.

"Call for you, says he's Dr. Dunne."

Chris nodded at the disappearing head and reached for his phone.

"Inspector Chambers."

"Morning Chris, Pat Dunne, got a minute?"

Chris instantly recognized the gruff no-nonsense voice of Vancouver's recently retired Coroner and found himself smiling as he responded.

"Pat, I thought you were on a permanent fishing trip. What can I do for you?"

"Fishing trip my ass. I may have retired as Vancouver's head meat cutter but I'm still keeping my hand in, mostly drop in clinic stuff. Some work for Corrections Canada... keeping busy you know, since Emily passed."

Chris realized then that he hadn't spoken to Dunne since his old friend's wife Emily's funeral a good six months ago and immediately regretted he hadn't at least called Pat during that time. Uncharacteristically, he found himself feeling a little uncomfortable with the man he'd worked and played with for over twenty years.

"Anyway, the reason I called was, the guys at the 'Old Blue Farts Club' were wondering if you'd be interested in joining our group, considering that you'll be hanging up your hat and heading for retirement too in three months or so. They asked me to give you a call and sound you out. Nothing like a bunch of old cops meeting every couple of weeks to whine and complain about the old days and how good it used to be. Wondered if you'd like to drop by and scout us out on Wednesday night. We meet next in Maple Ridge at the Seaside Pub about six if you're interested...don't have to decide now; you can give me a call on my cell and let me know."

Chris was vaguely aware of the old timers group, known in mixed company as the 'Alumni', and to its members themselves as the 'Old Blue Farts Club', that met every second week, but wasn't exactly enthralled at the thought of sitting around with a bunch of ancient cops reliving the past. On the other hand, Pat was a friend and it would be good to see some of the retirees again...besides, he was feeling uncomfortable about not having contacted Pat since Emily's funeral and he didn't want to turn his old friend down.

"Sounds like fun. I'll drop in on Wednesday if I can, I'll give you a call and let you know either way."

CHAPTER TWO

Mike looked over at Jim Simmons, and noting that the color had returned to his friend's face and his breathing came more easily, glanced toward the next flight of stairs.

"Ready?"

An exchange of nods and they began to climb, both men taking the opportunity to pull on latex gloves as they neared the landing of the next floor. They paused for a second letting their eyes get used to the poorly lit hallway, and then moved up to the door marked 42. Jim knocked.

As the door opened Mike pulled a sheet of paper out of his jacket and compared the man who stood before them to the photocopied photograph in his hand.

"Clifford Weston? Police, I'm Detective Stanovich and this is Staff Sergeant Simmons."

A frightened, trapped look came over the man's face as soon as the words were out of Mike's mouth and there was no need for a verbal confirmation of his identity.

Weston was a perfect fit for the profile of a repeat child offender. His nervous sweat stunk of it. Mike neatly folded the paper and put it back into his jacket pocket and both men stepped inside while their unnerved prey abruptly stumbled backward to allow them entry.

Mike looked briefly at Jim. The two men had been over the plan again and again. Jim was in charge; it was his area of expertise - he was the Crime Scene man and the handwriting expert. Mike was the muscle in this one. They were ready, and they didn't need to communicate further between themselves.

Mike grasped Weston in a headlock and Jim applied the cloth he'd removed from the small plastic bag he'd taken from his jacket pocket and applied it to the startled man's face, covering both his nose and mouth firmly.

Weston began to struggle as his senses took in the chemical effect from the saturated cloth, but was out in seconds. Mike gently lowered the limp form to the floor as Jim opened the garbage bag, reached inside and passed him a pair of white coveralls and two sets of white booties. He and Mike both got into coveralls and slipped the booties over their shoes, and then Mike lifted Weston's inert form slightly and watched dispassionately as Jim went to work. The older man quickly placed the cloth back into the plastic bag and sealed and pocketed it then moved about the dingy room precisely, slowly and with great care. He took no extra steps, having surveyed the room on entry and having already set up the scenario of what would be required to complete the job and gone over what needed to be done. First he crossed to the wall housing the only window in the room. Little light filtered through the filthy, almost opaque window, but it was enough for him to see the wall electrical outlet near the floor.

An old standing lamp with a frayed shade was plugged into it. Jim removed the plug from the socket then let the end of the cord fall to the floor before moving across the room to pick up a butcher knife from beside the sink.

He then carried the knife across the room to where Mike held Weston and firmly placed it into the man's right hand and curled the fingers around the hilt before setting the knife down on the floor.

Jim then took an envelope out of his shirt pocket, tipped the pen that was inside out into his gloved hand, and repeated the procedure of transferring the unconscious man's prints onto the pen before slipping it back into the envelope and returning it to his pocket.

He then retrieved the knife and moved back across the room toward the lamp where he bent down and used the knife to cut off the electrical cord attached to the lamp at the bottom of its base. This left him with several feet of electrical cord which he tossed onto the unmade bed.

Jim left the knife on the floor by the outlet, and then crossed toward the small kitchen table where he pulled the envelope back out of his pocket and tipped its contents out into the centre of the table. He then folded the envelope and put it back into his shirt pocket before picking up the single rickety wooden kitchen chair and carrying that across the room until it was directly below the bare light which hung down on a couple of feet of cord from the ceiling, in the center of the room.

He then retrieved the cord from the bed and climbed carefully up onto the chair and, under Mike's watchful eyes, attached one end of the cord securely to the metal plate in the ceiling, before knotting it several times along the two-foot length of electrical wire leading to the bulb itself. He then pulled firmly on the lamp cord that was now dangling below the bulb to test its resistance and, satisfied that it would hold the weight of a suspended body, nodded toward Mike.

The big man shifted the dead weight in his arms, moving it over to the chair. Mike then lifted the limp form a good eighteen inches, until Weston's feet were touching the seat of the chair. He gave an audible groan from the effort it took, and Jim quickly looped the cord around Weston's neck and knotted it tightly, before stepping down off the chair to assist Mike in holding Weston in position on the chair. Jim briefly let his eyes run over the scene they had just staged before tapping the chair backward with his foot until it flipped over. Then satisfied, he turned to Mike.

"Okay, let him down, gently now. We don't want the cord to break or rip out of the ceiling up top... and we don't want him to break his neck, we want him to strangle Shouldn't take long.

Mike did as he was told and was surprised when the light fixture took the full weight and, although some of the plaster flaked away at the base of the fixture, absorbed the strain. Weston began to gurgle softly and his feet jerked briefly, but Jim had been right, it didn't take long.

Jim ignored Weston as he moved over to the table, pulled out his wallet, opened it and retrieved his masterpiece, the perfectly forged suicide note unquestionably signed by Weston. Without reading it, he placed it on the table and turned to look at Mike, then reconsidered and turned back to read.

'I can no longer live with myself. I want to quit, but I can't. I'm going to do it again, I know it. It's better this way.'

Jim had carefully studied and mastered several examples of Weston's handwriting, and no one would ever question the signature and if they ever did, any expert would tell them it was genuine. He then took a quick look around the room, before he motioned to Mike and they left as they had come, cracking the door to ensure that the hallway was empty before stepping out and removing their protective gear, then placing it back into the garbage bag.

* * * * *

The stench got stronger as they neared the door marked with the number 14 and Wayne was inwardly battling to ignore it as he tried to prepare himself mentally for what was on the other side. The manager was fumbling with keys on a chain attached to his belt and seemed to be unaware of how bad the smell was until he opened the door.

It hit them full force the instant the door cracked free of the frame and all three of them took an involuntary half step backward. Bill nudged the manager aside and looked inside briefly. His experienced gaze took in the makeup of the small room quickly. He spotted the body on the bed and instantly determined that it had been dead for several days.

Having seen what he expected, he immediately

reached for the door and pulled it shut, before turning to the manager.

"Go on back down. We'll talk to you in a bit."

Once the manager had shuffled out of earshot, Bill turned his attention to Wayne.

"Let Dispatch know what we have. Have them send us a crime scene team and let the ambulance guys know we are going to need them to pick up a body when forensics is through. Make sure that they tell the crew to have a couple of spray bombs; we're going to need them."

Wayne pulled his portable from its holster and, glad to have something to take his mind off the lingering smell, did what had been asked of him. Bill, always the Training Officer, listened to ensure Wayne had understood and was carrying out his instructions properly. At the same time, he reached under his tunic into his shirt pocket and pulled out a cigar, which he promptly lit. As he exhaled, Wayne finished the transmission and turned to look directly at him, raising his eyebrows slightly before he spoke.

"I didn't know you smoked."

Bill grinned before releasing a considerable cloud of smoke.

"Only in times such as these."

Nodding toward the cigar in his hand, he looked over at Wayne, fixing his eyes with a questioning stare.

"Want one?"

* * * * *

Chris had finished dealing with his e-mails and in doing so was now up to date on the current investigations ongoing within IHIT. It was the usual assortment of murder investigations; eight simple, know who did it, tie up the loose ends, get a confession if possible, and forward to Crown Council with a recommendation to charge; and three no suspects yet scenarios.

Two of the latter were gang related. It was only a matter of time before suspects would be nailed down in those as well, but preparing airtight charges when it came to them would be decidedly more difficult and would take much more time. The last was the rape and murder of a thirteen-year-old North Vancouver girl which had occurred the night before and was in the initial stages of investigation.

He selected a button on his intercom and pushed.

"Don, where are they on this one from last night?"

The question had been anticipated and the response was immediate.

"Our crime scene team is still there, haven't removed the body; the crime scene itself is pretty well virgin as yet. Sharma has your car warmed up and is waiting for you in the garage."

Although they had only been working together for little over a year, LaRue knew his boss well and had little doubt as to how Chris expected their working relationship to perform on a day-to-day basis. As soon as he had received his transfer to the new unit he had done his homework, as he had always done when his career led him into a new area of police work, and he knew as much about Chris's background and habits as anyone within his own force did. He knew exactly what Chris wanted in a second-in-charge.

IHIT had been first proposed as a means to ensure that murder investigations in the greater Vancouver area were being coordinated among the various local police agencies. This to ensure that none of the historic problems of failing to share information or failure to seek input from other police departments who were responsible for the close geographical areas that were adjacent to a murder crime scene were eradicated. IHIT was supposed to remove the ability of the murderer to take advantage of the limited resources, experience and manpower of the smaller law enforcement entities, and of the tendency of smaller forces to attempt to take on more than they could be reasonably expected to handle.

There had been precedents in Vancouver for this type of joint force police work. As a detective, Chris had been part of two of the previous creations; first Joint Forces and then the Coordinated Law Enforcement Unit or CLEU. These had both consisted of shared manpower and resources of the R.C.M.P. and the Vancouver Police Force, and were involved primarily with the investigation of organized crime.

IHIT had been a natural progression in the process, expanding to include all the police agencies within the greater Vancouver area. It differed however, in that it took on the limited scope of murder. Other specialized squads had also been formed to deal with other areas of police work.

When Chris had been approached to become a part of IHIT, he had been pleased to be considered. It was without doubt an elite unit that was being formed and it was made clear to him that a promotion went with the move. Later, he had been pleasantly surprised to learn that he was to be placed in charge of the team if he accepted.

Normally the top position in these joint forces initiatives was held by a member of the R.C.M.P., for all the best reasons; senior force, best equipped, more experience.

However, in this instance the 'powers that be' had, uncharacteristically, decided that they were simply going to look for the best man for the job, and that man would be selected from whichever of the participating forces that happened to have him.

At the time, it was lost on no one, Chris especially, that this decision was going to be a sore point for the R.C.M.P. members who participated in the new unit…but he saw it as a challenge to be overcome, not a hindrance as some others might have done. He had fully experienced what he called "Scarlet Fever" within the federal police force during his years of working with and around them. They were the biggest.

They considered themselves to be the best. They were, in their red serge, after all, Canada's most recognized symbol.

To Chris however, they were no different from most dedicated cops; very capable, and very well trained. As with any other force, there was the odd exception. His previous working experience with members of the federal force had taught him that the Mounties did deserve the in-house reputation of occasionally, and with some exceptions, being pompous asses who thought that they knew it all. However, joint operations between fellow cops soon overcame and buried that problem for good, as earned mutual respect overcame the 'ivory tower' mentality that seemed to resonate from the red serge uniform.

After accepting the position, Chris had taken his first step to move that process along by requesting an R.C.M.P. member as his number two man in the team. He'd made it clear that he was not a paper man but expected to be hands on in the new unit and that he would require an organized, super-efficient subordinate who could ensure that the day to day operation of the team utilized the optimum in both manpower and resources.

He fortified his request with the explanation that he felt a senior N.C.O., R.C.M.P detachment head, would have the qualifications he was seeking in a second-in-command for the unit.

He'd gotten exactly what he'd asked for in Staff Sergeant Don LaRue.

* * * * *

Mike eased his Nissan Titan into the short driveway of Jim's high-end White Rock townhouse and shut the truck off. There had been little conversation between the twosome since they'd left Weston's room, and Mike suddenly felt like he needed to talk before he started the long drive home to his empty Vancouver west-end apartment.

It wasn't that his conscience was bothering him. He had no problem there, but his years of service had made him a certain type of man, with a structured, reasonable and honest approach to everything he did. Until a short while ago, executing people had not been part of the accepted activities in his life, at least not in cold blood and with premeditation, and he had found that it was taking some getting used to.

He had been on the other side of that fence all his life, and although he hadn't crossed that line easily and without a great deal of thought, the act itself understandably troubled him. He was the type of man who required occasional support from others that he trusted, to enable him to accept this decidedly different episode in his life.

Jim had been lost in his own thoughts during the ride to his home. Not having second thoughts about what the two men had just done, he had made his decision on that at the start of their enterprise and was very sure that it had been the right one, but simply ensuring in his own mind that he had covered all the bases at the scene and that the job had been clean and tidy.

Jim was the kind of man that lived a clean and tidy life and often gave grave consideration to anything he was about to do, or had done.

Now as he became conscious of the fact that the vehicle had stopped he was drawn out of these thoughts and realized that he was home. He looked over at Mike and smiled as he spoke.

"Drink?"

The response indicated to Jim that the offer was both expected and appreciated.

"Thought you'd never ask."

Jim nodded and opened the passenger door to get out.

"Just let me grab a smoke before we go in...don't smoke inside and I could use one right now."

Mike stifled a grin as he glanced across the hood of the

Titan at the other man.

"You know you really should give those up and start working out."

Jim nodded and pointedly slipped a smoke between his lips and lit up as they neared the front porch. His words were slightly muffled by the cigarette in his mouth.

"Any time now."

CHAPTER THREE

Bill waited until Wayne had fired up the proffered cigar and coughed out a couple of healthy clouds of smoke before he pushed the door open for the second time and the two men entered the filthy room. Once inside the smell hit them again and Bill moved purposely but carefully across to the only window and after a slight struggle was able to reef it wide open. He immediately crossed back to the door and closed it firmly, then turned to his white faced rookie partner, and with uncharacteristic empathy, inquired as to his condition.

"You okay to start?"

Wayne, still white as a sheet, took a deep drag on the cigar and nodded.

They slipped on surgical gloves, and Bill shifted his attention back to the bed and the putrefying form lying on it. Notebook in hand, he began to write, concentrating on the general condition of the room, the placement of the sparse furnishings and the ballpark dimensions.

Once he had completed a rough diagram he approached the bed and took a closer look at the body. There were no obvious marks or wounds that would indicate anything other than a natural death, but of course the advancing stage of decomposition of the corpse could well disguise any of these signs. Additionally, the body would have to be flipped to check the other side.

This was not something Bill was prepared to do at this point in the initial investigation. His gaze shifted from the body to the small night table next to the bed and he pointed out the prescription bottles arrayed there to Wayne.

"Those will need to be seized. Don't move them or anything else in the room, and don't touch anything until the crime scene boys have finished, but once they are done check each one before you bag them and write down what they are and who provided the prescriptions. See if there are any more in the room and do the same with them once forensics is finished."

He moved as he spoke, kneeling and pulling out his flashlight which he then switched on to illuminate the pill bottle nearest him. As he read, a smile formed on his face.

"Well now, things are looking up; this might be a simple one after all."

He motioned Wayne over and directed the younger cop's attention to the bottle illuminated in the flashlight beam.

"For the heart, obviously this guy had a condition. Note down the name of our friend here from the prescription and run a check on him. I'm going to give the issuing Doctor a call and see if we can't get this over with in a hurry."

Wayne gave him a questioning look and Bill nodded at the bottle.

"Prescription was issued by Dr. Patrick Dunne, same with the rest of these I'll wager...Dunne was our Coroner until just recently when he retired. I assume the Academy taught you that if a Doctor agrees to 'certify death' in a sudden death, no autopsy is needed; a short report completes the investigation. If the forensic team finds nothing untoward, and, based on my experience I think that will happen, this is going to be a simple one. All they will do is take photos of the crime scene and be on their way. I'll call Dunne to see if he'll certify if forensics comes up with a blank, while you find out who our friend here is."

* * * * *

Chris found his unmarked silver Ford Crown Vic running and waiting for him just inside the closed overhead door of the parking garage beneath the IHIT offices. He popped open the passenger door and acknowledged the man behind the wheel with a curt nod.

"Morning, Ravi. Let's pick up a coffee on the way please. Could I have an up…"

Delta Detective Constable Ravinder Sharma was already holding a manila folder out for his boss and Chris didn't bother to finish his request as he accepted the folder and placed it on the dash in front of him, before he reached for his seat belt.

The instant he did so, Sharma hit the door opener affixed to the Crown Vic's sun visor and waited only until the big grey steel door had raised high enough to accommodate the unmarked police car before his foot hit the accelerator and they broke outside into the overcast and still drizzling morning sky.

* * * * *

Bill briefed the CSI team when they arrived. He and Wayne then moved to the corner of the room furthest from the bed and its occupant while forensics did their thing.

As Bill had envisioned, a physical check of the body satisfied the team that the death appeared to be natural and that, coupled with the information provided by Bill that death was to be Certified by none other than the retired city coroner, was sufficient to restrict their thrust to quickly completing a photographic and video history of the room and it's contents as it had been found by the police who had first arrived on the scene.

The ambulance crew had arrived to remove the body and was standing by in the hall, spray bombs in hand as they waited by their body trolley for the forensics crew to finish and leave. Twenty minutes later Bill and Wayne watched them body-bag the corpse and place it onto the waiting trolley before wheeling it into the hall. Wayne felt himself gag as the trolley was tilted by its handlers for the trip down the stairs and its contents flowed fluid-like to the lower end of the bag with an audible 'sloshing' sound.

That and the lessening efficiency of the residue of the aerosol bombs that had been earlier sprayed by the ambulance team left him with no desire whatsoever to spend any more time than absolutely necessary in the room.

Despite no outward sign that Bill seriously shared his misery, the older man was no more interested in dragging out their stay in room than Wayne was.

As soon as the two of them were left alone they moved quickly to finalize the investigation by first bagging the valuables, one man's gold colored ring with unknown clear stone; one man's Timex wristwatch, gold in color, provided by the ambulance crew who had kindly removed them from the corpse at their request, after liberally spraying the room with the aerosol bombs specifically designed to deal with the aftermath of a body left long enough to commence purification, then searching the room for anything else that could be classed as valuables and anything that might be of interest in relation to further confirming the identity of the body.

Using the landline in the dimly lit hall Wayne had learned that the deceased man was one Archie Bates, white male, 42 years of age, recently released after completing twelve years in a Québec Federal prison for the sexual molestation of no less than ten prepubescent males.

The man's criminal history went on for several pages, the highlights of which were the fact that he had served two previous federal sentences for exactly the same crime and had spent most of his adult life in jail as a result of repeat offences. When he passed this information on to Bill, the older cop nodded unsurprised.

"Ah yes… yet another outstanding example of the 'revolving door' policy of our esteemed Canadian Justice

System. I'd say we had some 'divine' intervention in that system in this case and justice has finally been served; no thanks to the system itself. Now let's just pop down to the Manager's rat hole and get the rest of the info we need for this report, and then on to a well deserved lunch, before we write it up!"

* * * * *

Jim placed his cigarette butt into the small coffee can tucked into a corner of the porch and then unlocked the front door to his townhouse and waved Mike inside.

"Excuse the mess...since Kay died; I haven't had much interest in day to day life around here. I try to spend as little time at home as possible. The kids think I should sell it and get something else and they're probably right."

Mike followed Jim's lead in, slipping his shoes off and leaving them on the mat by the door before passing his damp coat and hat over to be hung to dry. He then trailed Jim through the hallway into the kitchen as his host flipped light switches here and there which filled the place with a brightness that was in sheer contrast to the gloomy day outside.

He observed no sign of 'mess' but found what he could see of the townhouse very much like the man who owned it, clean and tidy.

He knew that Jim had lost his wife Kay to cancer two years previously and that he had two grown and married children who lived in the lower mainland area. Jim spoke of them and his two grandchildren often, and the family seemed close.

Jim fished a bottle of scotch out of the cupboard above the fridge and poured two generous portions into tumblers before handing one to Mike. They touched glasses and each took a swig in salute, then Jim picked up the phone and dialed from memory.

The call was answered on the second ring.

"Pat, Jim. That problem I told you about has sorted itself out and I'll be able to make the meeting on Wednesday, so I'll see you then."

Mike raised his glass to his mouth and welcomed the taste as the liquor went down and began the process of warming his chilled body.

* * * * *

The body of thirteen-year-old Sandra Rollins had been dumped in heavy bush off a logging road in North Vancouver and Ravi, well aware that Chris was fussy about his wheels, took great care in parking his boss's assigned unmarked police unit in a somewhat level spot near at least eight other emergency vehicles, many of which had obviously been first responders, and as such, had been haphazardly left wherever they could be pulled safely off the overgrown rain soaked roadway.

Although the rain had stopped for the moment and the sun was doing its best to peek its way between the now fluffier clouds, the roadway itself was a mucky mess at this point as a result of the comings and goings of emergency vehicles, including a good sized Fire Rescue unit, over the past few hours.

A very young uniformed North Vancouver Mountie who had been divesting himself of his rain slicker as he watched them drive up the roadway, approached them as soon as they parked, and having already recognized the car as a police unit, smiled as he neared Chris who was sliding out of the passenger door. Chris had taken his badge holder out of his pocket before exiting the car and now opened it and folded it back onto itself to expose his badge before slipping it into his top jacket pocket. When the Mountie reached Chris his gaze first traveled over the badge and then to Chris's face as his smile broadened.

"Good morning, sir. I'll need your names and ranks please."

Ravi joined them after securing Chris's unmarked unit and pulling white coveralls and gloves out of the trunk. Once the Mountie had recorded the information requested into his open notebook he closed it and put it into his pocket before addressing Chris.

"You'll be IHIT then sir. The dump scene is just down that little path behind the marked unit with the four-ways on over there... about fifty feet along the path; you'll see it once you get there."

Chris thanked the constable and joined Ravi at the back of the car. Ravi handed him a set of the disposable coveralls and gloves and began to slip into his as Chris took off his jacket and shifted his badge to the top overall pocket before dropping the jacket into the trunk and climbing into the coveralls.

* * * * *

Kevin Connolly, 'Irish' to those who knew him well, reached out to hammer the snooze button for at least the sixth time and in so doing, over-balanced and rolled off the bed onto the carpeted, but none the less, cement floor of the bedroom in his west end Vancouver apartment.

He winced as his shoulder took the brunt of the fall, then let out a string of expletives before forcing his bloodshot eyes open and welcoming a new day.

At 56 years of age, Kevin had been a 'Police Beat' newspaper reporter for as long as most people, including him, could remember, and definitely one of the old school. As such it only seemed fitting that he would suffer from the three best know habits of that particular species: working nights, smoking heavily and never far from a drink. Other things, of course, followed in the wake of this particular lifestyle and career choice, a few of which were three divorces with no kids produced, very little cash in the bank, and a somewhat disheveled appearance even when he was trying to look his best.

Morning for Kevin was never the best of times, and today was no exception. However, he did manage to drag his stocky five foot eight frame up off the floor, shut off the damned alarm and fire up his first smoke of the day before heading unsteadily toward the bathroom and the shower that he hoping would help to make his eyes open at least half way.

* * * * *

Retired Vancouver Police Detective Phil Harder took a sip from his rapidly cooling coffee and stretched his slim six foot four-inch body as best he could within the confines of the driver's seat of the unmarked four door police car.
His attention never left the door of the cheap Granville Street Hotel, turned rooming house, as he, not for the first time, found himself wondering why the hell he had chosen to accept going back to work for the Vancouver Police Force on a contract basis after retiring at fifty-five.

He sure as hell didn't need the money and you'd think he'd have better things to do with what time he had left. Truth was though, that he didn't.

Divorced twice before he was fifty, Phil lived a simple life in his Burnaby apartment with only his cat Cecil for company and a few old police buddies to see every couple of weeks. He had no more than retired when he found out that he had lung cancer. It had been caught relatively early and after treatment he'd gone into remission but he didn't kid himself, he didn't have a lot of time left.

Phil wasn't the type to feel sorry for himself. Hell, he'd

lived a good life and he'd lived it his way, but sitting in front of the TV in his apartment was not how he wanted to spend the rest of his life. Realizing that, he'd jumped at the chance to accept a spot in the 'High risk Re-offenders Team' known simply as 'HROT', when it was offered to him.

Nothing particularly physically demanding, not much writing, next to no supervision, nothing long term with a six-month renewing contract…hell, it was a cop's dream; and Phil was a cop, had always been a cop, and would be a cop until the day he died.

* * * * *

Ravi, always deferential and somewhat protective of his boss and who loved to work with Chris, had held the yellow police tape strung across the entrance to the overgrown path up for Chris to duck under before he moved quickly in front of him to lead the way, carefully pushing aside the brush and tree limbs that were making a fair attempt at reclaiming the walkway.

Chris who didn't particularity harbor any desire to be a follower in much of anything gave a small sigh but accepted the inevitable and let Ravi lead the way.

About fifty feet along the path, now deep into the heavy growth, Ravi spotted the white tent through the bush to their right. Another uniformed Mountie, older this time, was standing just off the trail in front of a strip of yellow tape that clearly marked off a good-sized area with the tent as its center. He still wore his rain slicker although rays of sunshine had definitely broken through the cloud cover and the trees around them were almost finished releasing the final clinging droplets of water from their branches.

Once again, their names and ranks were recorded before the Mountie lifted the tape to enable them entry into the area of the restricted crime scene.

CHAPTER FOUR

A cloud of acrid blue smoke belched out of the back of Kevin's old yellow and rust-pitted Volkswagen Bug as he shut it off.

He was parked in front of the main VPF building, in a spot designated as a loading zone. He pulled a dilapidated 'PRESS' sign out of the glove compartment and slapped it against the front window before exiting the vehicle, knowing full well that the sign might not save him from a ticket but it would be enough to make a cop pause and in all probability recognize the car as his, and that very well might save him from a ticket.

Kevin liked cops and cops liked Kevin.

Kevin still drove the beat up Bug for many reasons, one of which was the state of his bank account, but primarily he kept it because it was unique and with few exceptions recognizable to every Vancouver cop on the force. He could, and had, parked the damn thing almost anywhere in Vancouver and done so very nearly 100% of the time without penalty.

On the very rare occasions that he had received a ticket, by the time he got to court to fight it the officer who had issued it, inevitably, had learned of the error of his ways and the case had been dismissed due to a plea of lack of evidence on the part of the officer.

Such was life in Kevin's world and he loved it.

After shoving his police scanner under the passenger seat he left the car unlocked as usual--who the hell would want to steal it--and climbed up the stairs, taking a last deep drag from his cigarette and stomping the butt out before exhaling slowly.

He then pulled open one of the big brass doors that provided public access to the building and made his way inside.

A few seconds later he was standing at the Report Center front counter scrolling through the Nightly Occurrence Reports, something he did on an almost daily basis. After all his years in the business, he knew what to look for and having listened to his scanner for most of the night he had a couple of specific things he wanted more info on. Not that these reports that were available to the public actually held anything of value, but if you knew how to read them they were often the key that opened the door to a great deal of very interesting information.

As he had expected, there was nothing major to be found in Vancouver's overnights, but there was a brief report on the sudden death on Fraser and he paused when he came across it.

The address hit him first; he recognized it as one used by Corrections to dump ex-cons into on release programs and this piqued his interest. What really hit him, though, was the fact that the body had belonged to Archie Bates…now that was interesting.

The name Archie Bates was very familiar to him. Not a common name to be sure and Phil seriously doubted that there was more than one man with that name living in Vancouver. Bates had been released from prison just three weeks ago after serving his full sentence for several sexual molestations and the police had thought him bad enough and likely enough to re-offend that they had run one of those 'warn the public' bits on him shortly after his release.

Kevin had been at the press conference set up by Police at the time that was used to kick off the campaign. There would be a story in this one, he was sure.

* * * * *

Phil involuntarily reached over to spin the dial to turn down the music as the front door of the rooming house opened and his quarry stepped outside.

He remained motionless as he watched Barry Hertzog carefully survey the area before strolling slowly but purposefully south along the sidewalk. He waited until Hertzog was about thirty feet along before he turned the ignition to fire up the police car. Simultaneously he reached for the mike under the dash and broadcast.

"174...he's on the move."

His call was acknowledged but Phil's attention never left Hertzog as he continued to watch him move down the sidewalk. The man's pace had quickened, his stride lengthened, and his attention was firmly directed toward the path ahead.

Phil had a feeling about this trip. The hair on the back of his neck went up and he felt his body stiffen. All his years of experience told him that it was different than previous outings...it had purpose.

Phil watched Hertzog approach the intersection and turn right to cross the road before he pulled away from the curb and let the car move slowly toward the intersection. He had watched this man long enough to know where he would probably be headed first. His guess was confirmed when as he pulled up to the intersection, he spotted Hertzog sitting on the bus stop bench mid-block.

Phil eased the unmarked unit into the curb and didn't have long to wait before a bus pulled up and Hertzog boarded it. As the bus pulled out, Phil dropped in behind it and followed it across the Granville Street Bridge and up to Broadway.

Here Hertzog got off the bus and sat down on the bench, obviously prepared to wait for another bus.

Phil checked traffic, which was fairly heavy, then made

a wide right turn and drove past Hertzog in the far lane allowing other vehicles to come between them, before he switched into the curb lane and pulled into the tail end of a loading zone toward the other end of the block. He slapped the Ford into park and adjusted his right outside mirror slightly until he had a clear view of Hertzog sitting on the bench.

Phil reached over to pull a bus schedule out of the glove compartment and ran his finger down the list slowly until he found what he wanted, then tossed the schedule back where he'd gotten it.

The next scheduled bus was an express headed for the University of British Columbia. A chill went through Phil, for he knew that Hertzog liked to select his victims from students on university campuses and always spent a good deal of time studying a proposed victim's movements and patterns before he made the determination to attack them.

* * * * *

Chris noted that Ravi had now dropped back into step behind him and pulled out his notebook as the two of them approached the figures in white working under the protective cover that had been pitched directly over the body.

The investigation had reached the point that only his IHIT CSI and IHIT investigative staff were inside the perimeter of the crime scene now, with the exterior protected by the local R.C.M.P. Detachment members.

While CSI was taking center stage at the moment, there was no doubt in anyone's mind as to who was in charge of the investigation now that he was on the scene.

All those gathered under the cover stopped what they were doing and turned to face him. Chris had been silently identifying the individuals in white as he approached. He noted that the turnout from his office was a full complement and contained some of his best.

"Continue please. Jeff and Gordon, if I could see you both briefly."

Chris stood just outside the covered area and Jeff, the Staff Sergeant in charge of his IHIT CSI squad, and Gordon, who was one of his most experienced Detective Sergeants moved to join him. Ravi hovered a few feet away, writing studiously in his notebook.

Chris knew both of these men very well and was confident that he didn't need to make itemized inquiries of them. They would provide him with a thorough overview without prompting. Glancing at Jeff, he paused to pull out his own notebook and fished a pen out from under the coveralls before speaking.

"Jeff?"

Without hesitation the Staff Sergeant began to speak in a clipped monotone that Chris had learned to appreciate.

"It's a dump site, probably a couple of days old, know more after the autopsy. Strangled with her blouse, probably the cause of death, also several shallow stab wounds to the chest area, none of which appear to be serious enough to cause death and appear to have been inflicted pre-mortem.

Raped first and we have sperm. Because of the stab wounds, the method of transport and the crime scene itself will likely have blood traces, so we've got DNA running both ways even at this early stage…that's about it so far.

We are about finished with the body and will be moving out to sweep the perimeter, probably the length of the path and the roadway where it meets the pathway as well, although rain and emergency vehicles have torn that up pretty badly.

I did, however, get casts of every tire and footprint I could find when I arrived on the scene and at that time there were only three Police units, an Ambulance and a Fire Rescue truck here. You might want to thank that nice young Mountie out front if he's still there. He had the foresight to treat the situation seriously before he confirmed the body and did a laudable job of protecting the roadway at the path from as many of the pounding feet and wheels as could be expected. Depending on the weather we should be wrapping up by late tomorrow afternoon, barring surprises."

Chris nodded and asked only one question.

"Was she wrapped in anything?"

"If she was, the killer took it with him when he left, but I doubt it...no sign of her being wrapped up in anything. We've got a few fibers that may well tie her into the crime scene or more likely the vehicle used. We'll be starting to forward you tidbits of info, probably as early as tomorrow afternoon, and then time and science will take its course."

Chris finished his notes and thanked Jeff, then turned toward Gordon.

"What is your agenda and time frame?"

Gordon glanced toward Jeff then spoke.

"I've taken a statement from the couple who found the body and sent them on their way. We think we've got her identified, missing people's report, filed two days ago. Once we finish up here and she's autopsied, we'll get the positive ID. If it is her, she was a chronic runaway who has been bounced around from foster home to foster home for the past six years. The local detachment members are doing all the door to door inquiries along the road on the way up here.

We should have those by morning, and as you've already noticed they are protecting the crime scene perimeter until we wrap up.

We'll have a team here around the clock until Jeff's guys are done, and a team at the autopsy. I'm thinking we'll probably wrap up the initial stage by late tomorrow afternoon too, if Jeff is finished by then. I've scheduled a meeting with the team for 09:00 hours the day after tomorrow and we'll be able to pool our information and see what we have."

* * * * *

Kevin stepped out of the elevator and walked directly down the hall to the doorway marked 'Detective Division – FRAUD'. He didn't knock, simply turned the knob and walked in. The room was divided into four main cubicles and Kevin made for the one directly across from the entrance and popped his head into it.

Detective Colin Hamstead, a twenty-five-year veteran of the force was sitting at his desk, his feet propped up on the corner and the chair tilted well back. His hands, fingers intertwined, were crossed over his ample stomach and the strain that the well-earned expanse was causing on his none too clean shirt was clearly demonstrated by the stressed buttons struggling to hold it together.

The cop was half dozing and Kevin grinned as he kicked the bottom of the chair and Colin's arms flew out instinctively to maintain his balance.

"Top of the morning to you, Colin me lad."

Colin regained his composure quickly, shifting his feet off the desk and moving forward in the chair. He gave Kevin his best dirty look and shook his head before he spoke.

"I have to be here...what the hell is your excuse for being up at this time of day your stupid bastard?"

Kevin moved around the desk and flopped into the chair facing his old friend and drinking buddy. He and Colin went back a long way and were, in every sense, comfortable in each other's company. He took his steno pad out of his jacket and lifted one of Colin's pens up off the desk and held it up to the other man.

"Why, my job of course. You know, the dedicated reporter nosing out his story."

He paused and placed the pad down onto the desk.

"With the able assistance of his old friend the cop, of

course..."

CHAPTER FIVE

Phil tailed the bus containing his quarry all the way out to UBC, just as he had anticipated. Hertzog left the bus just inside the university grounds and Phil updated dispatch on his location then parked the car and began to shadow him on foot.

Phil wasn't concerned about being spotted by his quarry, there was plenty of foot traffic in the public areas that Hertzog preferred, but he was hard pressed to keep Hertzog in sight at all times.

Luckily, the ex-con was in no hurry as he meandered through the throngs of students who were moving between classes, hanging around in small groups, talking and enjoying the break in the weather.

Hertzog seemed to be strolling aimlessly for a good twenty minutes. Then Phil saw him slow his pace and center his attention on a pair of female students who were standing in the doorway of one of the faculty buildings.

The con paused for a few seconds, his eyes riveted on the two girls, then he suddenly swiveled his head from left to right, rapidly taking in his surroundings. Phil recognized the change in his quarry's demeanor; he'd seen the same thing happen before when a perp reached a decision about committing himself to an illegal act.

A chill swept through the policeman.

Hertzog had picked a prospective target and Phil knew it. Although Hertzog had looked directly at him in his sweep of the area, the con's head had continued to turn past the policeman in a steady movement and there had been no hesitation in the motion.

Phil was sure that he hadn't been made, but he moved to a better position anyway, seeking out a spot where he could remain motionless for a period of time without attracting attention.

He selected a small covered area attached to a building that allowed him to use a group of talking students as a screen between himself and Hertzog.

One man attempting to conduct surveillance on his own for any length of time without being spotted was damn near impossible and Phil knew it. The demand for 24-hour coverage on the dangerous and likely to re-offend types was a hell of a drain on any Police Department's manpower and resources, however, and Vancouver was far from the only police force that had no choice but to pay lip service to the task.

Phil knew the odds; he'd known the situation before he signed on and he'd accepted it. Some of the other old-timers that shared his duty bitched and whined continuously about the lack of manpower and equipment provided for the task of watching these bastards, but not Phil. He was good at it and he was good at reading the minds of his quarry. He knew that Hertzog had made his initial choice and if the con's attention stayed directed where it was now, for another twenty minutes, it would be as good as etched in stone.

* * * * *

Chris had Ravi drive him to the West Vancouver Crown Council's office once they had cleared the dump site. He had a scheduled meeting with the Senior Crown Council with regard to a case that had taken place in West Van's jurisdiction that the team had taken on four months ago.

His guys had wrapped it up and Chris would, as he always did, deliver the file and its recommendations for charges and explain it personally to the prosecuting representative of the crown.

To date, each of the cases investigated and compiled by

his unit had resulted in charges that led to convictions, something that Chris was very proud of. The thought of some inept Crown Council screwing up one of his cases haunted him and he ensured that he was a very strong contingent in each of the cases as they were being brought before the courts. He also sat through each trial whenever he could, offering advice to the Crown as he saw fit.

Although Chris, like any other policeman, was frustrated on a regular basis by the sentences the courts handed down upon conviction, he did relish the convictions themselves, both from the point of view of removing the bastards from the streets, however briefly, and because it reflected well on him and his unit as a whole.

Ravi, who had some follow up interviewing to do in West Vancouver relating to another case, would pick him up once he was finished.

* * * * *

Kevin sat listening intently to the one-sided conversation that Colin was conducting on the phone. From the gist of it, he wasn't going to get much out of it, but he still had the satisfaction of knowing that he would be made aware of details that no other reporter would have a hope of getting.

Colin was listening to the other party on the phone and making a few notes onto the lined pad on his desk blotter. Kevin was beginning to feel the strain of not being able to have a smoke. He pushed the craving aside and looked directly at Colin as his friend put the phone back into its cradle, and began to speak to him.

"Yep, it was 'the' Archie Bates...nothing untoward, natural causes, heart attack. Looks like the bastard finally got his just desserts."

Kevin grinned and stood up. The craving for a smoke was stronger now and he was eager to get out of the building and fire up. He had been hoping for more than 'natural causes' as a cause of death, but the history of the individual involved and the fact that he had been recently published as a concern to the police would be enough to justify a good sized piece in the morning paper. He was pleased with the info he had received from Colin; he had what he needed for his story. It was time to leave.

"Thank you old son...as usual you have confirmed my suspicions. Nothing juicy this time mind, but still a good yarn."

Colin grunted and raised an arm to wave him out of the office.

"Away with you...and that pen in your jacket pocket belongs to me...kindly leave it where you found it."

* * * * *

The group of students that had served to shield him from Hertzog broke up and Phil had to shift his own position to take advantage of some light shrubbery to aid in his concealment from any prying eyes.

He needn't have worried; Hertzog had not taken his attention off the two young women he was so intently observing.

Ten of the twenty minutes that Phil had mentally designated as necessary to confirm his thoughts had passed. The two girls that Hertzog was watching laughed loud enough for Phil to hear, embraced briefly and then split up.

One girl remained where they had been standing, waving to the other who had now begun to move away at a trot, obviously late for something.

Phil glued his eyes on Hertzog. He had been waiting for this to happen and was intent on catching Hertzog's reaction to the separation of the two girls.

Hertzog didn't move and Phil knew what that meant.

Unconsciously his body had become rigid as he awaited Hertzog's reaction and he felt himself releasing that rigidity and slumping slightly as his mind gripped the reality of the situation.

Phil had a decision to make now and he had to make it quickly, basing his conclusion on the facts that were now before him.

Did he contact the UBC Mountie detachment and tell them what he knew was about to take place, or did he pass it to the group?

He kept both Hertzog and the girl in view while he toyed with the problem that he knew he had little time to consider. The sound of his cell phone ringing took precedence over his thoughts and he reached for it and answered.

The call was from his supervising sergeant.

"Phil, it's me, got a scheduling change for you. Bates has had the decency to drop dead, so you have Allison for tomorrow instead, same time..."

Phil acknowledged the message and closed the phone to terminate the call. His eyes rested squarely on Hertzog and he made up his mind before he opened the phone again and dialed.

The call was answered immediately.

"How about dinner tonight at my place, say about seven."

The man on the other end responded as soon as the words were out.

"Sounds good, see you then."

Phil felt the tension leave his body now that the decision had been made and acted upon.

He knew he was right. Now all that was left was to keep an eye on Hertzog for the remainder of his shift and ensure that the girl was safe from attack during that period of time. His relief was coming on in six hours and although he wouldn't be able to give him all the facts of what had transpired he would be able to give him enough to sharpen the man's senses and cause him to keep the surveillance tight.

* * * * *

Off shift and back home, Phil dropped the bowl of moist cat food down in front of Cecil and stroked the cat a couple of times before dumping the empty can into the garbage and returning the can opener to the kitchen drawer.

He then reached for his glass and drained it before picking up the bottle to refresh it with scotch. He was mid-pour when the doorbell rang. He set the bottle back down on the counter and crossed the small kitchen to the little hallway at the front door to his apartment, pulling out his wallet as he moved.

The smell of the pizza hit him as soon as he had released the latch and opened the door. It made him realize that he hadn't eaten since breakfast and not much then. Money and pizza having changed hands he closed the door and moved across to the small stove to pull open the oven which he had preheated and ready. He slipped the pizza inside, box and all, and went back to the bottle to complete the pouring of his refill.

That done, he lifted it to his mouth and took a good portion inside and savored it before he swallowed.

He found himself smiling, alone there with Cecil, as he realized that although he couldn't remember when he had last eaten and was suddenly starving, and hadn't slept properly in days, and should be dead on his feet, he felt charged and very much alive. In fact, he hadn't felt this good in years.

Damn it was great to be doing the right thing and to be sharing that with friends.

The call of the door bell shattered the silence yet again and he turned to answer it.

* * * * *

Kevin had completed filing his stories, and was headed for the door when he heard the familiar voice behind him.

"My God…is it a ghost I'm seeing?"

He grinned and wheeled to face his editor.

"And well you should ask…say I."

Kevin was on very good terms with his editor. They went back a long way and although Kevin approached his job in what could be, nicely termed, a definitely unique manner and was virtually impossible to supervise, he was very good at it and although neither would admit it, both men recognized that fact.

Kevin rarely came into the office, preferring to file his stories electronically, but from time to time would drop in to delve into the line of eight filing cabinets that he kept in the sparsely furnished space that the paper allotted him as his own. He kept the cabinets locked when he was not using them and many in the office secretly wondered what they contained. Kevin always treated such curiosity as an invasion into his private space and dismissed it without comment.

When in the office, Kevin normally spent only as long as was necessary to accomplish the task that had brought him there. He spoke briefly to those who spoke to him, but did not go out of his way to converse with anyone.

Some of the faces around him now were unrecognizable to him, and he was aware that many people had come onto the staff of the paper and left without him ever seeing them. This fact did not concern him in the least.

It was not unexpected of him to spin around now and walk away from his editor without another word, and that is exactly what he did. His editor was not affronted by Kevin's actions.

* * * * *

The remnants of the pizza lay in the box sitting on the kitchen table between Phil and his guest, and the bottle which sat beside the box and had been three-quarters full upon the other man's arrival was now looking close to empty.

Phil had explained his take on Hertzog and given his reasons for having reached the decision he had. Both men had agreed that Phil's assessment was sound and had moved on to the next logical step.

Phil was listening intently as the other man spoke

"Well you know him best of all. We've been over his file and nothing leaps out at me...what do you think?"

Phil drained the bottle and leaned back in his chair as he tossed the swallow down before putting his empty glass onto the table.

"Not really my area of expertise, but it seems to me that it has to be some form of accidental death. This guy is fairly young, only 34 years old and he keeps himself in pretty good shape, runs every day..."

The other man cut him off.

"Where does he run?"

"Stanley Park, sea wall mostly."

"Isn't a lot of the wall blocked off still from all the storm damage?"

Phil nodded and raised his arms slightly as he answered.

"Ya, but nobody pays much attention to the signs and barriers. Hertzog runs early in the morning, usually between two and four. I don't think he likes to be around other people much."

A chuckle from across the table caused Phil to stare directly at the other man who followed the outburst with an observation.

"It's a little dangerous to be running down there in the dark, even if you carry a flashlight, which I'm sure he does; a man could get seriously injured that way, perhaps even die.

I'll talk it over with Jim before we go that route but it looks the best to me. He'll have to set it up though, as he's the man to ensure that it passes for an accident."

CHAPTER SIX

Chris retrieved the paper from the front porch of his Pitt Meadows townhouse and carried it inside, glancing over the front page as he closed the door then moved toward the kitchen where Janet was putting breakfast on the table. He dropped the paper in the center of the table as he sat down and eagerly reached for his knife and fork.

Janet sat down across from him and began to eat. Chris spoke around some sausage and eggs.

"Pat gave me a call and asked me if I'd be interested in joining a bunch of the old timers at their bi-weekly meeting...they have a group of retirees that meet and relive the past...call it the 'Alumni' in public and the 'Old Blue Farts Club' between themselves."

He let the sentence die and looked up from his plate to catch her response. Janet met his gaze and rested her fork.

"But you haven't retired yet."

Chris nodded and shoveled in another mouthful, chewed and swallowed before responding.

"No, but I will be in a few months. This invite was sort of a chance for me to see if I wanted to make it a regular thing after I retired. Pat was kind enough to offer me the chance to join; it would give me an opportunity to see him again. I realized when he called, that I haven't talked to him since the funeral, and I hate to say no..."

Once again Chris let it hang and helped himself to another bite. Janet didn't respond for a few seconds, taking a sip of coffee and clearing her mouth by swallowing before she spoke.

"Do you think that you would be interested in going after you retire? You will have a lot of spare time on your hands and if Pat is a part of it, I'm sure you'll enjoy yourself if you decide to go."

Chris nodded.

"True enough...I thought I'd pop in tonight for a bit and see how it goes. They meet alternately every two weeks, in Maple Ridge and White Rock. Tonight it's in Maple Ridge at the Seaside Pub, so I wouldn't have far to go."

Janet set her coffee cup down and shrugged.

"Maybe you should go."

* * * * *

Kevin couldn't keep his mind on the task a hand. He was listlessly pushing around poorly formed Macdonald's scrambled eggs and shoving them into the syrup and Pancakes on his plate.

He had been like this many times in his life and he recognized the sensation for what it was.

He had a great story on the tip of his tongue, but he couldn't quite see it, and he would feel like this until he did.

He gave up on what was left of breakfast and got up to leave. The day had been forecast as cloudy with sunny breaks and seemed to be holding true. He climbed into his Bug and fired her up, then worked his way out of the parking lot and onto the street.

He had traveled a good two blocks before he realized that he was headed toward Police Headquarters, when he should have been headed home. His work day was over.

Even with the realization, he continued on and tried very hard to see whatever was on the tip of his tongue, because he knew that was why he was heading to the cop shop. That was exactly where he needed to go.

Now, if he could only figure out why, before he got there!

* * * * *

Pat Dunne was sitting alone at the table when Jim ground out his cigarette on the sidewalk then entered the Tim Horton's and spotted him. Pat motioned to the cup across from him and Jim nodded and moved toward the table. As he slipped into the booth Pat spoke.

"Double-double, I hope that's OK?

Jim nodded and picked the coffee up, raising it straight to his lips for a sample. It was still hot. He took a big gulp of the coffee before he spoke.

"What's up?"

From force of habit Pat glanced around the room, and satisfied that the booth he had chosen was out of earshot from the rest of the patrons, he began to speak.

He outlined the situation on Hertzog pretty much as Phil had given it to him, then awaited Jim's response. Jim on his part took the time to weigh what he had heard carefully before he responded.

"I think what you propose is reasonable...although it will be complicated to set up and we don't seem to have much time here, if Phil is correct in his assessment. Something I don't doubt for a second by the way..."

Pat nodded in agreement and waited for Jim to continue. After a few moments of thought and a contemplative sip at his coffee the ex-IDENT Staff Sergeant pursed his lips and set the cup down.

"This will require muscle again and that means we will have to give it to someone that has just finished a job and, having just finished one is fully expecting to be out of that end of it for a reasonable period of time. It's a lot to expect of him; asking him to step in right away again. It's also a risky thing to do."

He idly ran his fingertip around the rim of his cup, purposely giving time for his words sink in before he continued.

'The main pillars of ensuring that we pull this little exercise of ours off successfully are firstly, that no one man should do more than one incident per month and that its important to compartmentalize these individual jobs and secondly, to carry them out on a strictly need to know basis. I'm not only not sure that we can reasonably expect this man to take on another one right away like this. I also find myself questioning whether or not to do so could be accepted as a reasonable risk. On top of that is the fact that we've done two in three weeks and this one would be three in three weeks. If we continue to push the envelope, are we taking the risk that someone is going to notice the frequency of the acts and put it together?"

Pat nodded his head in agreement.

"Are you suggesting that we pass this one up then, because if you are, I can tell you now that Phil is going to have a conniption?"

Jim cut him off, his tone touched with a hint of belligerence.

"No, I'm not…But I am saying that I don't particularly like it and it scares the hell out of me."

Pat grinned, more to lighten the atmosphere than because he found the topic amusing.

He said nothing for a moment, letting Jim's words sink in.

"I happen to share your anxiety, the only difference being that I've spoken to Phil about this and you haven't. Phil wants this done, and he wants it done yesterday."

Jim lowered his head slightly and studied his coffee.

"And he has every reason to feel that way…Okay, I'll raise it with the man we need for the job and we'll take it from there."

Satisfied, Pat leaned back into the booth. The two men studied each other for a few seconds then Pat spoke.

"I know that I don't need to emphasize that I need to have an answer quickly on this..."

Jim raised his voice significantly in reply.

"No shit!"

* * * * *

Chris reached for the paper that he'd dropped earlier in the center of the kitchen table and, as was his practice, removed the sports section before he passed the remainder of the paper to Janet.

He had finish catching up on the game scores for the past 24 hours and was part way into a story bemoaning the current injury list for the B.C. Lions football team, when Janet spoke.

"Well, there's one less of those parasites for people to worry about anyway."

Chris glanced over the top of his section of the paper with a quizzical expression pasted on his face. Noting it, she proceeded to read out loud to him the story on Archie Bates that had been printed that morning under Kevin Connolly's by-line. When she finished, he ginned across at her.

"See...there is a God."

* * * * *

Kevin sat in the Volkswagen, which was parked in his usual spot in front of the police station, for almost twenty minutes. He had finished two cigarettes in that time but still hadn't figured out why the hell he was there.

He was close to giving up when it hit him.

There was yet another story in this bullshit 'release the dangerous cons' situation. The public was pissed off and scared about what was happening, but in reality, due to the fact that their information source for facts on the situation was, at least partially limited by where they lived in the lower mainland, they were only getting a sanitized view of it, only seeing the tip of the iceberg.

A person living in North Vancouver, for example, would certainly have a good chance of being aware of any dangerous people who were now at large in their own City, but probably not how many there were in New Westminster or Burnaby or elsewhere in the lower mainland. The media had tended to localize these threats, as did the Police.

What the hell would the public think if they knew the total number of these bastards currently loose in the greater Vancouver area? Once they found out, the shit was going to hit the fan for sure. How about, how many were loose in Canada as a whole? This story would play nationally he was sure.

There was the real story; and it was a blockbuster. In order to get the ball rolling, he would attempt to wake up the lower mainland to what was happening around them, and thereby, force a reaction and then, if he got the local public outrage that he expected, he could move the story nationally.

He tossed his third butt out of the window of the Volkswagen's driver's door, pitched his 'Press" sign against the inside of the windshield and exited the car.

* * * * *

Pat had just left the restaurant and entered his car when his cell phone began to vibrate. He fished it out and checked to see who was calling. When he saw that it was Chris he answered it.

"Yes Chris…"

"I just wanted to let you know that I will be there tonight."

Pat was pleased and his tone expressed that pleasure.

"Great, see you then."

* * * * *

Kevin found Colin seated behind his office desk. The remnants of a fast food breakfast were strewn about the surface of the desk and the overweight cop held the handset of his phone to his ear with his left hand as he scrawled notes onto his pad with his right. He acknowledged Kevin's arrival with a nod toward the seat facing his desk and Kevin dropped into it without comment.

The phone conversation droned on for a few more seconds then Colin dropped the handset back into its cradle and leaned back into his chair before he addressed Kevin.

"Back already Irish? What is it this time?"

Kevin leaned forward and planted his forearms on the edge of the desk.

"I'm thinking of doing a follow-up on that story I filed on the death of that prick Bates...kind of expanding on the whole idea of these dangerous bastards being dropped into our communities and left free to molest, rape, and murder at will. Seems to me that the average guy out there has probably got no idea just how many of them there are, what they have done, and exactly what they are likely going to do."

Colin's gaze met his and he shifted his heavy form around in his chair looking for a more comfortable spot.

"About time someone took an interest in the amount of bloody, raw sewage Corrections regularly pours out into our streets. How can I help?"

Kevin sat upright in his chair and took out his pad and pen before he answered.

"I know that the police set up surveillance on a lot of these guys once they get released. Who looks after that here in Vancouver?" Colin considered the question for a few seconds, then reached for his interdepartmental phone list and ran his finger down the third page. He made no comment to

Kevin as he picked up the phone and dialed.

"Lyle, Colin Hamstead. Look, do you know who is running the surveillance on the dangerous Correction release assholes? I think I heard that Jack Marshall has something to do with that...where is he working out of, do you have any idea?"

There was a pause, and then Colin continued.

"Next to the Property Office you say...any idea of what local they use?"

He brushed aside a hash brown wrapper that had been holding center stage on his note pad and wrote a number down.

"Thanks Lyle."

He hung up the phone and looked across at Kevin.

"You know Jack Marshall?

Kevin nodded, and Colin continued.

"Okay, grab the elevator and go down to the sub-basement. Apparently these guys are holed up in some broom-closet next to the Property Office. I'll give Jack a ring and let him know you're coming."

* * * * *

Pat settled back into the comfortably heated leather driver's seat of his Caddy Escalade and gave himself time to think before he flipped open the cell phone in his hand and dialed Mike's home number. It rang three times before going to the machine. His message was short.

"Mike...Pat. Can you come about 17:30 tonight...I need to talk to you before the others show up. Call me on my cell if you can't make it early."

CHAPTER SEVEN

Pat was pleased to note that Mike's silver Nissan Titan was already parked in the lot when he pulled into the pub. He honestly had no idea how Mike was going to react to what he had to tell him, and realized that he might need the full half-hour that he had allotted to the meeting to reach a satisfactory conclusion. He wasn't looking forward to the meeting with Mike, but he was looking forward to getting it over with.

As he entered, Pat glanced around the pub, noting that the crowd, as usual, was small, with maybe a quarter of the tables and booths occupied. He didn't have to look for Mike, knowing that the special table set-up that they were privileged to have awaiting their get-togethers would be situated, as usual, in the rear of the pub some distance away from the rest of the patrons and affording a spectacular view of the Fraser River on the other side of the dike as it meandered its way toward its mouth and the Pacific Ocean.

Three tables had been moved together and Pat noted that Mike, like most cops given the choice, had seated himself in a chair facing the room with his back to the wall. These seats against the wall always filled up first on their Wednesday night gatherings.

Pat slipped in behind the tables, taking a chair next to Mike and was pleased to see a large bottle of Perrier and a glass awaiting him. Mike waited until he had poured the glass full and had taken an appreciative sip from it before he began speaking.

"What's up?"

Pat set the glass on the coaster that had been provided, toyed with it for a second, then took a deep breath before meeting the other mans gaze directly.

"We need you for another job, as soon a possible...I know that it's a lot to ask and that the suggestion flies in the face of the basic guidelines that we laid out for this when we originally set up our process, but I'm afraid we really don't have any choice in this case."

The expression on Mike's face didn't change. He said nothing but there was no doubt in Pat's mind that he now held the other man's undivided attention. Without further comment on the unacceptability of what he was proposing, he gave Mike all the information he had in relation to Barry Hertzog and a very beautiful young lady who had been carefully selected for the starring role in a brutal rape and murder.

When he had finished Mike took a solid shot of his scotch and nodded.

"OK, I agree with you, with the same concerns, I might add. The sensible thing to do would be to wait for at least three or four weeks before I took part in another one, but you're right, this is my kind of job. We really don't have any choice on this, as I see it. We know that Hertzog will likely take a few days to watch this girl before he sets up his attack on her, but he sure as hell isn't going to wait three or four weeks and that girl is probably going to die if we don't remove the problem within the next few days."

Pat nodded and managed a shallow smile.

"I had a feeling you'd say that."

Mike finished the contents of his glass and signaled for another drink before he looked back at Pat.

"Will I be working with Jim again on this one?"

Pat shook his head.

"No, Jim will plan it, but you'll be with someone else this time."

* * * * *

Chris found lots of empty parking spaces to choose from when he pulled into the pub's lot. Obviously Wednesday nights were fairly quiet. He selected one next to the big black Cadillac ESV, which he recognized as belonging to Pat, and shoved the unmarked police unit into park.

Knowing Chris well, Pat fully expected him to be slightly early or smack on time and he wasn't disappointed. The big clock over the bar was registering five minutes to six when he spotted Chris coming through the door and got up to wave him over to where they were sitting. By this time there were eight men seated at the combined tables, and Chris recognized them all as he moved to join them. Hands were shaken, 'long time no see' was repeated and grins of recognition shared as he dropped into the seat against the wall that his old friend had saved for him. As he did, Pat grabbed a passing waiter to order a round with the addition of a rye and water that he knew was what Chris preferred to drink

The only one of the group who had not spent the majority of his working life as a cop was Pat. Chris knew, however, that his friend had paid his dues as far as the others were concerned; he had been a Mountie, and then a Vancouver cop before finishing his medical education and finally becoming Vancouver's Chief Coroner. He was accepted at the table as an ex-cop. Nobody questioned that.

* * * * *

An earlier trip down to the police station's sub-basement had left Kevin surprised to learn that Sergeant Marshall, unlike most NCOs in charge of small squads, had chosen to work late shifts rather than straight days.

The reporter knew how the system worked and was well aware that any such position in the Vancouver Force usually found its leader working banker's hours with weekends off. Not so, Jack Marshall.

This was why Kevin's Volkswagen was pulling up, shortly after seven in the evening to the front of the police station, with the aim of claiming its usual illegal parking spot.

* * * * *

Chris, as was his habit when knowing he had to drive later, carefully rationed his first drink, making it last for the first hour and a half without difficulty. He replaced it with a very weak copy at that point and knew it would be his last for the evening.

Never a heavy drinker, unlike most of the men at the table, Chris did not need to consume alcohol in order to enjoy any social occasion and, despite his earlier doubts, he found himself enjoying the comradeship of the ex-policemen very much.

It had taken him a good hour to manage to catch up on the lives of the men who sat around the table. It was at that point in the evening that reminiscing had begun in earnest, and he found himself participating eagerly with up-dates on what had happened since their retirement and laughing more than he had in months at the resurrected memories of times gone by.

* * * * *

Kevin found Marshall in a small office that was at the end of a dimly lit hallway that wound past the Property Room and around the corner before stopping abruptly.

He noted the cardboard sign reading 'HROT' that had been taped to the outside of the opaque glass in the top of the door and grinned inwardly before opening the door. This squad was obviously running on a shoe-string budget.

Jack Marshall had his head buried in a file when Kevin startled him by entering the small office. Marshall's reaction to his entry told Kevin that the door didn't get opened very often and, considering the location of the office and the subject of its endeavors, that seemed reasonable.

Jack was a fifty-six-year-old, six foot, 230-pound cop who had a full thirty years on the job. He had a good head of thick grey hair and would have accepted an age 55 retirement package a year ago if he'd hadn't just married his third wife, who happened to be twenty years his junior and loved to spend money.

Jack had been a sergeant for over twelve years and he knew that he was never going to be promoted again. Almost all of his time had been spent in the Patrol Division and he had snapped up the chance to set up and run the 'High Risk Re-offender Team' when the opportunity had presented itself. He wanted nothing more than to ride out the rest of his hitch right behind the desk he was sitting in and sincerely prayed that nothing untoward would present itself to prevent that eventuality. Although he always performed his duties to the best of his ability, ambition was a thing of the past, the very distance past, for Jack Marshall.

Colin had called and left him a message advising of Kevin's likely visit and he'd therefore been provided with the opportunity to give some thought to what the reporter had in mind before the meeting.

The more he had considered it, the more he had liked the idea, and it was for that reason that he didn't hesitate to close the file that he had been engrossed in when Kevin entered the office and offer the reporter the chair across the desk from his own.

* * * * *

Chris was still working on his second drink of the night by the time the table got around to ordering food. Of the eight other men sitting in their party, four were clearly showing the signs of over-consumption of alcohol and another two were working towards that point.

The main topic of conversation had become the open discussion of the situations of other retired members of the force: what they were doing, health problems, who had died, or moved away. Chris was amazed at how well the others were informed as to the day to day of lives of their retired comrades-in-arms.

From there the conversation shifted, not unexpectedly, to the insane situation of the continued release of dangerous offenders back into the public mainstream. Almost immediately, one of them suggested that the only answer to the problem was that someone ought to start knocking them off as soon as the corrections system spit them onto the street. The vast majority immediately nodded or voiced their agreement with the suggestion.

Chris, who didn't find the idea either surprising or without merit, made no comment, although he was somewhat taken aback at just how vehemently the group as a whole had accepted, and immediately supported, that particular answer as the best way to deal with the problem.

There was a slight lull in the conversation and Pat turned to look directly at Chris.

"How about it Chris, you get to deal with these bastards often enough when they get released and commit yet another murder. Do you agree with the premise that the world would be a lot better place without them?"

Almost as one, the others sitting around the table turned to look at Chris. They all seemed to be awaiting his response to the question.

A little uncomfortable at being the center of attention, Chris shrugged, and chose his words carefully.

"Well, the system sure as hell isn't perfect, and yes, the world would definitely be a better place without them, but I don't know that vigilante justice is the answer. The system needs to be tightened up and the death penalty should be brought back; at the very least the dangerous ones need to be kept inside for their natural lives."

There was general laughter and Pat raised his eyes to the heavens in mock prayer.

"Yes God, please hear this man's words! And how long have the majority of our fellow countrymen been expressing that sentiment. Fifty years or more. Hasn't happened, nor is it likely to."

Chris immediately thought back to his discussions on this specific problem with Janet, and he recognized just how laughable his lame answer to Pat's question must have seemed to the men sitting around the table.

"No argument there, every man here knows how ineffective and dangerous our court and parole systems are."

Chris's response carried with it the general outlook of a mainstream cop. It had satisfied the rest of the group, and he was no longer the center of attention. There were nods of agreement and a round of drinks arrived, bringing with it a return to more intimate conversations around the table.

As a cop Chris was well aware of how strong the bond was between fellow policemen. Within a couple of months of graduation from a Police Academy, almost every cop had formed a new outlook on the day to day world around him.

On the street he quickly learned that he really had only one guaranteed supporter and protector and that was another cop, any other cop and every other cop. It very quickly became an 'us against the world' philosophy that was reinforced again and again on the street.

Those who lived and worked closely around the cop's world - Firemen, Ambulance crews, Coroners, Crime reporters, Emergency Room Doctors, and even to some extent Judges - were aware of this tight bond, having witnessed what happened when an 'Officer needs help' or 'Officer down' call echoed across the police radio. The response from cops to that type of call was both frightening and undeniably exhilarating to experience first hand.

* * * * *

Before he made his request, Kevin carefully outlined what he had in mind to Marshall, who was listening intently.

"So what I need is a complete list of these guys, not just for the lower mainland but for all of Canada, as well as all the background you can pass on: their records, specifics of their crimes, sentences served, etc."

Marshall had already made up his mind to provide the reporter with whatever he needed, and the two men began the process without delay, their enthusiasm for the project coming from distinctly individual angles that were, none the less, matched in intensity.

* * * * *

Chris found himself studying the men at the table individually, glancing about him as he listened to the lively conversation, laughing and nodding in response, as he shifted his gaze to each face briefly.

As individually unique as they were, with some exceptions as in any field of endeavor, these men shared a clear vision of what a cop was. The vast majority of those exceptions, such as rookies who managed to fall through the cracks of the Academy training and early years of service or those who didn't fit the mold, left the force for one reason or another at some point early in their careers.

Chris shared the general view of these men's evaluations of the world they lived in; their distaste for the politics of any situation and their inherent determination to stand up for the little guy in society.

He knew that each of these men had, along with other

reasons, become a policeman with the intent of climbing up onto a white charger with the aim of serving and protecting his fellow man from those who would do him harm.

Time had hardened them, making them far more cynical than the mainstream. Their chosen career ensured that it was the inevitably seedy underbelly of everyday life they experienced first hand; the scum of the earth were everyday adversaries for them, and the weak and challenged often depended on their help for life itself.

All cops shared a common distaste for the lack of justice delivered by the court system, which undeniably leaned to the benefit of the accused and not the victim; a system that made a mockery of the common man's concept of right and fair-play. This distaste was fortified by Corrections and Parole systems that were inept at the best of times, and brutally uncaring for the safety of the public at their worst.

Chris understood where the bond between cops came from and so did anyone else who had taken the time to take a close look at the lives society proposed and expected policeman to live.

The men at the table with him exemplified all good cops; they cared about right and wrong and had spent their working lives trying to make an imperfect, but worthwhile system, better within the confines of liberal laws that hindered them at every turn, despite a bail system that ensured most accused were released and back on the street long before the police had completed their reports on the crimes that had brought about the original arrests.

It was a cliché, to be sure, but these men had literally put their lives on the line for their fellow man and for each other. Most had done it repeatedly and without hesitation, not for huge financial reward but because it was something that needed to be done and something that they had committed to do. They were, in every sense of the word, ordinary men, with all the human foibles and shortcomings of any other group of men, but they had somehow managed to override those accepted frailties and stepped above them to give the public what was expected of them.

As the evening wore on, he found himself wondering what these dangerous to reoffend convicts would think if they knew that a group of professional investigators, such as the men sitting around this table, totally agreed and supported the suggestion that such convicts should be killed the instant they were released from prison. Chris couldn't think of a more formidable group of adversaries.

He calculated the total number of years these men had given to their public service careers. He worked it out to be roughly 240 years. When you thought about it, it was amazing that these men had been able to do what they had, against the odds that they faced, day after day for all those years without cracking completely under the strain.

He felt a sense of pride at being one of them.

* * * * *

Marshall was providing Kevin with a wealth of information, and promising more to come.

The reporter had been furiously scribbling notes as the Sergeant kept up a verbal running flow of information and background on the parole system in general and specifically on how it related to the release of dangerous offenders. All the while the man was adding printed material to the pile on the desk in front of Kevin. It was growing higher at an alarming rate.

The sheer amount of information that Marshall was providing was astonishing and after a few minutes Kevin gave up any attempt to try and evaluate it as is flowed. Instead he began to concentrate on ensuring that he was get-ting it down in some form of a legible state so that he would be able to make sense of it later.

By the time he left Marshall's office he was wound up like a watch spring.

He was onto something good, and he could hardly wait to get started.

* * * * *

The waiters were clearing the last of the dishes off the table and after dinner drinks that had been ordered were arriving as Chris turned to Pat who was sitting next to him. He kept his voice down as he spoke.

"Some of these guys shouldn't be driving…"

Pat smiled and cut him off.

"No problem, we have a system in place. I'm the designated driver for each night we meet. I take anyone home who needs it and then bring them back in the morning for their cars. I make the decision as to who doesn't drive and no one gets to argue."

Relieved, Chris nodded and turned his attention back to the conversation buzzing around him.

CHAPTER EIGHT

Chris, as was his practice when he had a scheduled meeting on a recent case, got up early and did his best not to disturb Janet as he dressed and grabbed a coffee. He was on the road headed to his office just before six a.m., missing his usual breakfast with Janet but already mentally ordering his day as he drove.

Due to the hour traffic was lighter than he normally experienced on his trip in. He found the driving put little demand on his thoughts as he worked out how he was going to deal with the day ahead.

He was about halfway to the office and had the day all worked out when his cell phone rang. The call was about to destroy his now thoroughly organized agenda.

* * * * *

Phil was parked just inside the entrance to Stanley Park, watching the dashboard clock in his unmarked unit intently. The rain had slowed to a light mist over the past half hour, and he no longer had to use his wipers to clear the windshield as he glanced toward the seawall, then back to the clock.

It was time. He picked up his mike.

"174..."

There was slight delay before he received a response.

"Go ahead 174..."

"Looks like I've lost him, he hasn't come back off the seawall at his usual spot. I can't see any point in hanging here any longer; I'm going to head in."

"Ten-four, 174"

* * * * *

Kevin rubbed his eyes and placed the notepad down onto his desk.

He had come directly home to his west end apartment, when he'd finished getting his info from Marshall at about eight-thirty the night before. He had gone over the information again and again in his mind, and it was now after six in the morning. Having been at it for ten hours he should have been dead tired, but he wasn't. Despite the fact that he'd finished off two packs of smokes and most of a bottle of hooch in that time, he felt wide awake and wired.

Very little in life surprised Kevin any more, he had been at it for too long, but it had taken him this long to admit to himself that what he saw before him in the information, lists, and records provided by Marshall was truly incredible. He had expected it to provide him with enough fuel to get the topic a spot in the paper both locally and nationally over time, but he'd never expected it to be this horrific.

There was a story here alright...there was a whole bloody career!

* * * **

Mike found his hand shaking as he lifted his coffee from the cup holder of Roger Phillip's silver Camry and lifted it to his lips.

Roger, seated behind the wheel of the vehicle that was now parked in a Tim Horton's parking lot noted the other man's condition but made no comment as he used a napkin to wipe up the slight spill that had resulted from the movement of the unsteady cup.

They had been sitting in the lot for over an hour at Mike's request, each now in the process of finishing their second coffee. Roger, having sensed Mike's need to use that time to get back to some sense of normalcy, made no comment and simply accepted the fact. The conversation over that hour had consisted of very few words.

Mike had not been in the mood to talk, and Roger had no desire to know what exactly Mike had been doing before he returned to the car.

He had dropped Mike off at 03:30 in the morning and had, as earlier specified by Jim, waited in the Prospect Point parking lot in Stanley Park until Mike had returned.

He had asked Mike if everything had gone alright when the other man had suddenly appeared out of the darkness and slipped into the car beside him. Mike had nodded in response as he quickly stripped off his soaked gloves, toque, muddy black coveralls and running shoes and placed them into the garbage bag in the back seat of the car. Mike had then run a comb through his dripping hair and pulled on the dry red jacket and white runners that he had earlier placed on the back seat of the car.

By that time Roger had driven out of the park and into the centre of the city, where he stopped in an alley long enough for Mike to deposit the garbage bag into a dumpster, knowing full well that the contents would be worn by one or more street people before the day was out.

It wasn't until they had left the laneway that Mike had spoken, and then made only a simple request for a Tim Horton's stop. Roger had readily acceded to the other man's suggestion.

Roger was one of the founding members of the 'Old Farts Club'.

He had retired from the Vancouver Force over ten years ago and had been a more than willing participant in the organizing and implementing of the plan to remove from the streets some of the garbage that the system couldn't, or more truthfully wouldn't, protect society from.

From the start, he'd known that his active participation

would have to be of a supportive role. Years of soccer playing, and a horrific car accident on the job while taking part in a high speed chase in his Dog unit had cost him a set of completely functioning knees. It had also cost him his partner King, a four-year-old German Shepherd, who had been, in his estimation, the best partner he'd ever worked with.

At 67 years of age he was physically just a shell of the man he'd once been, but his mind was as sharp as ever.

The two men had known each other on the job for almost forty years, and both had been active soccer players for the VPF up until the time of Roger's car accident. In addition, they shared an interest in playing chess and had spent many hours at the game while Roger had been on the mend from his accident. In many ways, they knew each other better than their immediate families did.

This had been the first time that they had been on a job as a team, but they were very comfortable with each other and the fit was as smooth as hand and glove.

* * * * *

Chris had pulled the Crown Vic over to the curb and shoved it into park before taking the call. He recognized Ravi's voice instantly.

"Got a bad one boss...Mountie chased a car from Richmond into Vancouver and it ended with a dead suspect. Shot and killed the guy. Happened about a half hour ago, and by the time Richmond advised us several of their cars had gone to cover and from what I understand it's quite a mess. We've got cars there now...but very little info back from the scene as yet..."

Chris cut him off.

"Where?"

"South on Cambie from Marine...couple of blocks."

Chris hit the switches and his emergency equipment lit

up the unmarked car like a Christmas tree as he hammered it into drive and his siren began to shred the peace that had so recently surrounded him.

The tires screamed as he shot from the shoulder onto the road and Ravi could barely hear him speak over the noise created by siren and rubber.

"I'm on the way…meet me there and start whatever we need on the way…oh… and Ravi, let LaRue know I won't be in for the meeting this morning."

* * * * *

Back in the dingy basement office at VPF Headquarters, Phil handed Marshall his report covering the evening surveillance of Hertzog before he spoke.

"I don't like losing him this way. I think it would be a good idea to put out a bulletin to Patrol and see if someone can locate him to make sure he's not up to no good. It was raining pretty hard, and although he's run in the rain before, he might have quit early without completing his run. But I'd still like to get a line on him and make sure he's being a good boy. There is a description of him and the clothing he was wearing in the report."

Marshall nodded and reached for the phone. The call went out as a general broadcast at 06:20 hours.

Phil, having completed his part of the scenario, left the 'HROT' office, but instead of heading home he crossed the alley and dropped into the Chinese restaurant frequented by Vancouver's finest and ordered breakfast. He knew that Marshall was off duty at seven and it was his intention to return to the office after his boss had left.

* * * * *

It was 6:45 a.m. when Kevin flushed the contents of his

ashtray for the fourth time that night and returned to his small desk. He glanced over the notes he had been scribbling as he'd gone through the papers, and then eased himself back into the chair as he exhaled a deep cloud of smoke from his newest cigarette.

Almost 600 of the bastards nationally: 130 in the lower mainland alone. There was no way that the police could be keeping tabs on all these assholes.

Obviously, not all of them were going to re-offend again...a good chunk of them were well into old age, having served a wad of time for their crimes before recent release. A portion of them were in poor health. What the hell, however unlikely it was, some of them may even have been rehabilitated the last time through the revolving door...but Jesus...

* * * * *

Dawn was breaking as the first Parks Board truck traveled across the parking lot at Stanley Park's Second Beach and stopped before the temporary gate that prevented public access to the seawall at that point.

Once through the gate, the driver pulled it closed behind him and swung the chain and lock around so that it appeared to secure the gate once more. He left it unlocked with the intention of making life easier for the work crews that would shortly join him on the wall to continue their task of removing storm debris and repairing the wall itself.

He climbed into the truck and poured himself a cup of steaming coffee from his thermos before beginning his drive down the seawall to the jobsite he had left the afternoon before.

Although he was moving relatively slowly, he nearly ran over the portion of Barry Hertzog's lifeless, battered body that had ended up partially spread-eagled on the wall.

After its 300 foot drop down the steep rocky cliff from the temporary detour trail above, the carcass resembled a life sized crumpled puppet more than a human form. The makeshift path had been created over the past few months by hundreds of joggers and hikers in a successful, if unauthorized and dangerous, attempt to join the ends of the undamaged portions of the walkway while repairs were underway to the damaged area below.

The truck came to an abrupt stop with the front left wheel hanging over the Pacific and the hot coffee in his lap, which had significantly added to his shock as he fought for control of the steering wheel.

Once he had backed the truck up and had all four wheels on the seawall, the man looked back toward the crumpled form to confirm that he'd seen what he thought he'd seen, then he took a couple of deep breaths as he put the truck into park and reached for his mike to advise his dispatcher of his discovery.

The first of the early morning joggers were already moving along the illicit trail above him and one or two had paused to have a curious look downward over the cliff toward the strangely parked Parks Board truck with its slowly revolving yellow light, its headlights cutting out across the choppy water below.

CHAPTER NINE

Chris expected the worst as he ploughed his way through the building traffic toward the scene of the shooting. He was apprehensive about what he was going to find. He feared that the crime scene would be crawling with Mounties who had responded to their man's urgent radio messages after the incident had occurred and, quite understandably, their first concern was going to be for their man, not for protection of the crime scene.

Hopefully an R.C.M.P. supervisor had responded quickly, and with any luck, Vancouver units had gotten there fast enough to bring order to the initial chaos.

His heart went out to the Mountie involved. The cop was in a no win situation; the social atmosphere of 'support your local police' had disappeared years ago. The press, and consequently the public, would be crying foul long before the dust had settled on the crime scene. No other investigation ever garnered the attention of the press more strongly than one involving a cop shooting someone, and with few exceptions the press sought sensationalism over unbiased and fair reporting every time.

In this era of instant communication and instant gratification, no one wanted to wait for the results of a properly handled investigation. Rumors and accusations would be flowing freely by the time he reached the incident and it was his job to see to it that the situation was handled the way it needed to be to ensure that truth would prevail and the chips would fall exactly where they should.

He rounded the corner onto Cambie Street and his eyes strained through the mass of abandoned emergency vehicles with their flashing lights that covered the block ahead of him.

He worked his way through them as far as he could, edging his way toward the crime scene. As he drove he was looking for two things, at least one of his own team, and yellow tape. Please Lord, lots of yellow tape.

He felt relief flow through him as his eyes found both.

* * * * *

Mike had called Pat's cell as soon as Roger had dropped him off at home, then he'd poured and finished a stiff drink.

The call had been brief, consisting of a few words that had meaning to the two of them only. Once he hung up he realized that he was shivering uncontrollably. He ran himself a hot bath and poured another drink which he took with him into the bathroom.

The room was beginning to fill with clouds of steam as he quickly slipped out of his damp clothing and into the welcoming warmth of the tub.

* * * * *

Phil used his key to enter the 'HROT' office and flicked on the light switch. He crossed directly to the row of clipboards hanging on the wall beside Marshall's desk and pulled one off.

The board contained a daily updated account of the number and status of all the people that fell under the team's surveillance responsibility. Intelligence garnered from the surveillance work and other sources was evaluated by Marshall every 24 hours and listed in order of probability that the subjects were likely to re-offend.

Marshall used this list to assign the limited manpower he had under his control. In effect, this list was a divining rod aimed straight at the most dangerous of the people so that they could be kept under twenty-four-hour surveillance. It was the best way to utilize the resources of the team.

It was also an almost flawless way for anyone to be able to select which of these people was most likely to seriously victimize the general public; in other words, a perfect hit list for anyone interested in preventing just such a thing from taking place.

Phil removed the top page from the file, and carried it over to the copier. He made one copy before returning the original and hanging the clipboard back on the wall.

He glanced around the small office briefly to ensure that he would leave it as he had found it and hit the light switch before leaving.

He smiled to himself, knowing that a very young and beautiful girl would probably just be getting up and facing a new day with all the hopes and aspirations of the young, and that he had played a small part in seeing that she would very likely have a chance to fulfill them.

He'd had a very productive night, but he was tired and looking forward to a well deserved sleep.

*****

Kevin was just completing a list of the 'dangerous to re-offend' currently residing in the lower mainland in order of what appeared to him to be their relative chance of committing a new crime, based on the information he had on each, when his cell phone went off, vibrating half off the desk before he could grab it.

It was his editor and he reached for a pencil and pad and began to scribble as the other man spoke rapidly.

The list in front of him slipped from his thoughts as he listened intently.

"...on Cambie south of Marine, we've got a photographer on the scene, he'll see you there."

* * * * *

The two man marked Patrol unit slid in behind the Parks Board truck and the obviously upset operator was at the driver's door of the car before they could shut the police unit down.

The constable riding shotgun got out of the passenger side and approached the truck driver quickly, doing his best to ignore the verbal deluge coming from the man's mouth. He took him gently by the shoulders and eased him into the warmth of the back seat of the cruiser. He spoke soothingly as the other man gratefully leaned back and settled himself into the safe confines of the Police car.

"...Easy pal...you just take a few seconds to catch your breath...I'll be right back and we can talk."

The cop gently closed the door and moved across to join his partner, who was carefully examining what was left of Hertzog's shattered body. His moving form threw a shadow across the beams from the headlights of the police car in the slowly but steadily brightening light of the dawn. The cop examining the body began to speak.

"Dead. I'll cover him, you get the tape up down here...and better call for some backup to meet me up above and protect the top of the cliff - do that before you take a statement from the truck driver."

He was careful not to disturb the body unnecessarily as he searched for identification, and retrieved a wallet from a top pocket in the jogging suit Herzog had been running in. He rolled back onto his haunches and tilted the wallet toward the light thrown from the headlights of the police car and, recognizing a medical plan ID card, he pulled it out to examine it in the light.

"Barry James Hertzog...isn't that the guy who was just broadcast for location?"

His partner nodded down at him.

"Ya. Marshall was looking for him. I'll let him know we found him."

The cop on his haunches lifted his eyes upward toward the top of the bluff and spoke as much to himself as to his partner.

"Christ what a drop...you know, you'd think a guy would be bright enough not to go running up along the top of that cliff... especially in the dark and in the rain. Hell, there are warning signs posted all over the fucking place up there...talk about stupid."

* * * * *

Chris took in the activity around him as he identified himself to a group of black-attired uniformed Vancouver officers then ducked under the yellow tape to make a bee line for Ravi, who was clustered with a group of Vancouver CSI members clad in white coveralls standing about twenty feet behind an R.C.M.P. cruiser. The driver's door of the marked unit was wide open and its flashing lights were still operating.

About ten feet in front of the cruiser stood a second vehicle, a dark blue Chrysler 300 C. The driver's door of this vehicle was also open.

Below the door Chris could clearly see the outline of a body covered by a white plastic sheet. As he approached the group, Ravi acknowledged his presence with a nod then turned to the CSI members and finished speaking before turning his attention back to Chris.

Together they silently watched the white suits cross toward the crime scene, and then Chris addressed Ravi.

"Talk to me."

The younger policeman took a deep breath and began speaking. He knew his boss well and he knew what Chris wanted from him was a short, concise overview and an indication of what needed to be done first.

"It's not as bad as it could have been. The shooting appears to have been accidental; however, the victim was not armed. The suspect apparently slammed the door open against the Constable as she approached him, knocking her down. Her gun discharged as she hit the ground. The round struck him in the head and it looks like he died instantly. The scene had been contaminated somewhat, unfortunately; six R.C.M.P. cruisers responded to cover the chase and arrived before one of their Supervisors got here. Once he arrived though, he got them out of the area and kept it clear until our guys got here. It was a female member who fired the shot..."

Chris cut him off.

"Where are the Mounties - who's got the gun?"

Chris knew that upon the arrival of Vancouver Police at the crime scene the R.C.M.P. members would have instantly congregated together to use each other as moral support and form a protective circle around the Constable involved in the incident, in what to them would be an unfamiliar landscape.

There would have been nothing untoward about such a response. It would be a subconscious and very natural reaction. He had both seen and experienced it before. Sure, they were all cops, but when one police force finds itself under scrutiny in another force's jurisdiction, they stick together like glue.

"Their supervisor has the gun...and when I saw them last, they were all near the supervisor's Suburban, which is parked over there behind the ambulance. I've identified myself to the supervisor; he's a Sergeant, name of Greg Landers. I told him you were on your way. He's been reasonably co-operative, but cautiously guarded to this point, I'd say."

Chris nodded.

"Do we have any of our IHIT R.C.M.P. members here?"

Ravi nodded.

"Ya...John Bernier is here. He's over with the Mounties, I think."

Chris wasn't surprised; IHIT might be a joint taskforce, but a Mountie's' loyalty to his own wasn't going to be transferred from his force to another without clearly defined boundaries. A situation like this definitely crossed those boundaries.

"Ask him to come and see me, please."

Ravi nodded and moved off quickly to carry out Chris's request, relieved that his report appeared to have been received as satisfactory, and that the follow-up questions had been few.

CHAPTER TEN

Kevin was forced to park his Bug in a commercial lot on Marine and walk in toward the crime scene. He located the paper's photographer at the outer fringe of the throng of press that had begun to form just north of the yellow tape that stretched across Cambie just south of Marine Drive.

The tape had a great deal of support in its task of keeping the crime scene clear of unwanted bodies. Six uniformed Vancouver cops stood roughly equidistant across the roadway, their feet firmly planted a few inches behind the tape. Their purpose was plain to all and they weren't answering any questions.

Kevin got a quick update from the photographer and asked for a few specific shots of the area, before he turned his attention to the emergency response people moving about the crime scene.

The figures were a block away, and several emergency vehicles obstructed his view but it took him only a few seconds to assess the situation. He noted one man who stood about twenty feet from the working forms of the crime scene men, and the khaki clad group of Mounties huddled together to one side of an R.C.M.P. supervisory unit that was partially concealed by an ambulance which was still exhibiting the flashes of its emergency lights.

He recognized Chris Chambers immediately. Though certainly not good friends, he and Chris went back a long way and there was a mutual respect between them that both men seemed to feel comfortable with. He turned his attention to surveying the scene again as he bided his time.

* * * * *

The initial police unit on the scene in Stanley Park had been substantially reinforced by other patrol units.

Both the area where the body had come to rest and the impromptu trail at the top of the cliff had been cordoned off with yellow police tape fortified by uniformed members, and the coroner had been notified of the situation and advised to attend once photos of the accident scene had been taken by Vancouver's on-call crime scene unit.

Initial investigation of the area at the top of the cliff by the assigned officers had given them no reason to assume that the incident was anything more than an unfortunate accident.

The trail at that point, if it could be called a trail, was a muddy, slippery mess; tree roots and boulders had been exposed by the heavy rains earlier in the morning and were an obvious tripping danger.

Even in the daylight the trail was extremely treacherous. There was a narrowing of the makeshift path at the top of the cliff and clear skid marks over the side of the bank that indicated the originating point of the fall.

It was obvious to both of the investigating cops that it had taken only one misplaced step to initiate the fatal tumble over the edge.

* * * * *

Ravi returned with R.C.M.P. Corporal John Bernier in tow. Chris moved across toward them, directing his attention toward John.

"How are they doing?"

Corporal Bernier didn't need to be advised as to who Chris was referring to.

"As well as can be expected under the circumstances, I guess."

Chris nodded and widened his gaze to cover both men

as he spoke.

"Here's how I see this going, let me know if you agree. John, I know that you are IHIT's press spokesman, but in this case I think I should look after that portion of things; it seems to me that it would be much better to have the press and public see this as a Vancouver Police headed investigation, and with me as spokesman that will be a given. I see you in a liaison position with the R.C.M.P. throughout the investigation."

Chris knew that John was very proud of being IHIT's press spokesperson, and he wanted understanding and agreement from John firmly in place before they commenced the investigation.

He saw the initial surprise register on Bernier's face as his words sunk in but he said nothing more, letting John think for a few seconds about what the overall implications of the situation were.

R.C.M.P. Corporal John Bernier was one of Chris's best and was extremely well liked by both the press and the public, but Chris knew that he was right on this point and he was sure that John would agree once he had given it some thought.

The first thing the Press, and thereby the public, did when a Police agency found itself in a position of having to investigate itself was to cry bias and scream for an independent investigation.

Having Chris as the spokesperson in this investigation would go a long way toward stifling that thrust and he was sure that John would see that. He could have made it an order, but he didn't work that way, and because he didn't his opinions and observations were greatly valued by the members of his team.

Each of his men, demonstrably, had a great deal of respect for his experience, and his management style, and they valued him even more for being a cop's cop.

John glanced from Chris to Ravi and back again; then

smiled.

"You don't miss much do you, Boss."

Chris shrugged and the two men facing him noted a change in the older man's demeanor as Chris mentally shifted gears.

It was time to get the show on the road.

"John, get your ass over there and ask the Sergeant to join us…it's time for you to start liaising. Oh, and make sure that he has the gun; it's time we relieved him of that. Ravi, you head out to the front of the tape and let the press know that I will be speaking with them in about forty-five minutes, then head back here."

* * * * *

As the Coroner's unmarked van arrived to remove Hertzog's remains, the backup CSI unit was in the final stages of examining and photographing the body and surrounding area and was preparing to move up to the top of the cliff to repeat the process there.

They had already discussed the scene with the Patrol team who would be writing up the initial report, and had confirmed to them that there was nothing they had found so far to indicate that the death had been anything other than an unfortunate, if predictable, accident.

They would, of course, have to finish up top to ensure that nothing untoward showed up there, but at the moment there wasn't a single cop on site who believed that the crime scene boys would find anything unusual up there either.

In addition, all of them were now aware of the earlier broadcast and knew that Hertzog had been under surveillance by 'HROT' at the time of the accident and, more importantly, they now had a good idea about why he had been under surveillance.

If you had taken the time to individually ask each cop

working on the call what he was thinking, you would have received a variety of responses, but all would echo a basic acceptance of the fact that this was 'the most fitting accidental death that they had ever seen'.

* * * * *

Chris found himself unconsciously making an initial assessment of the uniformed R.C.M.P. Sergeant who was walking back toward him in the company of his two IHIT men. He noted the highly polished boots and leather and the impeccable uniform. He also registered the grey hair below the cap and the wisely wrinkled features of the man.

Not for the first time, he realized that most of Canada's police agencies were reflecting what he saw coming toward him. Older experienced men, well past retirement age, at the helm; very few tested middle management supervisors and even fewer confident, Constables; so many young and inexperienced men on the street and little availability of 'aged in the barrel' backup available to provide support when it was needed.

It was a bad mix and it wasn't likely to get any better for a long time. He found himself wondering where all of the ten and fifteen year veterans had gone; the guys who had the street smarts and the experience to handle whatever was thrown at them, and handle it well.

Then he found himself assessing the Sergeant again.

Sergeant Greg Landers was in his late sixties or early seventies. He was an 'Old School' Mountie, that being reflected by both his stride and his dress, but Chris sensed that he was also a very good cop, probably with more experience and common sense than any other cop on the scene.

This assessment was confirmed as the men reached him and Sergeant Landers held out to him the sealed evidence bag containing the nine-millimeter pistol.

Chris took the bag and passed it directly to Ravi before he spoke.

"Thank you Sergeant. I'm Inspector Chambers. Chris."

He extended his right hand and Landers took it in his firm grip and shook it.

"Inspector."

Although he had extended the offer, Chris hadn't expected Landers to use his Christian name. He had anticipated that the Sergeant wouldn't consider that proper in the presence of junior members, and confirmation of the fact brought an instantaneous smile to Chris's face.

He liked this man.

"Let me begin by thanking you for protecting the scene upon your arrival - it couldn't have been easy under the circumstances."

Landers dismissed the remark with a brusque wave of his hand, treating it with the contempt he felt it deserved, but then returned Chris's smile with a broad one of his own that served to soften the action.

"These young fellows... tend to need a bit of a guiding hand from time to time."

Chris laughed and glanced at Ravi and then John before looking back at Landers to reply.

"Yes Sergeant, they do indeed."

He let the words dangle for effect for a few seconds then straightened.

"Now gentleman, let's get to work. John, you and Ravi get statements from all the R.C.M.P. members on scene so that the Sergeant can release these men to their duties as soon as possible. The Sergeant and I will get an initial statement from the Constable involved and see to it that she's removed from here as quickly as we can manage it... and Ravi, send me a CSI photographer. I may want some shots to record that Constable's physical condition."

John and Ravi moved off without further comment and

Chris turned to Landers after the two men had moved out of earshot.

"I assume she's in the ambulance. Perhaps you could give me a run down while we walk."

CHAPTER ELEVEN

Landers and Chris arrived at the back of the ambulance whose emergency lights had now been turned off. The walk had been relatively short, but Chris now had a good idea of the sequence of events leading up to the shooting. Landers had provided the scenario in clipped chronological segments, pausing between each to ensure that Chris had no questions before proceeding to the next.

Chris noted with satisfaction that there were only four R.C.M.P. members milling around their supervisor's SUV now, and that both Ravi and John had a Richmond member in their separate IHIT unmarked units. The taking of initial statements was well under way.

As they approached the Ambulance from behind, Chris dropped back slightly to let Landers take the lead and open the large rear door of the vehicle. He followed the Sergeant inside and pulled the door closed behind him.

Once inside the cramped quarters of the ambulance he noted that it held only two other occupants in the rear area. A uniformed ambulance attendant was speaking quietly with a uniformed female R.C.M.P. member, who was stretched out on the built-in, white-sheeted bed. The other ambulance attendant was in the front of the vehicle, behind the wheel making notes onto a clipboard that rested on his lap.

The attendant in the rear broke off his conversation as they entered the vehicle and Chris met his gaze.

"I wonder it you could give us a few moments alone with the patient, please?"

The attendant nodded and released the young Mountie's splinted and bandaged left hand, which he had been cradling as he spoke to her softly, then gently rested it on the cot at her left side and got up to move into the cab of the ambulance.

Landers moved forward and took the small stool next to the bed that the attendant had just vacated and Chris retrieved a second stool from its bracket on the wall and joined Landers beside the constable who was now pushing herself upright into a sitting position.

Chris watched her eyes flicker from Landers to him and noted the emotion that filled them. He knew that a multitude of feelings were flooding her reeling mind as she did her best to bring herself down from the shock, adrenalin rush, despair and a million other sensations that were the result of the chase and finality of death.

Landers smiled gently at her and rested his hand on hers as he spoke.

"Now then, Constable Frey, are you up to a few questions from Inspector Chambers here? Afterward we'll get busy taking steps that will get you home for some much needed rest."

* * * * *

Pat was already sipping on his second coffee when Jim Simmons entered the coffee shop and worked his way through the morning throng to join him in the booth at the back of the room.

When Pat saw the other man heading towards him he gave a wave of recognition, and reached into his pocket to pull out the list of names that Phil had provided him earlier.

He unfolded the document and placed it in the center of the table as Jim dropped into the booth across from him, then pushed it toward the other man as he reached for the coffee that Pat had ordered for him earlier.

"Hope it isn't cold...you're running a little late."

Jim smiled across at him.

"Cold or not, it's got to be better than what I had at home. Never could make a good cup of coffee...relied on Kay for that"

Pat waited for him to test the coffee's temperature before he pushed the document closer.

"Damn list never seems to get any shorter"

Jim nodded, slipping his reading glasses on with his right hand as he picked the document up with his left, and began to scan it.

Pat turned back to his own cup of java and enjoyed a couple of mouthfuls as he waited for Jim to work his way through the list.

When Jim had removed his glasses and leaned back into the high-backed seat, he fixed his gaze squarely on Pat and shook his head slowly.

"No, it doesn't. We don't seem to even be making a dent in it, and that's despite our recently increased level of activity. Considering what we already have in the works, it's getting to be a bit much, which is something I've been meaning to discuss with you by the way."

Both men glanced around the room before Pat; satisfied that they would not be overheard, spoke again.

"You and everyone else. It's beginning to be a little overwhelming - we seem to be losing control of the whole thing...a 'best laid plans of mice and men' sort of thing."

His words hung in the air, with neither man sure exactly where the answer to the dilemma lay. Finally, Jim broke the silence.

"I've been giving it a lot of thought recently, and I think as cops we've been conditioned to take immediate action in emergencies, dealing with any problem quickly and without a great deal of thought for our own safety...it's a hard habit to break. One look at these lists and we dive in with both hands. Hard not to."

Pat gave the observation some thought before responding.

"I think you've got something, and if you're right, perhaps you've supplied the answer to the problem as well."

Jim gave him a quizzical look.

"How so?"

Pat took a sip from his cup, then reached across the table and picked up the list.

"Perhaps we shouldn't be looking at the list every few days...maybe every couple of weeks or just once per month. There will probably be the odd emergency, as we saw with the last one, but if not we wouldn't even have the information to act on until another calendar month had gone by."

Jim stared blankly at him for a few seconds, and then Pat saw some of the concern begin to drain from the other man's face as he nodded.

"You know, I think you've hit the nail on the head...it would force us to pace ourselves. Maybe we should raise the idea at the next dinner."

* * * * *

In Chris's absence Staff Sergeant LaRue was chairing the morning meeting. Normally Chris chaired these case situation meetings, but occasionally he was unable attend.

It was in these rare instances that LaRue found himself in the chair at the head of the table in the conference room at IHIT headquarters.

He did so with some trepidation, although he never allowed his inner turmoil to demonstrate itself in any way to the others around the table.

Even though LaRue outranked all of them in both police experience and actual rank structure, every man there, including LaRue was well aware that he was not considered a working member of the team as he lacked their homicide investigation specialty, but instead as a team administrator.

He sat at the head of the table because of his rank, and was merely a figurehead. Each man in the room knew that LaRue's job as replacement chairman for Chris was a relatively simple one. His purpose was to invite every member of the team to offer the latest information each held with regard to the specific investigative file that was opened before the Staff Sergeant, and to listen intently to what they had to say and make notes that he would then pass on to Chris when he returned to the office later in the day.

While all the other team members were more relaxed when LaRue was in the chair, relieved at not having to face Chris's ever questioning overview of their individual progress on the case being evaluated, the Staff Sergeant was very aware of his inability to pick out critical parts of each team member's report as Chris would have done had he been occupying the head of the table.

In these situations, LaRue was a glorified secretary, and he knew it. That knowledge irritated him, but what was of real concern to him was the fact that he was never sure if he was passing on to Chris what his boss would be looking for…it was uncharted territory for him in many ways and his normal confidence in his abilities to do his job well deserted him each time he sat in this chair.

The meeting lasted for just over an hour and by the time it was over LaRue's neat writing filled three pages of the legal pad in front of him.

He asked very few questions as each member of the team reported their progress in the investigation into the North Vancouver murder, always conscious of the fact that he was a mere observer in the exchanges that were taking place around him, and ever vigilant to ensure that he had garnered as concise as possible an evaluation from each of the team members to pass on to Chris later in the day.

* * * * *

Kevin made very few notes as Chris addressed the press from just outside the line of yellow tape. He knew that few relevant facts would be coming out at this point in the investigation, and that Chris was basically delivering a standard PR message. 'Unfortunate incident, under investigation, additional facts to be released as soon as available...'

Unlike many of the other reporters on the scene, the fact that Chris was acting as spokesman on this particular investigation by IHIT didn't surprise Kevin. He had recognized the reason for this unusual turn of events as soon as Chris approached the members of the press outside of the crime scene. He allowed himself a smile as the briefing came to an end and Chris met his gaze briefly.

Recognition passed between them in that second before Chris excused himself and slipped back under the tape to return to the crime scene.

Kevin moved away from the pack of reporters and made his way back down the roadway toward his car, his eyes moving over the array of police vehicles parked haphazardly on the street as he walked.

When he located the silver Crown Victoria that Chris was currently driving, he made his way over to it and slipped a folded note under the passenger windshield wiper before heading back to where he had parked his Bug.

He intended to stop off at Police Headquarters to go through the overnight incident reports for any stories that might be found, and then return home to file this story and anything else of value electronically from there.

He was confident that Chris, as requested in the note, would call him to provide him with more detailed information on the shooting incident in time for him to make his deadline for tomorrow's morning paper.

* * * * *

Jim fired up a cigarette and smiled as he watched Pat moving purposefully across the street toward the Medical Clinic where he was currently putting in a few days a week, then turned and crossed over to climb into his car. To say that he felt somewhat relieved after talking with Pat was an understatement.

By the time they had left the restaurant, both men had felt that they recognized the shortcomings of the way the program had begun to spin out of control and had reached a reasonable and effective way to bring it back under control. The conversation had then turned to ordinary everyday exchanges and each man had recognized the surge of relief apparent in the other as that topic was put behind them.

He was certain that the other members of the group would feel the same when the decision was put to them, and he found himself looking forward to bringing it forward at the next meeting. It felt very good to be in control again.

He was whistling softly as he pulled out of the parking lot.

* * * * *

When Chris finished speaking with the Richmond supervisor he paused long enough to shake the R.C.M.P. Sergeant's hand before slipping under the tape to move toward his unmarked unit.

Ravi was already sitting behind the wheel.

He had been too engrossed in sorting through and evaluating the written statements of the Mountie Constables to notice the paper under the windshield wiper, but Chris didn't miss it. He was unfolding it as he slipped into the passenger seat beside Ravi.

He read it, then refolded it and slipped it into his pocket before addressing Ravi.

"Give me a synopsis of the statements on the way in."

Ravi was ready for him and began a slow, thorough run through of the basic facts of the incident that had surfaced during his rapid review of the various statements provided by the R.C.M.P. members.

* * * * *

Kevin quickly became deeply engrossed in the files of the dangerous offenders as soon as he reached home, and was surprised to see that it was already eleven o'clock when his cell phone rang.

He recognized Chris's voice immediately and leaned back with relief as he spoke.

"Hi Chris, I was beginning to wonder if you got my note. I just wanted to get your angle on this before I wrote it up."

It was a short exchange, and each man got something specific from it.

Kevin got a couple of interesting facts about the shooting that no other reporter would get, plus a general evaluation as to what direction the investigation would take, and Chris got the opportunity to put out the message that he wanted delivered to the public in an unofficial, yet credible form.

It was an arrangement that had served both men well for many years and each understood and respected the other's limits in these exchanges, which had begun shortly before Chris had been promoted and assigned to IHIT.

Once he was off the phone, Kevin quickly wrote his article for the day and sent it on its way, and then he had a final smoke before climbing into bed to grab a few hours sleep.

* * * * *

When Pat broke for lunch, he took his white smock off, hung it on a hook and got into his heavy jacket, before leaving the clinic to head for his usual restaurant.

As he walked he withdrew his cell phone from the top pocket of his parka and checked to see if he had any messages. There was only one. He recognized the number as belonging to Roger Phillips and flipped the phone open and dialed to recover the message. It was brief.

"Pat, Roger...I'm a little concerned about Mike. I was hoping that I could meet you for lunch and talk about it. I have to go into town anyway, so I'll be in the neighborhood of the clinic about noon. If you get this message before you head out, please give me a call."

Pat cleared the message and dialed Roger's cell number. Roger answered on the first ring and they arranged the meet.

CHAPTER TWELVE

True to his word, Roger arrived within ten minutes of the call and joined Pat in the busy little restaurant. They ordered as soon as Roger sat down and although there was no way that they could guarantee that they would not be overheard, the din caused by the other customers made that an unlikely possibility.

As soon as the harried waitress left the table Roger began to speak.

"When I picked Mike up he seemed to me to be running on adrenalin. He wasn't interested in talking, unusual for him, and he was pretty shaky when I got him home. I was wondering if everything went okay; he indicated it had, but his condition didn't appear to support that conclusion."

Pat set his coffee down and shook his head.

"Strange, as far as I know it went very well. We have put him under quite a bit of pressure lately though. That might have something to do with it."

Despite Pat's assurance that all had gone well, the concern hadn't left Roger's features.

"Well something's definitely wrong there. He just wasn't himself."

Pat thought for a second, taking a drink from his cup before continuing.

"You guys are pretty close aren't you? You know he's on his own and has no one to talk to about this stuff. I was thinking maybe you could do some socializing with him, get him talking and see if you can find out what, if anything specific, is bothering him."

"That's what I had in mind, but I wanted to touch base

with you first to see if something had gone wrong and that was the reason he was so up-tight. I figured that I'd suggest he and I get together at his place for some chess on Saturday night. We used to play a lot and my wife is out with the girls on Saturday, so it would be a good time for me."

Pat nodded his agreement.

"Do that, and let me know what you find out."

* * * * *

It was nearly one in the afternoon when Chris found time to meet with LaRue and Ravi in the conference room to go over the review of the North Vancouver rape-murder and the initial progress on the R.C.M.P. shooting. He poured himself a cup of coffee before joining them.

They had preceded him into the room and were sitting across from one another at one end of the big oval table, having left the chair at the head of the table free for him.

He nodded at each in turn, stifling a smile as he noted the thick file folders with a neat stack of yellow legal sheets resting on top, piled in front of LaRue.

His Staff Sergeant did not like to be asked a question about something that he couldn't answer.

Ravi didn't even have his notebook out on the table, only a fresh scratch pad and a pen. Both men had coffee mugs in front of them and there was the smell of fresh coffee coming from the machine on the counter at the other end of the room.

Chris grimaced as he set his own mug down. He should have known that they would have a fresh pot on. It had to be better than the reheated concoction he had brought from his office.

He settled himself into his chair and laid his pad and pen on the table before he spoke.

"Okay, Don, let's do the rape-murder first. It's the older of the two files"

LaRue picked up the top two yellow sheets that had been sitting on the bulky files and removed the paperclip that joined them, placing it neatly on the table, then carefully aligned the clip with the tops of the file folders at a precise right angle. He cleared his throat and began to speak.

"She was thirteen years old, and had been bounced around from one foster home to another for the past four years. Mother is a crack-head; no father in the picture that we can find. Cause of death was strangulation; her blouse was knotted around her neck. Superficial stab wounds to the chest area - nothing that would cause death, but there will be blood residue at the crime scene. Coroner thinks that it is likely that she was raped and killed in a vehicle, and the body dumped shortly thereafter. She was sexually assaulted and we have semen. It's being run for DNA. It would appear that the body wasn't wrapped before it was dumped; we have some carpet fibers and pubic hair from the body that should tie in with the vehicle used, and probably provide more DNA evidence once we get a suspect. The girl was in foster care and had run away, not for the first time apparently, probably on the afternoon of the day that she was killed."

Chris interrupted him.

"Did she have access to a computer in the foster home?"

The color drained out of LaRue's face then was quickly replaced with a flush as the Staff Sergeant looked anxiously across at Ravi. Chris shifted his gaze from the two men to settle directly on the young Detective Constable, not wishing to make his 2 i/c any more uncomfortable than he already was.

It was, after all, a question that should be addressed to a field investigator, not an administrator.

Ravi paled slightly under their combined gaze and realizing that Ravi didn't have the answer either, Chris continued.

"She was thirteen years old. If she had access to a computer, she would be using it and we need to find out who and what she was interested in"

Ravi was already getting up out of his chair.

"Check with North Van to see if they have inquired as to the girl's ability to access a computer. If not, get the foster parents on the phone and find out. If she did, then get a warrant before you go over to pick it up. And Ravi, if there is any chance that she could have been using a computer, I want it in our forensic lab before the end of the day."

Ravi had the conference room door open to leave as Chris finished speaking.

"Don and I will wait for you to check with North Van, so let us know what they have to say. If you have to go for the computer, we will carry on without you; and if that is the case, ask Gordie to join us in here in your stead, so we can move on with this."

Chris glanced over at LaRue as the door closed behind Ravi.

"Don, do we have any suspects?"

LaRue shook his head.

"Not as yet."

Chris nodded.

"Has anyone checked with Jack Marshall to see if North Van has any HROT possibilities that we should be looking at?"

"Yes, Sgt. Clark has Marshall checking, we should hear back on that shortly."

The door opened and Detective Sergeant Gordon Clark entered the room. A smirk formed on the Staff Sergeant's face.

"It would appear that Ravi is off to North Van to seize a computer."

Chris chose to ignore the comment. He greeted Clark with a smile.

"Thanks for filling in Gordie. Did Ravi bring you up to speed before he left?"

Clark lowered his slight 5 foot 10-inch body into the chair recently vacated by Ravi and nodded before answering his boss.

"Yes...I'd already arranged to have the computer from the foster home scooped by North Van; they are holding if for us to pick up. Ravi must have missed that in my report; he did get in a little late for the meeting this morning. Anyway, we'll have it in a couple of hours if Ravi manages to beat rush hour traffic."

Chris had expected no less from the seasoned Vancouver Homicide Detective Sergeant and nodded before glancing at LaRue, noticing with some satisfaction that the smirk was no longer present on the Staff Sergeant's face. Gordie continued.

"Marshall got back to me a few minutes ago; he's given us three possible suspects from the HROT list and seems to think one of them would fit the bill perfectly, based on the M.O."

"Guy named Joe Fraser, Native Indian, 34 years old, released on parole two weeks ago after serving eight years for multiple rapes in the Regina area, all with superficial stab wounds to the chest area. Currently staying with his sister in North Van."

The Sergeant reached into his jacket and pulled out two pieces of folded paper and handed them across the table to Chris.

"That's the info from Marshall. The second page is from the North Van Mounties, guy's current address etc. They don't have anything specific on him since he got out, unfortunately. Manpower shortage - haven't even dropped in to see him. He has reported to his parole officer twice - every Monday at 11:00 am. I checked the data bank and we have his

DNA, so once we run what we got from the body we should be able to eliminate or arrest him."

Chris glanced over at LaRue.

"Put a rush on the lab for the DNA results, please, Don...have them to put it at the top of their list."

Chris then turned his attention to Gordie.

"He meets with his parole officer on Mondays?"

The Sergeant nodded.

"Let's you and I arrange to see his parole officer at 10:00 am...I want a look at what he has on him. See if you can arrange that. I'll be interested to see if the con arrives in a vehicle for his meeting with his Parole officer. Don, get hold of Jack Marshall. Thank him for his input, and tell him that perhaps he should let North Van know that it would be a good idea to assign someone to keep an eye on Joe Fraser over the weekend. No direct contact, they just need to make sure that we don't have a repeat performance from him. Jack Marshall is good at what he does...he's obviously got a gut feeling on this and I think he's probably right on the money."

Both LaRue and Clark nodded their agreement and Chris centered his gaze on Gordie.

"We don't need you for the other file. I was at the scene, and Don can bring me up to speed on any new developments."

* * * * *

Phil's thoughts were elsewhere as he exited his doctor's examining room and moved slowly down the hall toward the reception area.

He had been prepared for the news for some time now and had convinced himself that he had come to terms with it, but now he knew that he had only been fooling himself.

It took him a second to realize that the motherly leader of the battery of receptionists scurrying to and fro while safely ensconced behind the counter in the airy medical clinic had been speaking to him.

"It's very nice to see you again Mr. Harder."

The instant his eyes met hers he realized that she knew what his doctor had just told him and that she was trying in her way to let him know that she was sorry for his trouble. They had formed a sort of relationship over the past two years since he'd begun making his regular trip to his personal doctor's office to receive the results of his quarterly checks taken at the Cancer Clinic; a friendly one with banter that they both enjoyed.

Phil realized that the shock had hit him hard. The results had been fairly devastating. He drew from his inner strength and willed himself to shed the shuffling pace and stooped stature that had come over him just moments earlier.

Phil sensed that the woman was making a sincere attempt to let him know that she cared, and he forced a smile to his lips.

"And for me to see you too, Carolyn; you're a shimmering ray of sunshine on an otherwise grey day."

Phil felt his legs beginning to shake and he picked up his pace slightly, knowing he could not keep up the front that he'd managed to put on for her benefit much longer.

The door to the outside world seemed to be miles away but somehow he reached it and slipped through.

Although Phil didn't see it, he wouldn't have been surprised that tears had welled up in Carolyn's eyes as the door closed behind him.

* * * * *

It was almost two-thirty before Chris set his pen down on his pad of foolscap and leaned back in his chair.

"Okay Don, let me just summarize this quickly as I see it, and then you can tell me if you agree with my assessment."

Chris didn't miss the look of relief on the Staff Sergeant's face as LaRue eagerly folded the top cover of the file down over the sheaf of reports that were stacked inside.

Chris smiled and reached for his mug, then got up and headed for the coffee maker.

"Don't know about you, but I could use a fresh cup before I start."

LaRue returned the smile and quickly joined Chris at the machine. He returned to his seat with his fresh brew, but Chris remained on his feet slowly walking the room as he sipped from his mug.

"Ok, we've got GPS on the Constable's car, so we know exactly where she was throughout the chase. She stops the car in Richmond for excessive speed, runs the plate before she gets out of her car, and before she gets any info back he hammers it and the chase is initiated.

On two occasions during the chase she witnesses what she thinks are drugs being tossed from the vehicle 'which has now been confirmed' and before they are out of Richmond she gets notified that the vehicle is registered to a known drug dealer and is a "Code 5". So, she knows that she is chasing someone who may be armed and has a history of violence.

The Chrysler 300 C out-powers her Crown Vic considerably and she has her hands full just trying to keep this guy in sight. He is across the Knight Street Bridge and into Vancouver in a matter of minutes. She can hear the cover cars coming from Richmond but she knows that they are a long way off and will not be able to reach her quickly, and she is now out of her own jurisdiction and in unfamiliar territory. She probably realizes that her people are in touch with

Vancouver by this point and we are responding as well, but she has absolutely no idea what kind of help she will get from us or how soon it will come. So she has to face the fact that she's on her own."

Chris paused and glanced over at LaRue, who was following him with his eyes as he moved about the room. Their eyes met and LaRue nodded.

Chris took a gulp from his mug and downed it before he continued.

"The chase comes off the bridge and into a deserted commercial area where the suspect stops. The Constable tells the radio that she has him stopped again but she can't tell them where she is. She knows that they can pinpoint her location via GPS, so help is on the way but she has no idea what that help will be or how soon it will arrive. She opens her driver's door and steps out of the marked unit careful to remain behind the door. She pulls out her gun, and she uses the unit's PA system to order the driver out with his hands up.

She's trying to buy time now, simply praying for cover to arrive and hoping that the driver doesn't take off again. The suspect doesn't do anything for a few seconds; then she sees the backup lights on the Chrysler flicker slightly and the brake lights come on. She knows that the suspect has shifted out of Park and is now using the brakes to keep the vehicle motionless...in other words, she knows that he could take off at any second and is probably considering it.

She has two choices: get back into her car and have another chase; or, approach the vehicle and try to arrest the driver on her own. Adrenaline is hammering through her as a result of the chase and she's got to be scared of the situation she finds herself in, but she isn't about to let him get away at this point, so she gathers her courage and starts toward the suspect's car, watching the brake lights and the driver's door knowing that, despite the fact that she's got her spot-lights on, the suspect's view of her will be vastly improved once she moves into the beams of her own headlights. All her training tells her to stay behind the door in relative safety, and wait for help, but she has to make a split second decision and she makes it, putting her own safety aside. Her eyes don't leave the driver's door of the suspect's car...she convinces herself that he will not shoot before the door opens and she moves purposely toward the car shouting for him to come out of the vehicle with his hands up. She moves in an arc, trying to get a clearer view of the suspect within the vehicle, who is vaguely silhouetted in the glow from the dash lights, but the windows are tinted and she's having trouble making him out. She can't see the back of the car at this point, so she is not aware that the driver has put the vehicle back into park. She is only a few feet from the driver's door approaching it at right angle; her attention is glued to the suspect's silhouette as she moves closer.

Suddenly, she hears the roar of the engine as the suspect hammers the gas and she instinctively closes the short distance and uses her left hand to yank the door handle open before the vehicle can move. The suspect kicks the door fully open in that instant, in his haste to exit the car, and catches her full in the chest with it. As she falls backwards onto the pavement in shock and pain, her service weapon discharges, and the deed is done. We have a doctor's report on her injuries to confirm her version of how the final few seconds went down, plus photographs of the obvious bruising, and two of her fingers on her left hand were broken when the door hit her, plus damage on the door itself. As well, the reconstruction has determined that the trajectory of the bullet from the gun to the victim supports the fact that it came from approximately one foot off the ground. I've interviewed the Constable personally and I'm sure that she will make a credible witness. I'm going to recommend against any charges. I think we can be very confident that a Coroner's Inquest will accept accidental death and make quick work of it."

He paused and faced LaRue, who stated without hesitation.

"I agree."

*　*　*　*　*

Phil had unlocked and entered his silver Honda Civic ten minutes ago but he hadn't yet started the car. He sat slouched in the driver's seat, staring out at the grey sky as if mesmerized.

His thoughts are unconnected, bouncing about from topic to topic...things he needs to do...decisions he has to make...reflections on what had been and what is to come.

After awhile his mind went blank and he simply sat dejectedly for several minutes before he took a deep breath and managed to get hold of himself.

He needed to talk to someone, and a one-sided conversation with Cecil, good company that he was, wouldn't fill the bill this time. With some effort he worked his cell out of his jacket pocket and dialed.

The call to Pat Dunne's cell went unanswered and eventually a machine asked him to leave a message. The simple act of dialing the phone had brought him back to the real world and he realized that he should have known that Pat wouldn't answer his cell when he was working at the clinic, if he was busy with a patient.

He was pleased that his voice sounded quite normal as he left Pat a message.

"Pat, its Phil. Could you give me a call when you get a chance...I need some advice."

*　*　*　*　*

Chris was tiding up his desk in preparation to leave the office for the day when Ravi arrived back at the office with the seized computer. The darkly handsome young Delta Detective Constable paused at Chris's open door and grinned broadly as he held his find out proudly.

"Got it Boss"

Chris returned the grin as he was reaching for his coat.

"Get it to Jeff and tell him what we need…he's still in the CSI office, I asked him to wait for you. I want this worked on right away. I'll see you on Monday morning, barring any surprises."

CHAPTER THIRTEEN

Chris waited for the garage door to close fully before he opened the door that led into the townhouse proper. The instant he did so, his nostrils filled with the delectable smell of something cooking in the kitchen, and he felt the stress of the day beginning to leave his body.

There were a couple of good games being televised, and he was looking forward to the weekend.

* * * * *

It was a little after six by the time Pat finished with his last patient and was able to check his messages. He called Phil immediately, and they agreed to meet for dinner that night at a restaurant a few blocks from the clinic.

* * * * *

Kevin's alarm went off at six thirty. As he sat on the edge of his bed lighting a cigarette, he noticed that the small red button at the base of his home phone was flashing.

He took it off mute and checked for messages. There was only one message. It was Chris Chambers, providing him with a number and asking for a return call that evening.

Kevin made a note of the number on the scratch pad that he kept by his bed, then punched the button to erase the message, stretched and got up to head for the shower.

* * * * *

The features on Rosie Simpson's, (nee Fraser's), face

softened slightly and a smile formed on her lips as she looked out the second story living room window of the North Vancouver home she shared with her husband and two boys. She stood motionless for several minutes watching her brother Joe as he scrubbed furiously at the interior of her 2000 red Dodge caravan that was parked in the driveway in the front of the house.

She'd had more than a little difficulty in convincing her husband Carl to agree to let her brother move in with them after he was released from prison. Although she had not expressed it to her husband, she too had harbored concerns about taking her brother in, especially because of the two boys; but things seemed to be working out all right and over time she had become less anxious about the arrangement.

Joe had been given the in-law suite in the basement and, other than sharing meals with the family, seemed to spend most of his time quietly reading downstairs or on the family's computer, which was located in a small room next to his suite on the lower floor of the house.

He had left the basement infrequently, just to attend the required meetings with his parole officer and attend a couple of job interviews. On one other occasion he had asked if he could borrow her van for the afternoon to go to the library in order to select some more books.

He had promised her that he would clean the van for her that weekend by way of thanks, and she was very impressed with the diligence of the cleaning going on below her now.

She used the van to take the kids to and from school as well as for getting herself to and from work every weekday and she had to make other arrangements for the days when Joe had used it. It also meant that the van hadn't been available for him to clean until she had arrived home from work tonight.

She had been more than a little surprised to find Joe

waiting for her in the driveway when she pulled in with the kids from school. He had an impressive conglomeration of cleaning supplies all prepared to go and seemed very eager to get on with the job.

Although Rosie had not seen Joe for several years due to his incarceration, from what she remembered of their earlier life together she had not expected to see him work so hard cleaning the van.

He had been a haphazard worker at best, who had put little serious effort into anything he did, in his younger years.

It pleased her very much to see him working hard and she gave a little sigh of satisfaction as she watched him.

Maybe his time in prison had done him some good after all, and perhaps her offer to help him after he was released had been more appreciated than she had originally sensed.

* * * * *

Chris and Janet were about to sit down for dinner when the phone rang.

Chris took the call and when he recognized Kevin's voice he asked him to hang on for a second then covered the mouthpiece as he turned to face Janet.

"Can you put dinner on hold for a bit, honey…I need to deal with this."

Janet had slipped on oven mitts and was bending over the stove, about to open the oven door. She stood up and thought for a second then reached for the temperature control knob for the oven and dropped it from 375 degrees to 250 before she slipped off the mitts and nodded.

"No problem."

Chris smiled across at her and then held out the phone to her.

"I'll take it in the den…hang up for me please, once I

pick it up in there."

* * * * *

Pat was already comfortably ensconced in a back booth of the nearly empty restaurant, with a Perrier in front of him, when Phil arrived.

When he saw Phil come into the restaurant, he nodded toward the waitress hovering a few feet away from him and she smiled and moved across to the bar. She had a glass of scotch with water on the side sitting on the table before Phil eased himself into his seat.

* * * * *

Kevin sat on the edge of his bed staring at the phone he'd just hung up, then picked up his notepad and reviewed what he had written down as Chris had run through the info on the R.C.M.P. shooting. He flipped the pages over as he reviewed them and absorbed their content. When he had finished he got up and carried the pad over to his small desk, sat down and dug out a fresh note pad from the top drawer.

He glanced at the clock on the wall above the desk and decided that he had time to get the story into rough form before he headed down to Police Headquarters to review the daily incident reports, and that if he did that he would still have time to file the final copy for this story before the deadline for the weekend edition of the paper.

The R.C.M.P. piece would be separate from anything else he would file this evening. It was an exclusive that he knew would pull a good spot, probably front page. He would have to take extra care with it in order to protect his relationship with Chris, and that meant spending a fair amount of time on it, but the night was young.

In exchange for an unlimited exclusive story on the

shooting and resulting investigation, Chris had only asked that the information on the facts leading up to the death be written in such a way as to play up the human interest part that the rookie female R.C.M.P. member had played in the drama. He had asked that Kevin give good coverage to the emotions and courage the Constable had to deal with in order to bring to a conclusion a very frightening situation and that the injuries she had suffered physically, as well as emotionally, as a result of the accidental shooting would be made clear to the public in the article.

A more than fair exchange, as far as Kevin was concerned. It was exclusives like this that went a long way in making Kevin the best at what he did for a living, and he knew it.

* * * * *

Pat and Phil gave their orders for dinner to the waitress, and once she had left Phil began to speak.

"I went to my doctor today to get the results from my last visit to the Cancer Clinic. So much for remission...it's back with a vengeance, apparently, and I don't think I have a great deal of time left."

Pat set his Perrier down and leaned back in the booth.

"Jesus Phil...I'm sorry to hear that."

Phil took a good pull at his drink before he continued.

"I've given this a lot of thought. I'm not going to go through the treatment again, not only because the cancer is far more pervasive this time, but because I don't think there is much chance that it will do any good. I've had a full life and I'm ready to pull the plug"

He let his gaze meet Pat's fully. Pat sensed that the other man had more to say and didn't risk breaking into his train of thought by speaking himself.

Phil, who had some time to prepare the speech he was

giving to Pat, continued without hesitation.

"I want to ask a favor of you. I need something that I can take when I need to, so that I can simply go to bed and not wake up. I know it's a lot to ask, but I don't fancy eating my gun...I'd rather do what needs to be done and at the same time, salvage as much of my self respect as I can."

Pat nodded.

"Don't give it another thought. I'll have what you need by tomorrow."

Phil's relief was plain. It was done and he could let go of it now. Pat watched the other man visibly relax in front of his eyes. He was about to speak when Phil raised a hand to cut him off.

"There is one more favor I'd like to ask."

He looked around quickly to ensure that they could not be overheard.

"I want to become more directly involved in at least one, if not all, of the next little endeavors that we take on...kind of leave my mark on this world in a very positive manner before I go. I know that we had agreed that I was only to supply the intelligence and not jeopardize my position within HROT by getting involved with the actual solutions, but it's suddenly very important to me that I do more now... while I still can."

Pat was a little taken aback and didn't say anything for a few moments.

Phil seemed anxious to impress upon him the importance of what he was proposing, and began to speak again.

"I don't have a great deal of time left, so this needs to be fairly soon, I'm afraid. I think I should make it clear now that I'm prepared to take risks if that is necessary...after all, I have little to fear from getting caught."

Pat nodded in agreement and they sat silently for a few seconds.

"I understand completely. I'll discuss it with Jim, but you've got my vote."

* * * * *

Chris had turned on the small television set in the kitchen before they started to eat and as the news broadcast began he reached for the remote and turned the previously muted volume up.

From past experience Janet knew that Chris would be looking for some specific story to be covered and she made no comment as the top story of the night, a shooting of a suspect by the R.C.M.P, came on the screen.

* * * * *

Kevin was so impressed with the article on the shooting by the time that he had completed it that he decided to file it electronically with the paper before he left his apartment to head down to the police station.

It was good and he wanted to make sure that his editor got a chance read it through and arrange to place it well for the morning edition.

* * * * *

Phil couldn't remember when he had enjoyed a meal so much. He knew that it wasn't because of the meal itself, but more because he was at peace with the world and that he had made the right decision with regard to what needed to transpire in the time he had left.

The conversation passing between the two men had been casual throughout the meal and Pat knew as he watched the other man that he would do what he could to see to it that

Phil's final requests would be met. He had known this

man for a long time and he had a great deal of respect for him and had every intention of fulfilling those requests, one way or another.

* * * * *

Chris put the set on mute again and his eyes met Janet's across the table. Janet tilted her head in the direction of the television before she spoke.

"An IHIT investigation?"

Chris nodded and put his fork down on his empty plate, before using his napkin.

"Yep, about what I expected. Bloody sensation seeking reporters...that's why I had Kevin give me a call. I think the public will have a different slant on things after his story hits the papers tomorrow. I sure as hell hope so anyway."

* * * * *

Kevin was pleased to find his usual parking spot in front of the police station empty, and adroitly slid the little Bug into the slot in a haze of blue smoke. A few moments later he was scrolling his way through the daily incident reports in the report centre. He was disappointed to find that nothing in particular caught his interest but even more pleased that he had decided to get his exclusive on the R.C.M.P. shooting off to his editor before he'd left his apartment.

Finally satisfied that there was nothing worthwhile, he got up from the stool he had been using and returned his notebook and pen to his jacket pocket before leaving the report centre. As he headed for the door, he glanced at this watch and seeing that it was approaching seven thirty, decided to drop in and see if Marshall was around...perhaps he could get some more info on the 'likely to reoffend' story he was working on.

* * * * *

Pat gave Jim a call after leaving Phil outside the restaurant. He arranged to meet Jim the next day for brunch at the golf course near Jim's White Rock townhouse, a place where they met on a fairly regular basis.

He had not given Jim a reason for the meeting, and Jim hadn't asked for one.

* * * * *

Chris had gone through the facts of the R.C.M.P. shooting with Janet, and given her the gist of the information that he had already passed on to Kevin for publication in the morning paper. After, they sat down to watch a movie that Janet had pre-recorded earlier in the week, which both of them had been looking forward to.

He set up the entertainment centre in preparation for the movie while she poured them an after dinner drink.

* * * * *

Marshall looked up as Kevin entered the HROT broom closet of an office and they exchanged smiles as he waved Kevin into the chair on the other side of his desk

Kevin had no more than sat down when the door to the small office opened again and Phil walked in. Marshall looked from Phil to Kevin and back.

"You two know each other?"

Kevin stood up and extended his hand to Phil.

"Good to see you again Detective Harder. I thought you'd retired."

Phil grinned and shrugged his shoulders.

"Can't seem to stay away from this place, just putting in a few days a week with HROT to bolster my ineffective pension."

Phil turned his gaze toward Marshall.

"Thanks for letting me come in a little late."

Marshall cut him off with a flip of his hand.

"Not a problem, but you'd better get your ass out there. Old Jimmy will be worn out after 13 hours, not that he would ever admit it."

He reached for the car keys hanging on one of the hooks on the wall beside his desk and tossed them to Phil as he spoke.

"Same set up as last night."

Phil nodded to both men in turn and left the office.

Kevin dropped back into the chair across from Marshall and took his notepad and pen out of his jacket pocket and set them down on the desk in front of him. While he was doing this Marshall gave a deep sigh and made a half-hearted attempt to tidy up the surface of his desk, managing to clear a small area directly in front of himself. Kevin spoke first.

"I was upstairs and thought I'd drop in while I was here to see if you had anything new for me."

Marshall fished around in the remaining mess of paper on his desk and located a small note pad which he then held in his left hand while he put on his reading glasses with his right.

"As a matter of fact, I do. Made a couple of notes here earlier...thought you might drop in. Let me see..."

Kevin moved his pen to his notepad in preparation to jot down whatever information Marshall had to offer.

"First, you can take Barry Hertzog off your list; he was good enough to kill himself today."

Kevin interrupted the other man.

"I knew that there was something familiar about that name when I saw it in the incident reports upstairs, it rang a bell, but I couldn't place it...fell off a cliff in Stanley Park ...right?"

Marshall nodded.

"Yep, couldn't have happened to a nicer guy...I think this second thing will be of more interest to you though, but you'll have to take it 'off the record' for now. That okay with you?"

Intrigued, Kevin nodded his agreement and Marshall studied him for a second as if trying to make up his mind about whether or not he could trust him.

"Colin tells me that you can be trusted. You can use this later, but I thought you'd like to know before it breaks."

Even more intrigued, and now a little impatient, Kevin broke in.

"No problem, I won't use it until I get your go-ahead."

Marshall nodded.

"You know the North Van rape-murder that IHIT is working on? Well, it seems that one of our assholes is a prime suspect...guy named Joe Fraser"

He fished around in the stack of papers again and pulled out a few sheets that had been clipped together.

"Here is some info on him; I've given you as much background as I could get."

Kevin interrupted again.

"Chris Chamber's guys are working on this?"

Marshall nodded.

"Yep... it's IHIT's baby."

CHAPTER FOURTEEN

The pre-dawn skies were overcast, but the light rain had ceased. Phil took a sip from his coffee and then put the Styrofoam cup into the holder located in the Crown Vic's center console. He shifted his gaze from the small, dilapidated house to the clock in the dash, which read six forty-five, and he yawned.

When he had relieved Jimmy the night before the older ex-cop had told him that he would have a quiet night, as their current subject was suddenly becoming a very busy boy during the day and seemed to be sleeping away the nights of late.

This was a major change in the man's past habits, and Jimmy was becoming concerned about it.

Brad Allison was a 42-year-old sex murderer who had been recently released in Ontario after serving his full 15-year sentence and was therefore not controlled by any conditions of parole. When he got out he had moved to Vancouver, and they had inherited him.

Allison had kidnapped and raped a nine-year-old girl; then murdered her and cut her body up into several pieces before burying the parts in different locations.

Upon being arrested for the crime, he had worked out a plea bargain with the TO police based on his pleading guilty to a charge of second degree murder.

After some heavy negotiations, he had ended up getting 15 years in exchange for his showing the cops the various locations where he had buried the little girl's severed limbs, torso and head.

The deal had been struck, in the interest of giving the victim's family closure and the offer of the guilty plea.

Problem, from Jimmy's point of view at least, was the fact that the guy had spent his first two months in Vancouver drinking his nights away in various bars and sleeping all day, but had now shifted gear and was spending his days walking aimlessly through various residential areas, which contained several primary schools.

There had been no loitering near the schools as yet but his quarry's pace had repeatedly slowed each time he passed a school when the kids were outside.

Jimmy didn't like the change one damn bit, and he had told Phil so in no uncertain terms.

Phil didn't like the scenario either and when he was relieved and had returned his car to the station, he decided not to go directly home.

* * * * *

Chris had a game he wanted to watch at nine, so in order to respect their customary leisurely breakfast together, he and Janet were up by seven.

When Chris came out of the shower he could smell breakfast cooking and by the time he got into the kitchen Janet was setting the table. Chris gave her a smile then went to the front door to retrieve the thick weekend edition of the paper that was waiting on the porch of their townhouse.

It didn't take him long to find what he was looking for. The R.C.M.P. shooting story under Kevin's by-line had made the front page. He began to read the article while he walked back down the hall toward the kitchen.

* * * * *

As expected at eight o'clock on a Saturday morning, Ravi found the normally busy IHIT lab almost devoid of staff when he entered their office. Only Staff Sergeant Jeff Winters and a single member of the civilian VPF forensic scientific team were visible in the large, well lit room.

Winters was peering resolutely over the shoulder of the unit's computer geek as the civilian forensic scientist hammered away at the keyboard in front of her. Both were clad in white lab coats and were so involved in discussing the information in the windows that were popping up in the screen that they didn't notice Ravi's arrival.

Not wanting to disturb them, Ravi moved quietly up behind them and positioned himself where he could observe the screen and listen to them without interrupting their avid verbal exchange.

* * * * *

Marshall had still been in the office when Phil went in to return his car keys and drop off his report for the night. It appeared that Jack was just about to wrap up, so Phil went down the lane to the café behind the station and got a coffee and settled himself into a booth where he could sit for a half hour before returning to the HROT office.

* * * * *

Chris finished reading the article out loud as Janet had requested while she was dishing them up breakfast. As he put the paper down she spoke.

"Well that's sure as hell a different story from what we saw on the news last night. Do you and Kevin do this kind of thing often?"

Chris was very pleased at the way Kevin had put the story across and his expression showed it as he answered her.

"Not often enough, I'm beginning to think!"

They both laughed and then began to dig in.

* * * * *

Once Phil was inside the unoccupied HROT office, he went directly to the clip board on the peg beside Marshall's desk and removed the top sheet, photocopied it, replaced the original, and slipped the copy into his pocket.

Moments later he was getting into his car in the underground police lot.

As he pulled up to the automatic overhead door and waited for the pressure pad to do its work he fished his cell phone out and dialed.

* * * * *

It was a good five minutes before Staff Sergeant Winters noticed that Ravi had joined them in the lab. He did a double take.

"What the hell are you doing in here on a Saturday? Sneaking up on people…got nothing better to do?"

Ravi smiled his most disarming smile, one that most handsome men seem to adopt at an early age to dispel negative reactions, and responded.

"I was about to ask you the same thing."

With a wave of his hand, Winters dismissed the question as irrelevant and pointed back over his right shoulder in the general direction of the figure at the keyboard.

"Andrea has something you are going to want to see."

Ravi began to cross the short distance to the wide workspace in the center of the room.

He had taken no more than a few steps when his nostrils picked up the faint but striking perfume that he recognized as hers.

From a very early age, Ravi had never had any trouble getting any girl, or as he grew older, any woman he wanted. As a result, he had never given much thought to the need to have to pursue a female and he'd always felt supremely confident when first meeting any member of the opposite sex.

Not so when it came to Andrea Henderson.

It wasn't the first time he'd met a beautiful girl and found himself instantly in lust; which was what had happened the first time that he had met her. But there was something strangely unique about his reaction when it came to his first contact with Andrea. Oh the lust was there all right, but it wasn't as simple as that. There was something more, but try as he might, he hadn't been able to figure out quite what the difference was.

She was a relatively new hire for the Department, starting three weeks previously, and he had only briefly spoken to her twice in that time, but she had had an immediate and exceptional effect on him from day one that had shaken the hell out of him.

On both of the previous occasions their paths had crossed he hadn't even been able to manage to mumble more than a few words in her presence.

Just being around her caused him to feel like he was back in grade five, completely lacking in self confidence, when he had found himself faced with the blatant demand that he drop his pants for one of his friend's eighteen-year-old sister, once she had managed to corner him alone in the bathroom.

After the second occasion of being in Andrea's presence when the strange reaction had once again come over him, Ravi had spent some time trying to sort it out in his mind, but he hadn't been able to put his finger on exactly what it was about simply being in her presence that affected him so profoundly.

The sensation of feeling more than just a strong sexual interest was something new for him, and although it intrigued him, he wasn't particularly comfortable with it.

She was physically gorgeous, that was a given, but he had been with several women before her that could match her in the looks department and he already had an inkling that in Andrea's case there was more to it than that, much more.

At both meetings the change in Ravi's demeanor the minute the stunning girl came into sight was not missed by Chris, who had been highly surprised and more than a little amused at seeing the transformation in his usually confident junior team member.

Chris knew from experience, that damn near all females that he and Ravi met in the course of their duties started to drool the minute they set eyes on Ravi, and that the strikingly handsome man rarely seemed to notice, taking it in stride as commonplace. Therefore, after each of their contacts with Andrea, he hadn't been able to resist making a comment to Ravi about the noticeable effect that she obviously had on him. This, of course, had simply added to Ravi's consternation over the whole situation.

As the Staff Sergeant spoke, Andrea looked away from the screen in front of her and swiveled on the stool to half face Ravi. A wide smile formed on her face that seemed to him to be both warm and sincere. Ravi felt himself freeze in mid stride.

Only his eyes were moving now, from the long flowing, shimmering, pitch black hair that framed her face, the pert little nose, and huge dark brown eyes... down over those impressive mounds that the lab coat that was having great difficulty containing.

Realizing what he was doing he came to an abrupt stop, and managed a small smile of his own.

"Hi Andrea..."

She slid off the stool, lightly hitting the floor, and as she did her breasts bounced, and from Ravi's viewpoint, instantly put the already stressed, top button of the lab coat under what could only be described as extreme pressure.

Andrea was a tall woman, and standing she was only about six inches shorter than he was. Their eyes met and locked.

Ravi opened his mouth as if to speak but nothing came out. He cleared his throat and luckily Andrea spoke, taking the pressure off.

"Hi, Ravi. You'll want to have a look at this; I think we have what you were looking for."

Her voice was low pitched, slightly husky, but very feminine. He had noticed before that it brimmed with a deeply bewitching innocence. The combination of her undeniably great looks and the sound of her voice brought a slight flush to Ravi's face and he was immediately aware that the hot blood flushing his cheeks was beginning to surge into another part of his body as he moved up to join her in front of the computer resting on the work counter.

One thought passed through his mind as she began to speak again.

'Jesus... what is it about her?'

Jeff, who had been watching them from a distance, shook his head and mumbled half to himself.

"I knew that girl was going to be as distraction, the first time I saw her"

He grinned and moved across to a smaller work area against one wall of the lab where he seated himself and began pushing buttons on the control panel.

CHAPTER FIFTEEN

Pat found Jim inside the golf course dining room, seated in their usual booth. He took a look at what the buffet was offering as he crossed the room to join Jim. When he got close, Jim started to shift out of the booth to head for the buffet, but Pat waved him back into his seat.

"We might as well sit for a bit. Let's order coffee for now. Phil called me earlier and he's going to join us for brunch. He should be here shortly."

"Phil? Problem?"

Pat sat down and shook his head.

"Not sure, actually. His cancer is back, and the prognosis isn't good. He's decided that he wants to be more directly involved in our project, an active participant if you like, and there is a definite urgency to his interest now. Anyway, he's wired about it and needs to talk it out."

* * * * *

Kevin blindly hammered the snooze button for the third time that morning and turned over, breathing heavily. Resigned, he rolled back and reached for his cigarettes and fired one up.

As he sat on the edge of his bed idly scratching his crotch he found himself wondering what in God's name had convinced him it was a good idea to get up early on a Saturday to do some prep work on his potential HROT story.

* * * * *

Once the waitress had cleaned off the table and refilled

their coffees, Phil, who had been impatient throughout the meal and only played with his food, pushing it around the plate and eating little, made a quick check to ensure that no one was close enough to overhear their conversation.

He focused his attention on Jim; sure that he had already gained a great deal of ground on his plan with Pat.

"I don't know if Pat told you, but I don't have a great deal of time left and I'd really like to become directly involved in our projects from this point on."

Jim leaned back into the booth cushions and nodded.

"Yes. Sorry to hear about it, Phil, but I don't..."

Phil cut him off, his voice a little louder than he had intended.

"Just hear me out please. I've thought this through and I know what I've got to do, and that I have very little enough time left to do it."

Pat, who was sitting beside Jim in the booth, nudged him with his knee under the table. Jim, who had opened his mouth to speak, closed it and looked down at the table top.

Phil took a deep breath and continued.

"When we started, I know we all agreed that I shouldn't have any direct involvement in the solutions to the problems, in order not to jeopardize the position I had at HROT and the intelligence gathering ability that my position allowed.

He paused and the other two men nodded in acknowledgement.

"It was a sound decision at the time, but I know that Jack Marshall will accept my recommendation for a replacement for me if I quit, and I sure as hell have a reason to quit now if I want to, no one is going to question that. That means that we can preselect whomever we want to replace me at HROT, and that will ensure no interruption with the information that we need to operate."

Jim looked from Phil to Pat and put his coffee mug

down on the table.

"Ok, if you are sure, but it seems to me like change for the sake of change; you've played your part in this, God knows. You provide each target for us, why isn't that enough?"

Phil slouched slightly and shook his head.

"I'm not sure, but it isn't enough for me any more. I don't want to be just an organizer and planner."

He laid his big hands on the table in front of him and rolled them over, palms upward and stared down at them for a few seconds before continuing.

"I want the opportunity to finish these bastards myself. I need to kill the evil they possess personally, and I want to use these hands to end the horror of what they are. Before I die, I want to accomplish that and I know that if I do, I can go content. I'm asking you as friends to help me do what I know I must."

No one spoke for some time, each absorbing what Phil had said. Neither of them questioned Phil's initial statement. They knew that Phil was right about Marshall, he would accept any replacement recommended by Phil.

It was the intensity of Phil's plea to take part in the wet side of the program that was open to question. While his delivery had been powerful, each of them had to think it through carefully... this wasn't some sporting event they were discussing, and while friendship went a long way with this particular group, so did common sense.

In initially setting up the plan to act, Jim and Pat had very carefully selected the members of the group, each man being chosen first for his commitment to the idea and then on his ability to work within the team in a specific position based on experience and ability.

They had only taken the best of the best in each area, and only as many men as was necessary to accomplish the goals of the group. A small group who trusted each other implicitly and whose abilities and loyalty had been proven beyond doubt over many years.

It was Pat who finally broke the silence, looking first at Phil and then Jim.

"You know I've been worrying about Mike a little. He seems to be uneasy with his part in our activities lately, not without good reason, considering that he's been very much centre stage in that part of things. Perhaps this would be a good opportunity to give him a change? I'm sure Marshall would welcome him as Phil's replacement and Phil could shift to the other end of things to allow him to accomplish what he wants."

Jim picked up on the thought.

"That would mean we wouldn't have to bring anyone new into the group, we'd just be shifting the workload...I can ask Mike, but I honestly believe that he would jump at the chance for a change like this."

Relieved, Phil smiled and leaned back into the softness of the booth behind him.

"Thanks guys. I'll wait until you hear back from Mike before I talk to Marshall, but the sooner the better from my point of view. Now, there is another matter I think you need to know about..."

He reached into his Jacket and hauled out the neatly folded copy of the HROT priority surveillance list, opened it, and placed it on the table between them.

"I know we were going to wait a little before we moved again, but I'm afraid we have a very real urgency here."

* * * * *

As Andrea explained to Ravi what she had found on the seized hard drive, he was relieved to find himself shifting his attention to admiration for her professional abilities versus the powerful attraction to her physical attractiveness that had consumed him at the initial sight of her.

For her part, Andrea seemed oblivious to how she affected him, proudly rambling on, losing him often with technical jargon, but very pleased with the obvious surprise and admiration that her discovery was bringing to Ravi.

* * * * *

Kevin lifted his hands from the keyboard and leaned back slightly in his chair as he stretched.

He now had the entire list of HROT subjects entered into his laptop, and had broken down those in the lower mainland onto a separate second screen. Each list was now as up to date as he could make it. He had also removed both Bates and Hertzog from the local list.

He now began to familiarize himself with the records and background information on each of the subjects, trying to get a better overall understanding of the strange makeup of each of these monsters.

* * * * *

Phil passed on to Jim and Pat the conversation that he had with old Jimmy the night before and shared their concerns about Brad Allison's change in activity pattern. For emphasis, he took out his pen and circled Allison's name, which topped the list that Jack Marshall had recently updated.

"As you can see, Jack seems to see it the same way. I know you feel we've been moving too fast but isn't it just possible that we are over-reacting here?

Maybe you know something that I don't, but to my knowledge there hasn't even been a sniff of interest in what we've been doing. It seems to me that we should be more concerned about watching for any outside interest, rather than being overly concerned about the frequency of the incidents themselves."

Pat and Jim looked at each other, and then Jim took a sip from his cup and waved the waitress over.

He then asked in an undertone.

"You want to take him out now?"

The arrival of the waitress forced a brief cessation of the discussion and it wasn't until Jim had asked for refills and she'd gone for the pot that Phil answered.

"Yes I do, and if you agree, I have an idea as to how it can be done cleanly."

Fresh coffee arrived and the other two men took the opportunity provided by the interruption to silently evaluate Phil's suggestion.

* * * * *

Staff Sergeant Winters got up from his stool and turned to cross the room to where Andrea and Ravi stood at the workbench, still avidly involved in the secrets that the hard drive had provided.

He stood behind them listening to their excited exchanges for a few minutes and then cleared his throat loudly.

"I hesitate to interrupt, but I think that we should perhaps consider the fact that unlike the rest of us who managed to get a good night's sleep, Andrea has by now been working for 23 hours straight and should be seriously thinking about getting some nourishment and sleep soon.

Either that or I recommend that we should put in a call for the Paramedics before the repeated adrenalin rushes that have been keeping her going up to this point wear off and she collapses on us."

Ravi and Andrea stopped in mid verbal exchange and swiveled to face him.

He smiled at them.

"Seriously Andrea, you cracked the hard drive and it will be at least a couple of hours before we get the results on this DNA so that you can try for a match. Why don't you take a break? I can call you when it's done if you like. I know you'll want to do the comparisons yourself."

Ravi shifted his gaze to Andrea and, for the first time since he had entered the room, he registered the signs of exhaustion that were now clear on her beautiful features. He felt an unfamiliar surge of protective instinct fill him.

"Christ. You worked through the night on this?"

Andrea dropped back into a sitting position on the stool behind her and flashed him a weak smile.

"Well, it needed to be done and since I'm the only one here who could do it…"

Winters looked from Andrea to Ravi and smiled.

"I know she doesn't have a ride…she car pools with our handwriting guy and he drove yesterday. Maybe you could give her a lift home, Ravi?"

Ravi nodded instantly.

"Sure…I need to give my boss a call first and let him know what we have, but I'd be glad to."

Andrea stood up again. She rested her hand briefly on Ravi's arm and smiled.

"That would be great; I am feeling a little bushed. You go ahead and make your call. I'll just go and freshen up a bit."

* * * * *

In the middle of watching a game, Chris didn't even hear the phone ring, it wasn't until Janet came into the room and spoke that he turned his attention from the screen.

"It's Ravi."

She waited for him to mute the set and then reached out to pass him the phone. Chris eased himself out of the chair and stood up to take it from her. He couldn't hide the trace of irritation in his voice as he spoke.

"Yes?"

Ravi knew his boss too well to miss the undertone.

"Sorry for calling you at home boss, but I thought you would want to know, Andrea got into the hard drive and I think she's got exactly what you were looking for."

His words hung in the air for what, Chris eventually realized, would seem like a lifetime to Ravi who was waiting for a response on the other end of the line. Chris forced himself to put the game out of his mind and break the silence. When he spoke, any suggestion of annoyance was gone.

"That's great news Ravi. You were right to call...are you in the lab?"

"Yes."

"Can you put Andrea on please so she can bring me up to speed?"

Ravi glanced toward the back of the lab where a hallway led to the washrooms. He spotted Andrea headed towards him.

"She's been up all night and I'm going to take her home for a break, she has no transport. Staff Sergeant Winters asked me to give her a lift, she's really beat, and she still has to come back in a couple of hours to do the final DNA comparison work."

Chris almost laughed out loud as Ravi uncharacteristically rambled on, but he bit his tongue and let him run down before interrupting.

"OK Ravi, just put her on please. And Ravi, please give me a call when she has the results of the DNA work. Based on what we have now and the likelihood of a match with the DNA, we are likely going to have to move on this on short notice. We'll have to arrest him and get him behind bars without delay, if we get what I expect we will, and that means getting a take-down team together on a Saturday."

"Right Boss. I'll stick to her like glue and let you know as soon as we have anything on the DNA."

Tongue biting couldn't hack it. Chris did laugh out loud.

"You do that Ravi...now put her on, please."

CHAPTER SIXTEEN

Ravi held the passenger door of his mint, white over Nassau blue, 1966 Corvette Roadster open for Andrea who, as tired as she was, couldn't resist a beaming smile.

"Wow...I'm impressed! What a cool car. My dad would love to see this; he's an antique car nut."

He returned her smile and took her arm to help her inside.

"One of my weakness I'm afraid, I love classics."

He didn't miss the brief, but enticing, flash of long, firm, darkly tanned leg that was exposed below the skirt that had hiked slightly to allow entry into the white leather passenger seat of the low slung car.

When he slid into the driver's seat beside her he noted that she was taking in the impeccable interior of the car appreciatively. She seemed sincerely impressed with it, and as Ravi took a great deal of pride in the work that he had done on the car, her interest pleased him.

He glanced at her as he fitted the key into the ignition and turned the Vette's powerful motor over. It started instantly and the throaty rumble issuing from the big, finely tuned V8, by way of the side exhaust pipes, echoed around them in the secure confines of the Police underground parking garage.

"I have to admit that she's my first love. I've done a full frame-up restoration on her, only finished a couple of months back."

He eased the car out of its parking stall and moved slowly toward the pressure pad fronting the door at the far end of the garage, letting the car idle its way toward the entrance in first gear. When the door began to move up he turned to look at her.

"Where to?"

Andrea glanced at her watch and frowned.

"Well, we've only got a couple of hours or so. I live on the east side of Burnaby, a return trip would take us an hour...maybe we could just go for a bite to eat somewhere close and forget my place. A little food might be enough to get me back on my feet."

Ravi concentrated on pulling out into traffic safely before he answered her.

"I think a nap is as important as food at this point. You should try to get your head down, even if it's only for an hour."

He glanced at her briefly and realized that she was giving serious consideration to what he had said, and he took a chance.

"Look, my place in the west end is a lot closer, and while I'm sure as hell no gourmet cook, I could put together a couple of omelets for us pretty quickly and then you would have time to get a bit of a rest before we have to go back. What do you think?"

Andrea took a few seconds to answer, and although he was intent on his driving, he was aware that she was studying him intently as she contemplated the offer.

"I don't want to put you out, I'm sure that you have better things to be doing than babysitting me."

Ravi laughed.

"Not that I can think of. Besides, you wouldn't be putting me out, it would be my pleasure. My place it is then"

* * * * *

Phil finished outlining to Pat and Jim his plan for dealing with Allison, and then he lifted his cup to his lips and drained it.

"I know that this is a lot for you to digest in a short

time, but you guys are the experts and I would appreciate it if you would let me know what you think before tomorrow morning, Sunday being the best day of the week to pull it off. I'll head home and get some sleep now, give you a chance to kick my idea around. I'll be up and about in a few hours…give me a call if it's a go."

* * * * *

Chris was sure that the DNA would be a match.

Having missed a good portion of the game and his mind now firmly in work mode, he didn't bother to watch the last of it; instead he went into his den and dug out his phone list and began to make the calls that would give a heads-up to enough of his team to allow the formation, if necessary, of an effective take-down team for Fraser later that day.

* * * * *

Exhaustion was setting in for Andrea, and recognizing that, Ravi kept the conversation light, giving her a chance to relax as he drove. It didn't take long; fifteen minutes after leaving the station he was pulling the Vette into the underground parking area of one of the better west end high-rise apartment blocks.

He drove straight through to the back of the building and reached for the remote that opened one of the steel double-doors that were the only way to access his enclosed four -car garage from the outside. He waited until the door had opened fully, and then drove inside.

During the drive to his apartment, Ravi had become concerned about Andrea's physical condition. The fatigue was now clearly demonstrating itself and he was sure that she was no longer able to ignore it completely. He was pleased to note that her eyes had brightened and that she appeared to be taken aback at the size of the enclosed garage as they entered.

It was apparent to him that she had not expected the brightness of the lighting, the rows of impeccably polished red tool chests nor the massive work bench that filled the end of the room in front of them as they came to a stop.

It was unique, and nothing one would have expected to find in a west end high-rise underground parking area; an impressive professional workshop by anyone's standards. He was sure that she had never seen anything quite like it, at least not in private hands; it certainly couldn't be classified as your run of the mill home workshop.

Ravi hopped out of the driver's door and moved quickly around the front of the car to the space separating it from the big black vehicle next to it and opened the passenger door for her.

Andrea's skirt had ridden up a little further as she had relaxed into the comfortable leather bucket seat during the ride and Ravi was treated with another wide expanse of shapely golden legs as he reached in to help her out into the brightly lit room.

He gave her a smile and then led her around the two other vehicles in the garage - one of them draped by a dust cover - to the stainless steel door fronting the private elevator that was situated in the centre of the west wall.

Ravi inserted one of the keys from his ring into a slot in a small panel to the right of the door, and when he turned it the door opened silently in response. As it did, Andrea used her hand on his forearm to turn him until he was facing her and looked him straight in the eye.

"You on the take?"

Ravi flushed slightly, and then laughed as he took her hand and led her into the elevator. Once inside he pressed a button in a panel on the wall to his right and the door slid closed and began a very rapid, smooth climb.

"No...my family owns the building actually."

* * * * *

Phil had just left the golf course parking lot when he felt his cell begin to vibrate. He got it out and answered, and immediately recognized the voice of the retired VPF Deputy Chief on the other end.

He swore softly to himself as he remembered that he had agreed to do some electrical renovation work for the man that morning, and had totally forgotten about it.

"Shit...sorry Harry...things got a little crazy and it slipped my mind. Could we make it next Saturday?"

* * * * *

The elevator door opened directly into the large, airy and expensively furnished living area of the penthouse. Andrea took in the massive glass wall to the left which overlooked the large, professionally landscaped, patio area outside, and the expanse of the ocean and mountains in the distance.

It was an understatement to say that it was strikingly beautiful, even on this grey October day.

Ravi took her coat from her shoulders and placed it with his own overcoat and jacket in the closet to the left of the elevator door, then gave her a second to appreciate the view before he spoke.

"Have a look around if you want...I'll see about those omelets"

Andrea, who due to her lack of nourishment and sleep was feeling a little chilly, moved across the thick carpet to the far side of the room before turning her back to the large fireplace centered in the wall.

She relished the luxuriating warmth given off by the

large natural gas built-in unit as she watched Ravi disappear into another room.

Andrea stood there for a few minutes her dark eyes taking in the size of the room and appreciating the classic beauty of the furnishings.

* * * * *

Chris, distracted as he had been by the call from Ravi, had almost forgotten that he had one more phone call to make; something that he had planned to do after the game.

He hauled the phone book out of the top right drawer of his desk and flipped through until he found the number he wanted, and then dialed. He had the book halfway back into the drawer when the call was answered.

"Richmond R.C.M.P..."

Chris identified himself and asked for Sergeant Greg Landers. He was politely informed that the Sergeant was on the road at the moment but expected back shortly and would the Inspector like his voice mail?

Yes, the Inspector would.

He left his home and cell numbers.

* * * * *

It wasn't until she heard the banging of pans that Andrea crossed over to and through the doorway that Ravi had entered earlier.

She found him standing to one side of the huge stainless steel stove in the middle of the central island of the massive, professionally appointed and commercially equipped, kitchen. He was dicing green onions on a cutting board and the blue flicker of a gas flame showed below the large frying pan sitting on one of the stove's front burners.

The room was huge, all white and stainless steel, impeccably clean with nothing out of place. It looked as though it had never been used for the purpose for which it was designed and yet Ravi, a crisp white apron tied in place to protect him from spatter, seemed very much a home in it.

He saw her in the doorway and a smile broke out on his face.

"Make yourself at home. The rest of the place is through that door."

He pointed with the knife he was using at the doorway on the opposite side of the kitchen before turning his attention back to the preparation of the omelets.

"These will be ready in a jiffy... go ahead, take the grand tour, and meet me back in the dining room when you're finished."

Andrea's eyes didn't leave him as she moved across the room and through the doorway into what turned out to be a formal, elegantly furnished dining room which in turn gave way to a hallway that led to a full sized powder room, a large office/den, two good sized bedrooms with walk in closets and their own bathrooms, and finally into a huge three room master suite with a walk through built-in closet that led to a separate bathroom containing a steam room, four person Jacuzzi tub and well stocked exercise room.

One wall of each room was made entirely of glass which provided natural light and wide, unobstructed views of the city and vistas below.

* * * * *

The two New Westminster Police Constables both gave sighs of relief as they left the ancient hotel and climbed into their marked patrol unit that was sitting at the curb in front of the building.

It had taken them three hours to handle the suicide call and they were relieved to have only the reports left to do.

Clifford Weston was about to become another statistic; one more suicide to add to the daily Canadian average, and as suicides went, not a particularly distressing one for the veteran cops. If anything, it had been ironically satisfying for them...one more scumbag six feet under.

Although the report that they were about to put in wouldn't reflect it directly, both seasoned policemen were very much in agreement with the message contained in the suicide note.

Neither of them doubted for a second that society as a whole would be much better off without the likes of Mr. Weston, and that his decision to depart this world by his own hand had been a sound, if long overdue, one.

* * * * *

Andrea, surprised at just how hungry she had been and how good it had tasted, made short work of her omelet. Ravi beamed across the big table at her as she set her fork down and raised her large glass of orange juice to her lips to finish it off.

Ravi pushed his chair back and stood up as she used her napkin to gently pat her lips and he was standing behind her to pull out her chair by the time she dropped the napkin back onto her empty plate.

"That was awesome...you know your way around a kitchen. Thanks."

Ravi pushed the chair back under the table and smiled.

"Now I know why my mom gets so much satisfaction out of preparing food for others...it's very nice to watch someone eat what you make with such obvious pleasure. C'mon, I'll show you where you can crash"

Andrea followed him out into the hall and then down to the first of the bedrooms. He stood aside and waved her into the room.

"You will find a toothbrush and stuff in the bathroom, shower if you want, robes on the back of the bathroom door...I'll be cleaning up, just give me a shout when your Blackberry goes off and we'll head back in. Sleep well"

He flashed her broad grin and closed the door behind him as he left the room.

CHAPTER SEVENTEEN

As sound asleep as she was, Andrea's Blackberry woke her instantly.

She was momentarily disoriented in her strange environment but that passed quickly and she threw back the covers and sat up on the edge of the comfortable queen sized bed, grabbing the instrument and reading the message presented on the small screen as she did so.

She glanced at the clock on the bedside table, noting that she had only been asleep for just over an hour and a half.

Despite the fact that her rest had been short, the bed had been as comfortable as her own, if not more so, and she felt remarkably refreshed. She was both pleased and surprised by the fact.

She stood, and stretched her lithe naked body briefly before crossing the room to pick up the full length white silk robe that she had earlier left draped across the chair against the left wall.

A momentary shudder of pure delight shimmered through her body as she slipped into it and the silk engulfed her naked body. She found herself hugging it tightly around herself and enjoying the blissful feel of it for a few seconds, before belting the robe firmly and crossing to the bedroom door.

As she moved down the hallway, the deliciously sensuous material of the robe gently caressed her large firm breasts with each step she took. She felt herself shudder slightly at the almost electric sensation that radiated over her skin and was a little surprised to feel a definite surge of arousal course through her body.

When she glanced downward she flushed deeply.

Her nipples had reacted predictably to the richly stimulating material, and were very clearly fully erect, and plainly visible against the front of the fabric that was stretched tautly across the expanse of her ample chest.

Andrea found Ravi down the hall in the combination office/den, sitting in front of a computer screen at the big antique desk that dominated the spacious room.

He had his back to the door.

Conscious of her clearly outlined and obviously fully erect nipples through the thin material, she poked only her head through the door to speak to him.

"It's time…I'll be ready to go in about fifteen minutes."

And she was gone, hurrying back down the hallway to the bedroom before Ravi could respond.

* * * * *

Chris hadn't been able to get back into his usual weekend routine. He was impatiently waiting for the call from Ravi, and when the phone rang he picked up immediately.

"Yes."

Obviously the caller hadn't expected the abrupt greeting, as there was a slight pause before Chris heard the firm crisp voice, which he recognized as belonging to Landers, respond.

"Inspector Chambers…Sergeant Landers, Richmond R.C.M.P., returning your call."

Chris laughed before speaking.

"Right Sergeant … sorry, I was expecting another call. I just wanted to let you know that I've reached a decision as to what path the shooting incident will take and I wanted you to be the first to know.

It won't be made public for a day or two, but I will be recommending no charges and a Coroners Inquest. I'd appreciate it if you kept this to yourself until we release it, as it has to be presented to the public with care. Although, I did think that you might want to communicate my decision to one other person, and that would be fine with me…off the record of course."

He paused to wait for a response, which came instantly.

"That goes without saying sir, and may I say thank you sir… I very much appreciate your taking the time to call me, and I'm sure the other party will as well. If there is anything that I can ever do…"

Chris cut him off.

"Professional courtesy Sergeant, I'm sure you would have done the same if our roles had been reversed."

* * * * *

Ravi pulled a keyless entry remote from his pocket as the elevator door slipped silently open at the garage level. The headlights flashed and the horn sounded briefly on the shiny black Hummer which filled the middle parking spot in the brightly lit garage.

Andrea raised her eyebrows slightly and gave him an inquisitive look. Ravi opened the passenger door of the - at least to Andrea - somewhat intimidating vehicle and smiled as he waved her in.

"Company vehicle…don't like to take my baby out unless I know she's going to be safe. We could be in for a long night if you make a DNA match and I'll be happier knowing that she is safely home."

As the door opened behind them and Ravi backed out she noted that like the third vehicle in that garage, the Vette now had a dust cover over it too. She smiled to herself as the thought crossed her mind that the car really was his 'baby'.

Ravi quite clearly looked after what was important to him and she found that fact far more relevant to her than she would have expected it to be.

Not for the first time that day, she found herself blatantly studying him very carefully as he backed the big unit out of the garage and pressed the remote to bring the solid double-doors down.

* * * * *

After hanging the phone up, Sergeant Landers picked up the weekend paper that had been sitting on his desk.

He read the article under Kevin's by-line for the second time that day and smiled. It painted a very different picture of the shooting incident than that of the TV news reports that had been playing throughout the day.

Landers knew, without doubt, that Chris had played a part in Kevin's story; that was obvious by the appearance in the article, of some of the facts that had been utilized to set the stage in directing the reading public to a clear understanding of the events that had led up to the shooting itself.

There were facts in the article that could have only come from IHIT, and Landers knew only too well that nothing came from a unit like IHIT without the OIC giving it the go ahead.

He found himself very glad that Inspector Chris Chambers was OIC at IHIT.

The fact that a VPF Inspector had been put in charge of IHIT when the joint- force homicide team had been formed had been as repellent to him as it had been repellent to many senior R.C.M.P. members who had felt that a member of the senior force should have been put in charge of the new unit.

He now felt that that had been a very shortsighted and foolish position to take and readily admitted to himself that he was beginning to have a great deal of respect for this newly met law enforcement colleague.

* * * * *

Andrea had felt initial unease at the thought of riding within the confines of the heavy west end traffic in the big vehicle, but had determined within a few blocks of travel that Ravi, despite that fact that he gave considerable attention to the road in front of him, was not in the slightest intimidated by its size and drove through the busy arteries with confidence and seemingly little effort.

The quarter hour trip passed without incident and she was completely relaxed by the time Ravi squeezed the Hummer into one of the underground parking stalls in the secure parking lot below the IHIT building.

When he had placed the vehicle into park and turned off the ignition, she turned to face him.

"Thanks for looking after me; I really appreciate it."

Ravi studied her for a second before speaking.

"It was my pleasure…but do me a favor will you. Let's keep it to ourselves. I do my best to keep my private life, private. No one on the job knows how or where I live, and I'd prefer to keep it that way."

Andrea gave him a knowing smile and nodded.

"Sure…my lips are sealed."

Ravi got out of the Hummer and moved to open her door for her. As she stepped out she was for the first time fully conscious of him openly evaluating her body as she moved and she felt the return of the familiar warmth within her loins and breasts that the silk robe had magnified early in the day.

It pleased her that he obviously found her attractive, and she smiled.

"I assume that means that you've never invited anyone else on the job up to your place."

Ravi laughed as he hit the remote to lock the Hummer up.

"Actually, I've never had anybody other than family there... you were the first."

That pleased her too.

* * * * *

The ringing phone woke Phil, who was immediately, as was his habit when his sleep was disturbed, mentally alert and clear headed. Pat Dunne was on the other end of the line.

"Ok Phil it's on..."

A surge of relief filled Phil and he felt himself relax as Pat continued.

"...how about Jim and I drop over and pick you up about seven tonight. We could go out for dinner and discuss it."

* * * * *

Back in the lab, Andrea slipped into a fresh white lab coat and went immediately back to her workbench. She received an update from Sergeant Winters, who then promptly crossed to the wall mounted coat rack beside the door and switched his lab coat for his jacket.

"I've done my part. It's up to you now Andrea. Took longer than I thought, but maybe I can still salvage something out of my Saturday. Make sure you lock up before you go and I'll see you on Monday."

Now in her lab coat, Andrea was instantly all work, Ravi perched himself on a stool behind her and quietly watched as she concentrated fully on the task before her.

CHAPTER EIGHTEEN

Chris, who was impatiently awaiting Ravi's call, had been poor company for a good three hours, and as Janet cleared up the remains of a late lunch and loaded the dishwasher she shook her head.

"For heaven's sake. Instead of moping around, why don't you just give him a call?"

Chris, still seated at the kitchen table looked up from the coffee mug he'd been blankly studying and met her gaze. His strained features softened as he smiled across at her then drained the remainder of the lukewarm contents, before getting to his feet and placing it into the dishwasher. He then gave her a light peck on the cheek before answering.

"Sorry for screwing up your Saturday."

The ringing of the phone cut him off and Janet kissed him back then picked the handset up from its cradle on the counter and handed it to him.

* * * * *

Ravi hung up the phone and turned to face Andrea who was still flushed with the success of the DNA match.

He knew that the match was the clincher on the case and although the accomplishment had been definitely Andrea's, he was almost as pleased by it as she was.

Ravi let her savor the moment for a few seconds then glanced at his watch. Chris had decided to have the take-down team meet at the office at five. That gave him an hour.

"Look, I'd give you a lift home, but I've only got an hour. How about I get a patrol unit to drop you off..."

Andrea thought for a second, and then shook her head.

"No...I'm too wound up right now to go home. I know that this is probably pretty mundane stuff for you, but this is my first successful match on a real homicide case and it's going to take me a bit of time to get back to normal I'm afraid. I wish I could be with you guys when you make the arrest. It would be nice to put a face to this DNA and have the satisfaction of seeing him in cuffs."

Ravi understood how she felt. Although being a part of IHIT had given him the opportunity to build several cases from start to finish, his earlier time as a regular patrol cop had meant that he had on many occasions only been able to provide small parts of ongoing investigations: he had experienced the same feeling that Andrea was expressing now several times in his career.

There was nothing quite so satisfying for a cop as to be able to place the cuffs on a suspect after personally and painstakingly building a case against him from the ground up.

He studied her for a second, and then grinned.

"You know, that just might be possible...I'll be driving the Boss, so I'd definitely have to clear it with him first, but he's going to be very pleased with your match and might agree to let you take part in the take-down as one of the crime scene members ."

Andrea brightened appreciably.

"Do you really think so?"

"Well, you've only been with us for a few weeks and it's pretty early for you to be moving out of the lab for hands on crime scene work, but it would be a chance for you to get out into the field and gain some experience there...and you do have a personal interest in this now.

The Boss is always on about how IHIT is a team and we shouldn't forget how much we depend on the part that the lab and the Forensic Scientists play in our investigations and how we should keep them up to speed and thoroughly immerse them in our investigations from start to finish.

It's worth a try if you really want to go along. He's going to be busy on the phone for a bit getting things set up, but I could give him a call in a half hour and ask him if you like."

*****

Kevin was dumping the empty Chinese takeout containers into the garbage when the phone rang. He picked it up and was surprised to hear Chris's voice on the other end of the line.

They exchanged pleasantries briefly, and then Chris got into the reason for the call.

"That was a good article in the paper this morning; figure that I owe you one. I know that you don't have a paper coming out until Monday morning now, but if you aren't busy tonight, how would you like to observe and record the arrest of the bastard that is responsible for the recent murder-rape of the girl in North Vancouver? Not exactly an exclusive, no doubt some of the facts about the case will leak out to other media before Monday morning, but you'd have the full story and exclusive photos of us taking him off the street."

Seconds after Kevin had hung up the phone he was grabbing his coat.

*****

In addition to contacting the members of his own IHIT take-down team to confirm his earlier heads up call and specify a five o'clock meeting at the office and touching base with Kevin, Chris had made two other calls in rapid succession.

The first had been to the Duty Officer at the North Vancouver R.C.M.P. detachment and the second had been to the Watch Commander at the same detachment.

Having been briefed on the situation, the Duty Officer had immediately arranged for an R.C.M.P. Emergency Response Team to meet the IHIT take-down team at a shopping mall parking lot two blocks from the location they were hitting in North Van at seven o'clock.

The Watch Commander had arranged for two unmarked units to move into unobtrusive surveillance positions in front and back of the house where the suspect was living in a move to back up the one-man unmarked unit that had been dispatched earlier in the day to keep an eye on Fraser's movements.

The Watch Commander, who had put Chris on hold for a moment in order to contact the unit on site, had been able to assure Chris that Fraser was at the location and had been for several hours. He appeared to be alone; the rest of the family had gone out earlier in the day.

Chris was in his car and had almost reached the office when Ravi called him with a request to have Andrea join them on the take-down.

From his perspective she had earned the opportunity and he agreed.

* * * * *

Kevin cursed the call display function available on phones in this modern age.

He had spent a fruitless twenty minutes trying to track down the specific photographer that he wanted with him for the arrest and in frustration had finally put a call through to his editor at home.

Less than five minutes after he hung up from that call he received a call from the apologetic photographer, whose cell had apparently recovered from a drained battery only seconds before, and who said he would be pleased to meet Kevin at the location specified in North Vancouver at a quarter to seven that night.

* * * * *

Since Ravi had left to go upstairs to the IHIT office to get ready for the rest of the take-down team's arrival, Andrea had been attempting to immerse herself in some of the backlog that had built up in her inbox over the past few days.

She was mildly displeased with herself that the thought of going along on the arrest was far too stimulating to allow her to concentrate on anything major, but she took some satisfaction in the fact that, despite her minimal sleep over the past, God only knew how many hours, she felt awake and fully alert.

This was fortified by the realization that she had at least managed to deal with a few simple tasks and that the pile in her in-box was slowly diminishing.

While she worked she found herself repeatedly looking up at the big clock on the far wall, which seemed to be moving at a snail's pace, if at all.

She was still plodding along when Ravi entered the lab.

Andrea swiveled around on her stool at the sound of the door and smiled across at him. Up to now, she had never seen him in anything but a well tailored suit.

"Wow...quite a change. Very intimidating."

For a second Ravi didn't understand. Then catching sight of his reflection in the window across the room, he realized what she meant.

He was dressed for the take-down, all in black; cargo pants, T-shirt, bullet proof vest and jacket emblazoned with the word 'POLICE' in reflective white, front and back. The only part of the gear that he wasn't wearing was the black balaclava that he'd shoved into his jacket pocket before coming down to the lab.

He laughed, raised his arms and did a slow pirouette in the centre of the room.

"My Sunday best…definitely designed to impress."

Ravi dropped his arms to his sides and continued.

"Time to head out. Boss says you can ride over with us if you want, or go in the crime scene van with the forensic team if you'd rather. I told him that you were going to need a lift home when we finish and suggested maybe you should go with us. You won't need to bring anything, all the gear you'll require at the scene is in the van."

Andrea didn't answer immediately, reflecting on the fact that her arriving with the Boss might be frowned on by the other crime scene staff. Their eyes met and Ravi sensed what she was thinking and, while Andrea realized which choice Ravi wanted her to make, she was still weighing the pros and cons when he spoke again.

"The crime scene guys are going to know that you need a lift home after, so they wouldn't think it strange for you to ride over with the Boss and me."

The very fact that Ravi understood her discomfort confirmed in her own mind that she was correct in the assuming that riding with them would be inappropriate.

"I think it would be best if I went over in the van with them."

She could see the brief flash of disappointment that registered in Ravi's face as she spoke and as he opened his mouth to respond, she continued.

"But I'm sure that they would understand if I came back with you and the Boss…needing a ride home as I do."

* * * * *

Darkness had descended, and the sky was heavily overcast. The amalgamation of unmarked police units at the far end of the large parking lot might have gone unnoticed by most of the general public, but even under artificial light the clearly marked crime scene van would have drawn a good deal of attention to the area, so Chris had delegated it to a side street a block away from the mall.

Andrea and two veteran members of the IHIT forensic team, one a photography specialist and the other detailed as the 'exhibit man', both of whom were regular VPF members, were waiting inside exchanging small talk from time to time, but they were mainly concerned with the radio traffic that was taking place on the 'TAC" channel that Chris had specified for the take-down team.

* * * * *

As soon as he arrived in the lot Chris had detailed IHIT's Richmond R.C.M.P Corporal John Bernier to liaise with the R.C.M.P. Emergency Response Team and North Vancouver Mounties who would be taking part in the take down. He didn't want to keep the unit in the lot for any longer than was necessary, as that would make it more likely that their presence might be noticed and thereby blow the exercise.

He gave the Corporal only enough time to outline the plan of attack before he and Ravi, similarly dressed and outfitted, moved over to the group. His gaze flickered from man to man as he approached them and he was pleased to note that he recognized at least three men out of the group of eight that made up the Emergency Response unit, one of whom was the leader.

* * * * *

Pat and Jim picked up Phil in Pat's Caddie Escalade just before seven. Pat had driven only a few blocks when Jim nodded in the direction of a Chinese restaurant whose neon sign was flashing a smorgasbord advertisement in the next block.

"That will do nicely…you guys okay with Chinese?"

* * * * *

Kevin and his cameraman were crammed into the ancient yellow Bug that was surrounded by a small cloud of blue smoke. They pulled into the lot and moved directly across to the parked police units.

Chris caught the movement out of the corner of his eye and recognizing the Volkswagen, excused himself from the group of men that stood in the center of the vehicles and made his way over to Kevin's car as it rolled to a stop.

He addressed Kevin through the open driver's window without preamble.

"Follow my car in and stay put in yours until the door goes in, then go ahead and start taking pictures - but don't enter the house. I'll be going in with the Emergency Response Team, but I'll get back to you just as soon as the cuffs are on. We move in about five minutes"

* * * * *

The Chinese restaurant was busy, but not overly crowded. They were able to find a booth in the back that was out of earshot of the other tables.

All three of them ordered the smorgasbord then they headed off to assess the spread that was on offer before loading up with their individual preferences.

CHAPTER NINETEEN

Having been provided with the layout of the house and the surrounding neighborhood by the surveillance unit on site, Chris had been able to direct each of the individual units that moved in, to safe parking spots close to their specific target positions. The house was covered within a few seconds of their arrival, half of the Emergency Response members covering the back and Chris and Ravi rapidly following the other four up to the front door.

Once they were confirmed to be in position via radio earpieces Chris nodded to the burly young R.C.M.P. member holding the ram and the door went in with a single hit, frame shattering. He and Ravi followed the other four cops as they shot inside, loud shouts of 'POLICE' echoed off the hallway walls as they moved.

Kevin and his cameraman struggled out of the Volkswagen with Kevin shouting at the other man to hurry. A battery of camera flashes illuminated the sagging door and the porch area of the house.

The marked crime scene vehicle pulled up directly in front of the house and Andrea, similarly attired, followed the two white coverall clad men out onto the street.

While they opened the side and rear doors of the van in preparation for the removal of the gear that they would need, Andrea stood to one side of the vehicle.

Her attention was glued to the front of the house. She heard the sound of the first of two 'flash bang' grenades going off as the assault team entered the lower level of the house.

Although it seemed to Andrea like an eternity, it was only a matter of minutes before two members of the Emergency Response Team, each holding one of the suspect's handcuffed arm's, made their way through the hole that had been left by the removal of the door. They were followed by Chris.

Two thoughts crossed her mind as the camera flashes enveloped the scene in front of her in repeated eruptions of brightness.

The first was a result of her first glimpse of the suspect, a very small and dejected figure held firmly between the two big cops who were still clutching their imposing automatic weapons in their free hands.

He seemed so insignificant, not as she had envisioned him at all; she had expected him to look like the monster he was...how could it be that this pitiful little man had committed such a devastating crime?

Then, as the suspect was being handed over to two regularly uniformed Mounties for transport to the lockup, she found herself a little concerned and turned her attention back to the gaping, dimly lit doorway, wondering where Ravi was.

* * * * *

Phil waited in silence as the other two men finished eating.

Pat pushed his plate into the center of the table and raised his cup to his lips for a mouth clearing sip of hot green tea as he surveyed the room around them.

"Ok Phil, why don't you outline your plan again so we can work up exactly what kind of help you will need to pull it off smoothly."

* * * * *

Chris spoke briefly with the two Mounties who had taken custody of the prisoner, then crossed the lawn to the street where his car was parked and popped the trunk open.

He returned both his and Ravi's compact automatic rifles to their racks inside the trunk and locked them into place then selected a pair of plastic wrapped white coveralls and two packages each of similarly wrapped latex gloves and slip-over booties from three of the custom built equipment racks that took up most of the interior of the Crown Vic's trunk. These in hand, he closed the trunk and crossed over to where Andrea and the other members of the crime scene team were standing on the sidewalk next to their van.

He addressed the designated exhibit man.

"I'm going to head into the North Van detachment office and interview the suspect. Ravi will be in charge of the crime scene. He has copies of the warrant. I want any and all computers you find inside seized in addition to whatever else you find, plus I want hair and semen samples for a further DNA match and at least one good set of prints from both hands. Go ahead and get started. Ravi knows what we need. If you have any questions, ask him. Corporal Bernier will be in control of the exterior and will be staying with the crime scene until the owners return. He's going to be taking statements and seizing a vehicle or vehicles for shipment to our garage for forensics."

He turned his attention to Andrea, who had been studying the front of the house but who had now turned to face him directly at the mention of Ravi's name.

"You tag along, Andrea…these guys are two of the best and watching them work the crime scene will be good experience for you, help you to understand how we come up with all this stuff that you are continually asked to test."

Chris held out the gear that he had selected from the trunk of his car toward Andrea.

"Give these to Ravi please. He will be expecting them."

* * * * *

Phil finished speaking and leaned back. Jim glanced from him to Pat and back, and then set his cup down.

"Okay, just to make sure I've got this straight, let me run over it and you correct me if I go wrong."

Phil nodded and Jim went on.

"This needs to happen on a Sunday night because that's when this chap has the exclusive use of the laundry room in the basement to do his washing. He normally spends about two hours down there, from about seven to nine at night, and takes his heroin paraphernalia down with him and fixes while sitting on the couch beside the machines, and then drifts off, enjoying his high while the dryer does its job. While he's doing this he's clearly visible from the street with the use of binoculars, through a basement window. He's a loner, never had anybody accompany him when he does his wash and shoots up... right so far?"

Phil nodded in agreement. Jim continued.

"You'll need to have someone with you to ensure our boy doesn't wake up while you deal with the dryer. Pat has offered to look after that little problem by giving him a second injection with a 'hot cap' of pure Heroin."

As if on cue, Pat picked up the string and continued.

"Our boy will get a high he's not expecting and be comatose in no time. Setting up the wiring in the dryer so that it will start a fire when it's turned on again is something that you can handle by yourself using your electrical knowledge and experience as an arson investigator. We also need to have someone outside to distract old Jimmy during the period that you are setting up, and to act as lookout to ensure that we don't have any surprise visitors. That person will also have to drive you and me to and from the scene without being observed by Jimmy.

He will do that by dropping the two of us off in the back lane. We go in through the back basement door, then he gets hold of Jimmy by phone and arranges a meet a block away to provide him with the usual updated surveillance schedule for the next week, something that is a normal practice on Sunday nights, and in this case has to be done by one of our group to ensure that the timing is right. Larry Tenant can do that, as he only puts in weekend shifts with HROT. He will be working Sunday night and is in fact the man Marshall normally gets to drop off the schedules that he draws up on Friday nights to the working HROT team members, who are currently on assignment. Larry can easily arrange the meet with Jimmy to get him off the surveillance long enough for us to do what we need to unobserved and without raising any suspicion."

The other two men nodded and Jim took a sip of his now lukewarm tea before he resumed.

"Fatal house fires resulting from dryers are common enough to allow this to slip through as accidental if the scene is properly set, but for our purposes we have to ensure that the fire does only two things."

He swallowed.

"Firstly, it has to create enough smoke to do the job for which its intended, and secondly, although we expect the rest of the house to be unoccupied as usual at this time on a Sunday night, we don't want the fire to spread into the upper floors without allowing anyone else time to get out before they are at serious risk of having the fire overtake them. Nor do we want it to get out of control and spread to the neighboring houses. Because you and I will have to leave the basement before the fire gets too big, we will have to contact Larry by phone as soon as you are sure that it's got a good start, in order for him to end the meet and to give Jimmy sufficient time to get back to the front of the house to raise the alarm if necessary.

Then Larry can pick us up in the back lane where he dropped us off and get us to hell out of there. You will have one of the HROT portable radios with you so that we can monitor the channel for any calls he makes regarding the fire. As a backup to ensure that the fire is reported as soon as it's done its job and before it completely engulfs the house, we can call it in anonymously from one of the phone booths located at the next intersection, if Jimmy or someone else hasn't already reported it by that time."

* * * * *

Chris remained at the crime scene only long enough to satisfy himself that it was secure. While waiting, he took the opportunity to speak privately with Kevin away from the bustling police presence, and Kevin made furious notes in his bastard shorthand as Chris talked.

Uniformed North Vancouver R.C.M.P. members had taken over responsibility for control of the exterior, and by the time Chris had filled in the blanks for Kevin, the entire house was ringed with yellow police tape and was manned with sufficient personnel to ensure no one without authorization could gain access to the area.

The Emergency Response Team members had remained on the scene only long enough to ensure an arrest and to utilize a large commercial fan to clear out the remaining fumes resulting from the earlier explosion of the flash bangs. They had already cleared the location. Only IHIT staff remained within the immediate crime scene itself.

Satisfied, Chris, having cleared up a couple of remaining questions raised by Kevin, watched the reporter climb into the yellow beetle to join his photographer and waved as they pulled away.

He then got behind the wheel of his unmarked silver Crown Vic and headed for the North Vancouver R.C.M.P. Detachment where, as he had instructed, he knew he would find Fraser cooling his heels in an institutionally clean, but sparsely furnished and unadorned, interview room.

* * * * *

Ravi was waiting for the IHIT crime scene team just inside what was left of the front door. He nodded as the three of them paused to slip on booties before entering then led them into the living room just off the hallway.

Once they had joined him in the room, he pulled off his heavy outer jacket and laid it over the couch beside him, then stripped off his bullet proof vest and dropped it on top of the jacket.

As he turned around to face them Andrea couldn't help but notice the well-muscled upper body that the close fitting t-shirt, that was now his only remaining article of clothing above the waist served to emphasize, and her eyes sparkled a little as she reached out to hand him the protective crime scene garments that Chris had asked her to give to him.

Ravi, mind elsewhere, nodded his thanks and quickly slipped into the coveralls and a pair of the booties, then opened a package of gloves and put them on before placing the packaged spares into his pants pockets.

He was anxious to get downstairs and was going over in his mind how best to handle the crime scene, and what approach to take to ensure that they got through it quickly but thoroughly. He kept his thoughts to himself making no comment to the others.

The exhibit man and the photographer had slipped into latex gloves as well, and Andrea followed suit.

A few minutes later, Ravi was leading them single file downstairs, with Andrea bringing up the rear, to the lower level of the house where they had located and arrested Fraser.

* * * * *

Pat and Jim dropped Phil off at home just before nine.

Once inside, Phil took the time to give Cecil, who, meowing in greeting, always met him at the door whenever he returned from the outside world, a friendly scratch of greeting. He hung up his coat, flicked on the lights in the living room, and then went directly into the kitchen to pour himself a stiff scotch.

Drink in hand, he took a large slug from the glass before putting it down on the kitchen counter and opening the fridge to retrieve the open can of cat food from the top shelf. He removed the cover and transferred a good sized chunk into a small saucer, which he then deposited on the floor between the cat's water dish and bowl of dry cat food.

Cecil, who had followed him quietly into the kitchen and had watched the familiar process from a few feet away, made no move to go for the food until Phil had left the kitchen to go into the living room.

Phil settled himself comfortably into the big Lazy boy chair that, along with the large screen TV, dominated the room and took another hit from his glass prior to putting it down on the table beside him.

He felt more at peace than he had in months.

He picked up the glass again and savored the taste of the 25-year-old scotch as it filled his mouth.

He knew that over the past few hours he had fully come to terms with the return of his cancer and the resulting realization that every moment of time he had left was precious.

He also knew, without hesitation, exactly how to best spend that time.

* * * * *

Once he had arrived, Chris met briefly with the R.C.M.P. Watch Supervisor in the Sergeant's office at the Detachment.

The response of uniformed members at the house had been well orchestrated for such short notice and he wanted to let the Sergeant know that he appreciated it.

Primarily to reinforce the involvement of the local uniformed police in what was without question a high profile case, which Chris knew would be a good political move, but also to give credence to the thanks he had proffered to the Sergeant for the part that uniformed R.C.M.P. members had played in the successful arrest, Chris was also going to offer the man a chance to be present for the interview.

The obvious delight that registered in the man's eyes when Chris asked him to take part was more than sufficient to confirm for Chris that he had been right to make the overture. He had made a friend here, and the more friends IHIT made in the Detachments and Departments they served, the easier Chris's job became.

It was a little after nine-thirty when he and the Sergeant entered the room adjacent to the interview room and closed the door firmly behind them.

CHAPTER TWENTY

It was just after ten when Mike managed the second check-mate of the night. Roger had gotten the first.

It had been months since they had played chess and each of them had thoroughly enjoyed the evening. There had been little conversation during the play, normally the situation, but Roger had noticed that Mike had begun to relax after the first couple of hours and had, by the end of the second game seemed almost back to his old self.

They had been drinking tea while they played and as Roger began to put away the chess set, Mike moved into the small kitchen of his apartment, fished two snifters out of the cupboard and poured their ritual after play brandies. Roger heard the sound of the microwave indicating that the two glasses of golden amber fluid had been warmed and leaned back into the couch.

As Mike returned to the living room with them, Roger, who knew from past experience that Mike was normally a man of few words, but liked to talk after they had played chess, opened the conversation as his friend put the glasses down on the coffee table between them.

"God I enjoyed that. I've missed our games more than I realized."

Mike dropped into the chair across from him and smiled.

"Me too, seems like since we got started on our little project, we haven't had a lot of time for much else."

Roger nodded as he picked up his glass and cupped it in his hands, and lifted it to his nose to appreciate the aroma.

"Yes, I was saying much the same thing to Pat just the other day. He was telling me that you've been the busiest of all of us lately. I noticed the other night that you seemed to be kind of bushed, you still okay with this stuff?"

Mike sipped from his glass and shifted into a more comfortable position in his chair as he considered the question.

"Yes, I'm okay with it. It's just not as easy as I thought it would be I guess. I know that these guys deserve it and all that and that we are stopping them from hurting more people, but actually doing it is pretty rough, especially when I'm doing it alone. I don't mean physically, no problem there. I've been having dreams about the last one, not sleeping very well. That kind of thing"

"Pretty normal if you ask me. Have you told Pat or Jim about it?"

Mike lifted his gaze to his friend and shook his head slowly.

"No, I want to pull my weight. The two of them do all the planning after all. They do a lot more than I do."

Roger set his glass down and leaned forward.

"I'm sure that isn't how they see it. Okay with you if I talk to them about it? This is a team effort after all. Maybe you should take on a different role for a while"

Roger had been watching the other man's face carefully. It had brightened considerably with his last statement.

"Sure, I could do some of the driving, and I don't mind doing the heavy lifting and stuff. Just for a couple of weeks of so till I catch up on my sleep maybe"

* * * * *

Corporal John Bernier had, with the assistance of two of the outer perimeter R.C.M.P. constables, opened the yellow tape long enough to allow him to back the marked crime scene van into the driveway at the front of the house.

He then opened the rear barn doors of the vehicle and switched on the two bright rear-facing spotlights that were situated on the roof of the vehicle, above the doors. These served to illuminate the area at the rear of the van. He was now assisting the exhibit man to load and secure the substantially growing amount of evidence that was being brought out of the house to the van. To make the task as simple as possible, they were bringing the exhibits through the overhead garage door that gave them access to a small door that led directly into the basement area, where the on-site crime scene segment of the IHIT team had been concentrating its attention.

As each sealed and initialed piece of potential evidence was placed inside the secure metal cage in the rear of the crime scene vehicle, the exhibit man carefully re-locked the cage door. John stood by to ensure that the continuity of the evidence necessary for court purposes wasn't compromised in any way.

The exhibit man had just disappeared back into the garage to return to the basement when John caught the brief flicker of moving headlights in his peripheral vision. He walked to one side of the van and looked toward the yellow tape at the front of the driveway.

He observed one of the uniformed R.C.M.P Constables outside the perimeter speaking to the driver of a red Dodge Caravan that was stopped on the outside of the restrictive tape. Bernier closed and locked the back doors of the crime scene van and moved toward them.

By the time he reached the front of the vehicle, the driver's door of the Caravan was opening and a figure got out, standing to face the Constable. John quickened his pace to join them and as he did, caught the tail end of the conversation.

"This is my house…what's going on?"

John moved to take charge of the situation, pulling his

identification out and illuminating it with his flashlight as he joined the two men by the still open door.

"Mr. Simpson, I'm Corporal Bernier."

John, who had changed earlier out of his take -down garb and bullet proof vest, was wearing a jacket clearly marked 'Police' and a ball cap emblazoned with IHIT above the brim, but his clothing was black and Bernier knew that Simpson would be unfamiliar with it, being conditioned to seeing the khaki uniform of the R.C.M.P., which was standard garb for police who worked the streets in the City of North Vancouver.

He gave the man time to take a good look at his IHIT Identification Card and absorb the information on it. The R.C.M.P. Constable took a pace backward, obviously relieved at having Bernier step in. John pulled out a copy of the warrant from his inside jacket pocket and handed it to the other man.

"We've just arrested your brother-in-law, and I'm afraid your house has to be treated as a crime scene for now. We won't be able to allow you or your family inside until we have completed our work here; you'll have to find somewhere else to stay until we've finished, I'm afraid. We'll also need to take brief initial statements from you and your wife... is there someone that you could leave the children with for a couple of hours?"

Bernier had been carefully studying the other man's face and his body language as he spoke, watching as a variety of different emotions expressed themselves in Simpson's demeanor. He had continued to speak in a soft monotone until he recognized in the other man's features the reaction he was looking for.

Simpson slumped slightly and his mouth hung open limply for a few seconds, then he nodded.

"Yes...their grandmother can take them I guess...I could call."

John held out his cell phone to the other man.

"Here, use my phone. Perhaps at the same time you could arrange for yourself and your family to spend the night with her once we've got your statements out of the way. I think that we should be finished up here by morning and you and your family will be free to return home then."

* * * * *

Chris had years of experience in one-on-one interviewing, and more courses on the subject under his belt than he could count. As a practice, he always observed prospective suspects for a period of time before he joined them in the actual interrogation room and began to question them. The length of time he spent varied each time as each subject was unique.

He and the Sergeant were sitting in two of the three folding chairs facing the one-way glass window that took up the majority of the wall in the small observation room that allowed them to scrutinize the prisoner seated in the interview room next door. The third man in the room was a uniformed R.C.M.P Constable who was overseeing the operation of the video equipment that would be used to record the interview as soon as it got under way.

Although he could sense that the Sergeant was wondering why they had been sitting observing Fraser for over twenty minutes at this point, Chris made no attempt to justify it, and the Mountie said nothing. Chris had learned to trust his gut to tell him when the subject on the other side of the glass was ripe for the picking, and he never hurried the process.

Intently studying the prisoner on the other side of the glass, Chris didn't give the man beside him another thought. Joe Fraser's right leg had begun to bounce rhythmically up and down under the table and a film of a sweat had formed on his forehead under the harsh light. Chris smiled and stood up.

"Right Sergeant...if you could start the tape rolling, I think it's time this piece of shit spilled his guts."

Without being asked, the Constable flipped a switch on the video control panel which in turn caused a small light to turn from red to green, but Chris had already left the room and his attention was on the door just down the hall that led straight into the interview room itself.

Chris noted with satisfaction that Fraser literally jumped as he entered.

He crossed directly to the other side of the table, pulled out the single chair and sat down across from the suspect.

Having left his jacket in the adjoining observation room, he was clad in a black IHIT t-shirt and black cargo pants. The fact that Chris was now fifty-seven years old did nothing to diminish his basic presence.

While not a huge man, his six foot two inch, 190-pound frame was often imposing to others and he was aware of that fact and used it; more important was his ability to exhibit facial expressions that people found very intimidating, something that had served him well over his years as a cop.

On many occasions during his career just his presence and the look on his face as he entered, had been enough to bring a buzzing room full of people to expectant silence.

It was now having the same affect on Fraser; something that Chris was certain would be clearly apparent to the Sergeant inside the observation room next door, even though he would not be in a position to fully appreciate precisely what was causing that reaction in the suspect who was seated on the other side of the table from Chris.

Chris neither met the suspect's gaze nor spoke while he reached down with his right hand to pull his note book from the top pocket of his cargo pants. He dropped it down onto the table between himself and Fraser and slowly opened it to the page he wanted, then retrieved an eight by ten brown manila envelope out of another pocket and placed it unopened beside the note book, before resting both of his hands, palms down, on the desk in front of him.

Fraser dropped his eyes when Chris looked directly at him for the first time since entering the room, and Chris sat quietly waiting for the suspect to meet his gaze. He said nothing until that happened, and when he spoke it was in a deep but soft tone.

"I'm Inspector Chambers of the Vancouver Police, Joe, and although I know that you've already received a warning, I'm going to give it to you again."

Despite the now obvious layer of sweat covering Fraser's face, Chris could see the color drain from it as he gave him the official police warning, and when he had finished he waited for a few seconds before speaking again.

"Do you understand the warning that I have just given you, Joe?"

Fraser nodded slowly his head bowing again so that he was staring not at Chris but at the open note book and brown manila envelope sitting between them on the table. Chris gave it a second then continued.

"I need you to answer yes or no, Joe. If you don't understand it I can give it to you again."

Joe's head snapped up abruptly.

"I understand! I'm not stupid you know."

The expression on Chris's face didn't change, nor did his tone of voice.

"I know you aren't, Joe. Do you want a lawyer?"

"No I don't want a lawyer, why should I want a lawyer? I haven't done anything wrong...I told you, I'm not stupid."

"Okay Joe, no lawyer, but I think you've got some problems that we need to talk about. I'm not going to ask you to answer any questions for now, I just want you to hear me out before we try and get some of those problems off your chest. That all right with you?"

There was a perceptible softening of Chris's voice between this statement and the one that had preceded it. Fraser hadn't noticed it, but the Sergeant had and he had also observed the change in Fraser's posture that had occurred at the same time. The suspect had visibly relaxed and was now sitting more upright in his chair as he answered.

"No questions?"

Chris shook his head and allowed his facial expression to soften a little.

"No...just listen, and hear what I have to say."

Relieved, Fraser nodded.

"Okay."

Chris reached forward and shifted his note book closer to himself, leaving the envelope center-stage. When he spoke his voice was a soft, matter of fact, monotone.

"I'm investigating the death of a young girl; her name was Sandra Rollins."

The words hung in the air as Chris reached for the envelope and picked it up.

He took his time opening it, aware that Fraser couldn't take his eyes off of it, and withdrew several glossy color photographs which he then placed face up in a neat stack on the table next to his notebook.

His eyes met Fraser's briefly, and then he picked up the top picture from the stack and studied it briefly before putting it down squarely in front of Fraser.

"This was Sandra, in her last school picture. She was in grade eight."

Fraser lifted his eyes to meet Chris's appraising gaze. In so doing, he had avoided having to look directly at the picture in front of him.

"Why are you showing it to me? I don't know her."

Fraser badly wanted to look away from Chris's piercing

eyes, but he was even more afraid of looking at the picture. It was a staring contest that Chris couldn't lose and he held it for some time before answering.

"How do you know that you don't know her Joe? You didn't look at the picture."

Fraser sunk slightly down into his chair, bowing his head and covering his eyes with his hands.

Chris picked up the rest of the photographs and laid them out one after the other in a line across the centre of the table just above the school picture, commenting briefly on each as he laid them out.

"...and this is how she looked when we found her...when she was autopsied..."

As Chris had expected, Fraser, unable to face the pictures, refused to uncover his eyes.

"Why do you want to show me these pictures? I told you that I didn't know her."

Chris, who had been leaning forward, swept up the photographs in one swift motion and put them back into the envelope before he tilted back and shrugged his shoulders.

"Because that's my job, Joe. Because you did know her Joe. And because you did this to her. I know that because I have a large amount of evidence that proves you did it. I have that evidence because you made mistakes when you were with her, maybe because you hadn't intended it to go as far as it did, maybe because you had problems with her and things got out of hand...only you know why I have this mountain of evidence Joe."

Fraser slumped even lower into the chair and soft, rippling shudders began to move visibly through his shoulders.

He still hadn't removed his hands from his eyes.

Chris continued his voice barely above a whisper now.

"I know why you can't look at the pictures, Joe. I'm sure that you didn't want this to happen. I need to understand what happened, I need you to tell me what went wrong Joe…what did the girl do that caused you to leave me all that evidence…I really need to know."

Chris had his confession and he knew it. He said nothing as he watched the shuddering shoulders start to rise and fall in heavy heaves and the tears began to slip out from below the covering hands and trickle in streams down Fraser's cheeks.

"She wouldn't stop screaming…she wouldn't stop screaming…she just wouldn't stop screaming!"

Chris flipped open his notebook and pulled out a pen.

"Okay, Joe, just start at the beginning. First tell me how you found her."

Then the damn burst completely and Fraser began to sob uncontrollably.

Chris remained silent, knowing that at this point he couldn't have stopped the eventual outpouring of the entire story even if he had wanted to. It was only a matter of time now. He waited patiently for Fraser to gain enough control to allow him to begin speaking again. It wouldn't take long.

CHAPTER TWENTY-ONE

As soon as Roger left Mike's apartment building and got into his car, he glanced at his watch and then placed a call to Pat who answered on the second ring.

"Pat, Roger, I'm just leaving Mike's and I was right, this is getting to him. Apparently the last one he did on his own and he's had trouble sleeping since. I don't think that he's going to lose it or anything but he could sure as hell do with a bit of a rest."

"Okay, we have been using him a lot. To make things worse the last one he did was on short notice and as you said, he did it on his own. Do you think talking about it with you helped him?"

Roger paused before he answered.

"Yes, I do actually. He has no one really and I guess he hasn't been able to tell anyone he trusts about how he feels. It seemed to do him good to get it off his chest"

"Yes, I know what you mean, since Emily died, I've missed being able to talk things over with her...not that this particular topic would have been one that I'd have probably shared with her, but at least she would have been a around to use as a sounding board. Okay I'll talk it over with Jim and we'll somehow manage to make sure that Mike gets a break for a while."

* * * * *

Once he had ascertained that the suspect had been allowed the use of his sister's vehicle on several occasions, it hadn't taken long for Bernier to scoop the keys and arrange for the red Dodge Caravan to be picked up and towed to the IHIT garage.

He then handed the keys to his own unmarked unit to the exhibit man to pass on to Ravi, who was, now that Chris had gone, without transport, then swiftly arranged to have an unmarked car take the Simpson family off to grandma's house.

He was waiting in the driveway when it returned, minus the two boys, a half hour later. When the vehicle pulled up, John got into the front passenger seat then swiveled to face the couple seated in the back.

Her red eyes attested to the fact that Rosie had been crying and the space that separated the couple in the back seat made it clear to John that it had probably been a good thing that they had not been left alone up to this point, because the husband was staring blankly out of his window, and the anger he was attempting to suppress was registered clearly on his face.

"This won't take long; we just need a short statement from each of you, and the answers to a few questions."

It didn't surprise him that he received no more response from the back seat than a brief nod of acknowledgement from the wife.

* * * * *

Phil left the nearly empty bottle of Scotch on the table in the living room and got up somewhat unsteadily to make his way to bed, closing down the lights as he walked.

He was looking forward to tomorrow. It was going to be a busy day and he wanted to get a good night's sleep under his belt to ensure that he was fresh and ready to do it justice.

When he entered the bedroom, he found Cecil already stretched out on top of his bed. As usual, the cat was strategically positioned in the centre of the bed at the foot. He was fast asleep, and within minutes Phil had joined him.

* * * * *

Kevin knew that he had plenty of time to write up the story on the North Vancouver rape-murder in order to make his deadline for the Monday morning edition.

Despite that fact, he felt a compelling need to get it down while it was fresh in his mind, with the view to reworking it in the morning before he went into the office to go over the photos taken at the scene and personally select the ones that he wanted to run with the story.

At first, as he set to work at his small desk, he hadn't questioned the urgent need to get on with it, and it wasn't until he had everything set up to start that he paused and thought about the reasoning behind the unnecessary haste.

It wasn't because he expected to have to fight for good positioning of the story in the next paper run, and needed extra time and effort to ensure that. The story was good enough to win that battle on its own.

The reason why he was so wound up suddenly occurred to him. It was so obvious that he was surprised he hadn't thought of it earlier.

The Fraser rape-murder story was presenting him with the perfect vehicle to lodge the first segment of the much bigger story on the overall risk to the public by the systematic release of criminals that, even the liberal legal system itself was convinced, would very likely violently reoffend.

Kevin's mind began to work feverishly as he envisioned how the one story could well lead in to the second.

The fact that the Fraser story presented him with a natural launching mechanism for the much bigger story was undeniable. It could easily serve as a direct lead-in to what he had been working on with Marshall.

The quandary was; did he currently have enough background and research information on the bigger story to ensure that he was ready to crank out enough follow-up, meaty, rapid-fire articles to keep up the momentum, if he launched it now; or would he be risking having it become a single 'flash- in-the-pan' piece because he hadn't researched enough to provide the material that would afford him the opportunity to keep the pressure on.

Kevin was aware that the reading public could be very finicky, and was quite capable of losing concern in any specific theme very rapidly if their interest wasn't being piqued with repeated and emphatic infusions of fresh meat. Put simply, the longer a writer could hold the public's interest by fleshing out or expanding a theme, the less likely it was that some new story could grab their attention, and the longer and stronger the original story would play.

Although he knew that he would have to make a decision to go one way or the other with it within hours, he reasoned that either way the Fraser arrest was an important enough story to warrant his baby-sitting it through to the end. He would have done that anyway.

The question he had to answer very soon was: would he would be a fool to ignore the fact that it also presented him with the perfect tie-in to the dangerous re-offenders story that he had been researching of late and was extremely interested in pursuing?

He dismissed any thought of doing prep work on the rape-murder story before he knew which way he was going to angle it.

First, he had to work out in his mind whether he should be framing it in a way that would naturally set up the groundwork for the much larger and potentially explosive story, or just let it run on its own merit and wait until he was better prepared to make the best of the larger story, of which Fraser was a perfect example.

* * * * *

Chris had allowed Fraser to get the rape-murder off his chest without interruption at first, ensuring that his suspect had said more than enough to convince himself in his own mind that he had gone well past the point of no return, before he interjected with direct questions that would serve to tie the confession up neatly.

He had to sit silently through repeat bouts of the initial physical and mental breakdown by the prisoner, but as time went by, these had lessened in intensity and duration.

With a patience learned over years of interrogations, Chris had methodically, in the same soft voice, begun to ask direct questions that, one step at a time served to clarify omissions in the story as he adroitly directed Fraser through the process of reliving the entire horrific incident.

In the adjoining observation room, the Sergeant who had been watching the entire process develop had become so mesmerized by the scene as it unfolded in front of him, that he had entirely forgotten about the contents of the mug resting on the floor beside his chair.

At this point it was not longer relevant, in any case, as the contents had grown cold long before.

* * * * *

It was just after eleven o'clock when the unmarked police unit pulled into the public parking area that fronted the North Vancouver R.C.M.P. Detachment.

Bernier thanked, then dismissed the uniformed driver and led the Simpsons up to the front door of the building. He punched the intercom button in the panel beside the door, and within seconds they had been buzzed inside the lobby area.

The couple followed him like robots, still maintaining the silence between them that had settled in earlier.

John identified himself and spoke with the clerk who had slid back the small window that gave verbal access to the report counter area of the lobby. He arranged to have a Constable come out and take the Simpsons in tow, requesting that they be offered whatever refreshment was available and directing that they be then taken to an area where statements could be taken.

As an aside, he quietly asked the female Constable who'd responded to the request to stay with the couple until he could return to speak with them.

He watched the three of them disappear down a short hallway and through a door then he walked back to the report counter and asked directions to the interview room where Fraser was being interrogated. A few seconds later he entered the observation room next door to it and closed the door behind him.

There was a uniformed R.C.M.P. sergeant seated in a chair in front of the one-way mirror that separated the room from the ongoing interrogation, and the NCO shifted his gaze at the sound of the door closing and gave Bernier a look that clearly indicated he wasn't pleased with the interruption.

John presented his identification for the Sergeant's appraisal and extended his hand.

The look of displeasure on the Sergeants face disappeared and was replaced by a brief smile as he partially stood, took John's hand and shook it. Bernier then nodded in the direction of the one-way mirror.

"Mind if I join you until the Boss is finished?"

The Sergeant didn't answer, but simply indicated the chair bedside him that Chris had been using earlier by pointing to it as he turned his attention back to the scene unfolding in the room on the other side of the one-way glass.

John pulled off of his jacket and then draped it over the back of the chair that the Sergeant had indicated and dropped into it. As he began to watch and listen to the exchanges between Fraser and Chris it quickly became plain to him that, as he had expected, the confession was in its final stages.

Satisfied that the Simpsons would not have long to wait for Chris to be involved in taking their statements, John settled back into his chair and observed as Chris put the final touches on ensuring the completeness of the confession.

CHAPTER TWENTY-TWO

Kevin lifted his hands from the keyboard and stretched his legs, gently rolling his comfortably worn black leather chair back a short distance from the small desk.

His stared at the screen for a few seconds, and then he raised his hands and rubbed his eyes gently before reaching toward the ashtray and the burning cigarette, whose long ash demonstrated the intensity of his previous concentration on the material that Marshall had given him.

He sucked in a deep drag before grinding the butt out and exhaling.

It was going to be a hell of a lot of work, but he had enough to get started, and as long as Marshall kept him apprised of the additions to the list as they came in he was sure that he would be able to keep up the momentum of the overall story for as long as he could hold the reading public's interest.

This topic was going to play well nationally. He would need to discuss the whole thing with his editor and get him firmly onside before he launched it, that was a given, and he had to do that quickly in order to allow him time to make the Monday morning publishing deadline for his own paper and set up national coverage in as many newspapers as possible.

He had a hell of a lot of work to do.

* * * * *

Chris closed his notebook and put it back into his pants pocket, then stood up, reached for the envelope and looked down at Fraser's emotionally exhausted form.

"That's it for now Joe...I may have some more questions for you later."

Fraser gave only a small shift of his shoulders in response. Chris moved across to the interview room door and glanced in the direction of the one-way mirror.

There was a soft buzzing sound and the door popped free of the frame. Chris opened it and then closed it firmly behind him as he left the room. He walked down the hall to the door of the observation room and entered it.

He found John and the Sergeant facing him as he came inside. John was the first to speak.

"The sister and brother-in-law are waiting to give initial statements; I thought you might want to do it personally."

Chris thought for a second then shook his head.

"No, you can do it, but I will sit in."

He turned his attention to the Sergeant.

"I'd like the original tape as soon as you've made a copy."

The sergeant looked over at the Constable who was at the video control panel to be sure that the man had heard Chris's request, and received a nod from him. When he turned back to face Chris, the Inspector continued.

"Fraser's all yours now, Sergeant, lock him up. I would like to keep this to ourselves until the bastard makes his first court appearance on Monday morning. If it can be arranged, I'd like to hold a press conference here at ten Monday morning.

Would you see if your OIC would be willing to take part? John here is our IHIT spokesman and he'll arrange everything necessary for the conference itself, but perhaps your OIC would like to set the stage for the event as it starts. You know the kind of thing, the set up of the take-down team on short notice, etc."

The Sergeant grinned broadly.

"I'm sure he would, sir. I'll call and confirm with him

now and get back to you before you leave, but I'm sure he would."

Chris nodded.

"Good."

Chris then turned to speak to John.

"We'd better get the Simpsons out of the way...it's getting late."

He opened the door to leave, but before he did he turned back to the Sergeant.

"Oh and Sergeant...When you speak to him, would you tell your OIC that I would appreciate it if he would arrange to have you available for the news conference as well...I'm sure that you would be invaluable in helping us field the inevitable barrage or questions from the press."

The Sergeant beamed.

"Yes sir. I'd be pleased to help out anyway I can"

Chris nodded, and handshakes were exchanged then Bernier addressed the Sergeant.

"I'd be grateful if you could arrange for a car to drop the Simpsons off once we've taken their initial statements. Would that be possible?"

The Sergeant didn't hesitate.

"No problem."

After they had left the room and John had closed the door behind them, he met Chris's gaze and grinned.

"Share the glory, eh Boss?"

Chris laughed as they walked.

"Whenever I can Corporal...whenever I can. What goes around comes around."

* * * * *

Ravi waited until the last of the exhibits were safely locked up in the cage in the back of the crime scene van before he closed and secured the barn doors.

The exhibit man, who was already perched in the driver's seat of the vehicle, had turned off the auxiliary lighting on the rear of the van leaving the driveway in front of the garage door, that was now closed, poorly illuminated by the single light situated above the door itself.

Ravi moved to where the wide side door had been pulled open and joined the rest of the team, who were in the process of peeling off their protective outer clothing and dumping them into a garbage bag that sat on the pavement between them.

Ravi reached inside the vehicle to toss his jacket and bulletproof vest onto the back seat then glanced at his watch and turned to face the exhibit man behind the wheel.

"You guys might as well head in to the office and stow the exhibits. It's getting late and we've done everything that couldn't wait...time to call it a day. I'll take Andrea with me...she needs a lift home and I've got John's car to get back to the office. I've had the front doorway boarded up, but I want to recheck the exterior of the house to make sure it's secure before we turn it over to the Mounties. No need for you to hang around any longer."

* * * * *

The Watch Commander was waiting for Chris and John when they finished interviewing the Simpsons and led them out of the interview room. Without speaking he took the couple in tow and turned them over to the female R.C.M.P. member who had been working in the office earlier and who had been detailed to drive the couple home back to the grandmother's place where they had arranged to spend the night.

Once they had left, he turned to face Chris and John.

He grinned as he handed Chris the original copy of Fraser's taped confession.

"My boss will be pleased to take part in the press conference and, although it will cost him overtime which is something that he is a bastard about under normal circumstances, he has ordered me to be present to assist as required."

Chris valued the honesty and he laughed.

"Thank you Sergeant. I appreciate that."

The three men shook hands again before Chris and John left the building. Once seated in Chris's silver Crown Vic, with John behind the wheel beside him, Chris reached for his cell and placed a call to Ravi.

John was rolling out onto the street from the detachment parking lot as the call was picked up. Bernier concentrated on his driving, as he knew that the Boss was particular not only about his car, but also about how it was driven.

He only half listened to Chris's side of the telephone conversation as they headed back towards the Simpson house.

Chris closed the phone and returned it to his pocket.

"Never mind the house. They are in the process of clearing it…take us back to the office and I'll drop you there. It's been one hell of a long day for everyone and it's time to close it down. There's nothing left that can't wait until Monday."

Chris went over the confession process with Fraser in his mind for a few minutes and they drove in silence.

"You won't have any trouble setting up the conference for Monday morning at ten will you, John?"

Bernier shook his head.

"No, I can get that done in the morning. Something this hot, a few phone calls and it's a done deal."

* * * * *

Once she was back into her street clothes and had retrieved her purse from the van, Ravi had taken Andrea over to the dark blue unmarked Crown Vic that had been driven to the scene earlier by John, opened the passenger door for her and asked her to wait until he had spoken briefly with the Mounties who now had the responsibility of protecting the crime scene.

When he returned, he dropped into the driver's seat beside her and shoved the key into the ignition but didn't turn it; instead he turned to look at her.

"I know you must be beat, but I was wondering if you would like to stop off for a bite to eat before I take you home. I know this place here in North Van…great food if you like Indian."

Andrea took a second to consider the suggestion before she replied.

"Well I'm off tomorrow and I don't have any plans, so I can sleep in as late as I want…and yes I love Indian food, so I'd enjoy that very much…but I'm afraid I'm not really dressed for it. We could stop in for a fast food pickup if you are hungry"

Ravi grinned broadly.

"Not to worry. We can use a private room. There will be just us and the waiter. And, I think that I can guarantee you that there will be no problem with what either of us is wearing."

A quizzical expression covered Andrea's face, but she didn't say anything.

* * * * *

Cecil leaped off the bed in a panic as a stabbing chest pain awakened Phil from a deep sleep and he lurched upward off bed and struggled for breath.

Seconds later Phil experienced a coughing fit. He

swung his legs around to place his feet on the floor and struggled to get himself into a sitting position.

He managed to switch on the lamp on his bedside table and yanked a couple of tissues from the box beside it and covered his mouth with one hand while he reached for the glass of water that he kept there at night with the other. He raised it to his lips and was able to get a little water down between bouts of coughing.

He couldn't help but notice the sprinkling of blood that colored the tissue as he removed it from his mouth and his shoulders sagged. The water helped and although it took a few minutes, he was finally able to get his breathing back to some semblance of normalcy.

He sat there quietly for a little longer then glanced over at Cecil who was standing watching him from the doorway of the bedroom.

"Sorry old friend. If it makes you feel any better, I think if scared me a hell of lot more than it did you and I'm afraid it's going to be all downhill from here."

CHAPTER TWENTY-THREE

Kevin was oblivious of the time when he called his editor, and the reception on the other end hadn't been very welcoming initially. However, they were still talking a half hour later, and the tone had changed perceptibly.

He had his editor squarely on side and they arranged to meet at the office in the morning to get things set up for a full fledged story to break in all the nationally affiliated papers on Monday.

By the time he put the phone down, he was charged and any thought of getting some sleep was dismissed out of hand. He had a lot to do if he wanted to be ready for the meeting in the morning and he was so wound up that he couldn't have slept anyway.

* * * * *

Ravi extended his left hand to help Andrea out of the car as he held the door open for her with his right. Andrea took in the front of the restaurant he'd parked in front of as he locked the car, her eyes moved from the impressive structure to the vehicles that were parked near the building.

She turned slightly to face him.

"I don't know about this; pretty high-class and I don't see a car around that isn't worth a small fortune."

Ravi laughed and held out his arm for her to take.

"No fear, trust me."

She accepted the proffered arm with a hint of hesitation and then fell into step beside him. He held the door open to lead her inside.

He paused then indicated one of the expensively upholstered chairs in the large foyer and she sat down in it somewhat uncertainly as he turned and moved across the room to speak to the tux-attired Maître d'.

She noted that the smile didn't fade as Ravi approached the man. If anything it had expanded. Their conversation was brief and Ravi soon returned offering his arm.

It was then that Andrea remembered the name of the restaurant that she'd paid little attention to when she was outside…it had been one word, 'Sharma's'.

She took Ravi's arm as she stood up but held him firmly in place with it as he moved to follow the Maître d' who had crossed to a doorway behind the busy bar.

"I don't suppose that this restaurant happens to be part of the family business too?"

Ravi smiled in response, but said nothing as he turned and led her towards the door that was now being held open for them.

He led her inside and once he had closed the door firmly behind them they followed the imposing, tux -clad form, up a broad, richly carpeted, stairway and directly into a large expensively furnished dining room, with highly polished dark wood walls, dominated by a massive stone fireplace.

As Ravi seated her at one end of the large table in the centre of the room then settled into the chair closest to hers, the tux clad figure moved rapidly and silently about the room.

The fireplace flickered into life and delivered a warm glow to the room almost instantly. The subdued indirect lighting became a little brighter and the muted sound of soft music filled the air.

Andrea was speechless as she took it all in. Her eyes met Ravi's as the tux appeared beside her.

"Your waiter will be here shortly to take your order… would you care for a drink while you wait?"

Ravi replied.

"It's been a long day Mani, but a very good one for me how about we celebrate with a bottle of champagne?"

Andrea smiled and nodded slowly.

"Why not...it's already completely surreal to me. I must be dreaming, and if I am, champagne will fit the bill nicely."

The tux disappeared.

Once the door at the top of the stairs had closed behind him, they were alone. Ravi, who had been thoroughly enjoying her reaction so far, held her eyes with his momentarily, and then he stood up and moved to the back of her chair.

"I'm sure my lady would like the opportunity to freshen up, as would I. The powder room awaits, please follow me."

Andrea waited for him to pull her chair back and then gratefully picked up her purse before following him to a hidden door in the far wall of the room. She hadn't known there was a doorway there; it was constructed in such a way as to be almost invisible unless one knew of its existence.

It opened onto a short hallway with two doors leading off of it. The one on the right was marked with the 'Ladies' insignia. Ravi held it open for her with a smile, then turned on his heel and crossed to its opposite, on the other side of the hall.

Andrea found herself surrounded by dazzling, brightly lit white marble.

As a 'powder room' it was more than impressive, but by this point, Andrea was past the point of being surprised at her new surroundings.

She knew that she wasn't going to be able to do much with her appearance, considering how long she had been wearing the same clothes, and how little sleep she'd had over the past two days, but she welcomed the chance to clean up and do what she could to become at least half-way presentable.

* * * * *

Despite arriving home fairly late, Chris wasn't surprised to find Janet waiting up for him when he got home.

She greeted him at the door, clad in the old robe that she preferred to wear around the house despite his attempts to get her to replace it with a newer model. He'd become resigned to seeing the garment until it literally fell apart.

She kissed him as he finished taking off his shoes and hanging up his jacket in the hallway closet. She then headed into the kitchen, her voice trailing behind her as he followed.

"Kept your dinner in the oven for you...I hope it hasn't dried out too much. Why don't you grab a quick shower and I'll get it out for you. I left a martini in the fridge for you. I'll bring it to you in the bathroom. I'm sure you could use it about now."

Not for the first time in their relationship Chris pondered just how lucky he was to have her; as he watched her walk away, he reminded himself that he didn't tell her how he felt anywhere near as often as she deserved to hear it.

* * * * *

Ravi was already seated in his chair when Andrea returned to the dining room. He stood as she came through the door, and then moved to the back of her chair.

As she crossed the room Andrea noted that a champagne ice bucket was standing between their chairs and that a large, napkin-wrapped bottle was resting comfortably inside.

Once Ravi had pushed her chair in for her he returned to his own and lifted the already opened bottle from its receptacle and filled the two glasses that had appeared during her absence, along with china and silver utensils.

Having finished pouring, Ravi handed her a bubbling glass and raised his in toast. His eyes held hers for a second.

"To getting better acquainted."

Andrea smiled and let her glass touch his briefly. Once they had drunk, he set his glass down.

"I took the liberty of ordering for you, I hope you don't mind. I've arranged for an assortment of dishes, so you will have plenty of choice."

Andrea savored the taste of the excellent champagne briefly before answering him.

"Not at all. I'll be very happy if I don't need to make any more decisions today, I've already made more than my share I think."

Ravi smiled broadly and gave her a wink.

"So does that mean that you trust me to make them for you for the rest of the night?"

Andrea laughed and shook her head.

"On second thought, I may still have to make a few of my own."

Ravi's face took on a more serious expression.

"Andrea, I've really enjoyed your company today, and I want to get to know you better, much better. I'm not quite sure why I've enjoyed it so much, it's all been kind of a whirlwind and a blur, aside from the fact that you are, without doubt, one of the most stunningly beautiful girls that I've ever met, and you are intelligent, articulate, funny, well-read…"

Andrea rested her hand on top of his.

"Ravi let's not move too fast here."

She saw the disappointment register in his face and she continued before he had a chance to respond.

"Don't get me wrong, I know what you are feeling, because I feel the same way. I'm sure that there would be no use in my denying that the physical attraction that I already have for you is extremely strong; strong enough that I'm sure you have already sensed it. It has built up so fast that I quite honestly didn't even see it coming, but we've only know each other for a very short time and it's all really kind of mind-boggling for me at this point. I like you very much, but this is moving far too strongly and quickly for me, and I need time to get to know you a lot better before we start any sort of a relationship. Although, to be honest, it's something that I have a strange feeling might work. For the first time in my life I think I really understand what people mean when they say that a girl has been 'swept off her feet', so please be patient with me until I have had at least enough time to catch my breath."

Ravi was impressed with her honesty and with the depth of feeling that she had expressed. He carefully considered what she said before he responded.

"I think you should know that I feel the same way, although I couldn't have expressed it as well as you have. Suffice to say, I'm very relieved that you don't think I'm a complete idiot for falling for you as heavily and quickly as I have. This has never happened to me before and to be honest I've been scared that I was going to blow it; something that's never even entered my mind before I met you. I'm on virgin ground here."

They laughed together and then Ravi continued.

"Excuse the pun. I'll give you all the time you need, but I would be less than honest with you if I didn't tell you up front that I sincerely dread the thought of having to say goodnight or goodbye to you. I really don't want to be without you at all right now."

There was a soft knock and a split second later two waiters entered the room and began pushing a very large trolley across the room towards the table.

The mood was lost and they made no more than small talk while the numerous covered silver dishes were artfully arranged between them on the table. The waiters worked quickly, uncovering each dish with a flourish before stepping back. The older of the two addressed Ravi.

"Will you be requiring anything else Mr. Sharma?"

Ravi shook his head and they disappeared as silently as they had arrived, and he and Andrea were alone again.

Andrea gaped at the massive amount of food displayed between them and then shook her head in disbelief.

"We are only two people in this room, are we not?"

Ravi took in the multitude of dishes laid out before them and laughed.

"I think that they may be trying to impress us. Mind you, it's nothing compared to the spread they put on when we have family dinners here."

* * * * *

Kevin had been at it for two hours, and the level of the liquor in the bottle that had been unopened when he'd started work was well below the halfway point as was the fresh pack of smokes that had initially joined the bottle when he'd returned to his desk to work.

A pall of smoke filled the room and his astray was overflowing with butts.

Despite the general disarray spread across the small desk, he had managed to separate his notes and the various printed material and information on the dangerous offenders into somewhat ordered piles based on their specific content and was beginning to feel that he had at least reached a good starting point in his attempt to fully understand exactly what he had to work with.

* * * * *

By the time that they had finished eating the main

course and had each selected one of the numerous desserts, despite the fact that they were each stuffed, both Ravi and Andrea were completely relaxed.

The fact that they had both been able to confess their feelings for each other had, without doubt, also helped the process along.

A hovering waiter made a move to refresh Ravi's champagne glass but he held his hand over it and shook his head.

"Not for me...I have to drive, and two is my limit."

He raised his eyes and let them meet Andrea's.

"You can though if you want...you don't have any driving to do."

Andrea, who was already feeling the effect of the three glasses of bubbly that she had already consumed, shook her head.

"No...I think I'll pass. I may not have to drive, but I would like to be able to stand up."

They laughed together as the waiter repeated his by now familiar disappearing act. The good food, drink and the lack of sleep was really beginning to register on Andrea and she had to stifle a yawn as she relaxed into the welcoming warmth of her deeply cushioned chair.

Ravi studied her for a few seconds then chose his words carefully.

"Look, you really are beat...and since you've tentatively given me carte blanche when it comes to making decisions for you for the rest of the night, I have a suggestion..."

Andrea had taken time before saying anything, as if she, too, wanted to choose her words very carefully.

"Could it be that you have some ingenious plan to look after me for the rest of the night?"

Ravi put on his most ingratiating grin.

"Well, now that you ask...only a suggestion mind you,

but my place is a lot closer than yours and you did mention that you have nothing special planned for tomorrow, and I do have a very large Jacuzzi tub...and..."

Andrea cut him off.

"And I'm very much in need of fresh clothes and I don't have a bathing suit to wear in the Jacuzzi, which sounds absolutely wonderful by the way, and..."

Ravi held up his hand.

"Easily solved. I think that I can guarantee a change of clothes and a bathing suit. My little sister, Ana, who is also my best friend and closest confidant, keeps an apartment in the building. Although she's rarely there as she travels a great deal, it is well stocked with clothes. I know she wouldn't mind your borrowing what you need...she's about your size, if I am any judge of it. I've always prided myself on my ability to ascertain the fine points of the female form very accurately, even when clothed. She hasn't been quite as well endowed by Mother Nature in some areas of the female anatomy as you have, but she tends to have various sizes of clothing around because she's continually worried about gaining weight and about having to look her best at all times. Simply solves your problems, don't ya think?"

She was studying him carefully but said nothing.

Ravi decided to strengthen his position before he lost the battle.

"You would, of course, have exclusive use of your own room."

Andrea relented and answered him.

"No pressure?"

Ravi beamed and raised his right hand forming his fingers carefully.

"Scout's honor."

"Alright, but I've got to call and let my parents know that I won't be home tonight. If I don't, they will worry and I'll never hear the end of it. They don't seem to realize that

I'm a big girl now."

* * * * *

It was a good hour before Phil had managed to stop the repeated fits of coughing and was able to begin to breathe comfortably. There were several tissues spattered with blood on the night table by that point.

Cecil had rejoined him on the bed, but the cat seemed unable to settle back down to sleep. He kept watching Phil as if in anticipation of yet another round of coughing and Phil was in no way sure that he wasn't right.

Phil finally felt strong enough to get up and he scooped up the tissues and carried them into the kitchen and dumped them into the garbage, then poured himself a drink before returning to the bedroom with it. He shoved his pillows up against the headboard and sat down on the bed then leaned back against them.

By the time he had finished the drink he was ready to try getting back to sleep again.

CHAPTER TWENTY-FOUR

Once he had the unmarked police unit safely inside the private enclosed garage of his apartment high rise, Ravi helped Andrea out and they crossed to the elevator hand in hand.

He inserted his key into the panel to the right of the big stainless steel door and when it slid silently open they moved inside. Ravi touched a button in the control panel to close the door and they immediately began to move upward.

The elevator stopped seconds later. Ravi lead Andrea out into a wide brightly-lit corridor and crossed directly to a doorway that was marked 200 in polished brass numerals placed to one side of the doorbell pushbutton.

By the time they reached the door, Ravi had already fished out his ring of keys and selected one which he pushed into the lock. The door opened and they stepped inside. He flicked a couple of switches beside the door and the entire apartment flooded with light.

"Go ahead ...her bedroom is the door straight ahead down the hall on the right side. I'll join you as soon as I shut the alarm system down."

Andrea moved down the hall, glancing to her right through open double doors of the living room as she passed. It was expensively decorated and almost as large as Ravi's, but done in a completely different style; modern in design where his was more classic.

She found the bedroom door and opened it. He had joined her in time to turn the overhead light on. Andrea immediately liked the room; it was large, airy and simply but elegantly furnished.

Ravi crossed the room and opened a double door that

led into a large walk in closet and flicked another light switch on.

When Andrea joined him inside the closet, her mouth dropped open. It was a woman's dream come true and she had never seen anything like it. It was huge and stocked floor to ceiling with clothes and shoes of every kind and color imaginable.

"You say that she doesn't spend a lot of time here?"

He laughed and shook his head.

"Only a few days a month…go ahead and help yourself, you probably have a better idea than I do as to what you need."

Andrea was mesmerized by the selection afforded.

"Are you sure she wouldn't mind? There is nothing cheap in here…"

Ravi put his hands on her shoulders and turned her gently to face him.

"Well, I've never done this before, so I can't rely on past experience, and I could give her call and ask her if you are really concerned about it, but she and I are very close and I can assure you that she would tell you to help yourself if she was here with us now."

Andrea still hesitated and Ravi pulled out his cell phone and flipped it open.

Andrea held up her hand to stop him.

"No…if you are sure she won't mind."

Ravi smiled and walked out of the room, his voice trailing behind him.

"I doubt if she'd even notice to tell you the truth, but I will tell her next time I talk to her. I'll leave her a note to let her know. She's going to be back early Monday morning and I'll talk to her about it then.

Check the dressers for swim suits…underwear, nighties and that type of thing, you'll find an assortment of new stuff still in the wrapper if I know my little sister, and I do. This is a perfect opportunity for me to water her plants. I'm already a day behind in my duties in that department and I'm sure to catch hell for it when she gets back if I don't."

Andrea could hear him rummaging around in a cupboard and then the sound of running water filtered into the room.

She sighed and set herself to the task ahead of her.

* * * * *

Retired VPF Corporal Barry Newton pulled on his driving gloves and floored the black GMC pickup.

Although tonight had been the first time that he had driven this specific vehicle; the short trip to the top of the ridge had been enough for him to get a feel for it; after twenty years spent in the Accident Investigation Section of the Vancouver Police Traffic Division, he was very confident in his ability to accomplish the task ahead.

As he entered the sharp right curve at the top of the hill he hammered the brakes causing the truck to slew sideways slightly as it fought for traction on the roadway that was now beginning to reflect the effect of the drizzling rain upon its surface.

A sharp burst of fear filled him just before the truck came to a stop with the left front corner of the bumper lightly kissing the wooden guardrail.

The sensation was short-lived and he showed no outward sign of it as he opened the driver's door and stepped out onto the pavement.

* * * * *

Ravi was surprised to find Andrea still at it when he returned. Before he could open his mouth she raised a finger and cut him off.

"You have absolutely no idea how hard this is...so please, just keep quiet and find something else to keep yourself occupied with while I finish. How about seeing if you can find me a bathing suit? That should keep you busy for a bit."

Ravi laughed and went to do her bidding.

She soon joined him in the bedroom with a dress of some kind draped over her arm. He had finally managed to locate the swim suit department in one of the many dresser drawers, and was trying to make a choice from the considerable colors and styles.

Andrea was able to locate both panties and a nightie which were still, as he had predicted, enclosed in their original packaging. She selected one of each but didn't take the matching bra. She would have to rinse her own out and let it dry overnight, but she could live with that.

Moments later they were stepping back out of the elevator and into Ravi's living room. He helped her out of her coat and hung it up with his own, then turned back to face her. She studied the toned outline of his chest and abdomen under the tight-fitting black t-shirt.

Her gaze was so intense that Ravi spread his arms slightly and gave her a questioning look.

"Something wrong?"

Andrea shook her head slowly and raised her eyes to meet his.

"No, not from where I'm standing, but I'm not so sure that this was such a good idea."

Ravi laughed and raised his right arm, repeating the promise he'd made earlier in the evening.

"Scout's honor!"

Her responding laughter was deep and heartfelt.

They stood there laughing, a few feet apart and feeling quite content enjoying the moment until Ravi broke the spell by shifting his head around to his raised armpit and giving it an audible sniff.

"Don't know about you, but I could sure use a shower."

Andrea nodded and turned around to walk toward the hallway.

"Me too...how about I meet you back here in ten minutes and I'll let you introduce me to that big Jacuzzi tub."

As she walked, she tossed her head then swiveled it back to look over her shoulder at him and smiled.

"You did mention something about a Jacuzzi, didn't you?"

Ravi grinned.

"So I did. Ten minutes, then."

He stood motionless, appreciating the view, until she had disappeared from sight.

Although he had never considered himself an ass man, Ravi had always had a sincere appreciation for a muscular, well formed female ass, and what was moving away from him at the moment, was a very muscular, and well -formed female ass indeed.

* * * * *

Jim Simmons, a cigarette dangling from his lips, appeared out of the darkness to Barry's left, and shone the bright beam of his flashlight into the other man's face.

He held it there.

"You crazy old son of a bitch...you almost went over."

His voice softened slightly as he continued.

"You okay?"

Barry glared at him.

"Right as rain...and if you'd care to remember exactly which one of us is the accident reconstruction expert here, you might just decide to get the hell out of my way. We don't have all night you know. Those forecasted rolling thunder and lighting storms aren't far away…half hour from now this place is going to be hit by one hell of a deluge."

He chuckled to himself.

"Gonna wash this area clean as a whistle, and going to leave a very difficult to read accident scene, I'm afraid."

He climbed back into the truck and held the wheel firmly in position, while reversing about fifty feet, then got out again.   Jim had moved along with the truck on foot and he was beside Barry when he exited the vehicle, leaving the driver's door wide open. He had just left the vehicle when he spotted the taillights inching toward him.

Pat had backed his Escalade up to where they were standing. They heard the tailgate popping open and saw the flash of the interior lights come on as the big door lifted. They moved as one to the back of Pat's vehicle.

Pat joined them and began to remove the plastic sheet that contained the unconscious man.

"Seems so peaceful doesn't he? Quite a surprise for him to find out that the fourteen-year-old boy that he was planning to pick up in Squamish and take up to Whistler for a day of skiing and a night of sex turned out to be us instead."

He voice was laced with grim satisfaction as he continued.

"I'll never forget the look on his face when we identified ourselves."

Between the three of them, they manhandled the limp form into the driver's seat of the pickup and Barry locked the seatbelt into place over the inert, shallowly breathing form. He then pulled the release to pop the hood before he moved around to the front of the GMC.

Pat Dunne who, like the other two, was wearing latex gloves, now moved up to the open door of the GMC. He was holding an unopened bottle of Vodka in his left hand. He reached in and took the man's right hand firmly in his own and wrapped the pliable fingers around the bottle twice, pressing the fingertips firmly each time.

Pat then unscrewed the lid from the full bottle of Vodka and tossed it onto the floor on the passenger side of the truck before lifting the bottle to the parted and listless lips. He poured about half of the bottle down the struggling but defenseless throat, ensuring that the majority of it went down before pouring the remaining liquor down the front of the figure. He then let the empty bottle follow the course that the lid had taken, hearing it hit the floor.

Barry's voice drifted across to Jim.

"You love playing with that damn flashlight of yours so much Jim, how about making yourself useful for a change and bringing it over here.

Jim hurried over to him and held the light where Barry directed watching absently as the other man worked. It took no more than a few minutes and suddenly the engine of the big pickup roared to full power.

Barry took Jim's arm and led him away from the truck over to where Pat was standing, then turned and walked back to close the still open driver's door of the GMC. He climbed up onto the step below the door and reaching through the window to take a firm hold on the gear shift lever.

He glanced behind him briefly then took a deep breath and slammed the lever down into drive then swiveled to get into a position to jump off the truck.

There was a hell of a noise as the full power of the big diesel motor completed its connection to the driveline. The truck seemed to hesitate then grab, sending Barry sailing wildly free of the step, through the air and crumpling to the ground.

And then the truck was gone, making matchsticks out of the old rotten wooden barrier as it slammed through and hurtled out and over the cliff.

Despite Barry's pronounced limp, the three of them piled rapidly into the idling Escalade and were already on their way down the hill before the GMC hammered itself into the sharp, ragged outcropping of rock three hundred and fifty feet below, exploding in a blinding flash before rolling forward and dropping another fifty feet to land on the railway tracks below.

CHAPTER TWENTY-FIVE

Andrea came back into the living room only ten minutes behind schedule. As she entered the room she found herself somewhat self-consciously clutching the front of the robe which, despite the bikini beneath it, was having the same affect on her nipples as it had earlier in the day.

Ravi was standing in front of the fireplace. He was dressed in a robe made of the same color and material as hers, but in a more masculine cut. The rich, golden brown of his skin contrasted starkly with the material.

The effect of it wasn't lost on her and she felt her nipples register a new hit of stimulation.

Ravi smiled at her, then walked over and offered his hand. Andrea hesitated for a second, and then took it and as she did, she noticed Ravi's gaze drop briefly to a single well defined nipple.

He openly appreciated the view for just a second, then let his eyes meet hers, smiled and led her down the hall toward the master bedroom.

* * * * *

The Escalade pulled to a stop in Barry's driveway.

Jim picked up the small pile of slip-over booties that they had removed after wearing them at the scene of the accident, and tossed them into the back of the SUV on top of the plastic sheet in the cargo area, then got out the passenger door and turned to assist Barry out.

By the time he had pushed the door shut Pat had joined them and they each took an arm and helped a now badly limping Barry toward the front door.

Once inside the house with the door shut behind them Pat raised his voice from the mumbling monotone that he had been using all the way from the SUV to the door to a blistering pitch.

"Stupid ass! You think you're twenty years old or something? Could have broken your damn leg!"

He glanced from Barry to Jim.

"Here, help me get him over to the couch. I'd better have a closer look at him; don't think his ankle is broken, but he's sure as hell sprained it badly."

* * * *

Andrea, still clutching the front her robe, watched Ravi as he bent over to adjust the jets of the big Jacuzzi to his satisfaction and then get up to light several candles in the corner of the room, before dimming the overhead lights.

The illumination from the two spotlights built into the walls of the tub below the bubbling surface highlighted the effervescence given off by the powerful jets and created a beautiful effect on the walls of the entire room, which was in near darkness.

The storm had rolled in over the city and the floor to ceiling glass wall across from the tub began to showcase an impressive thunder and lightning performance for them.

Andrea's nostrils picked up just a hint of a lavender scent wafting across from the surface of the tub and she took in a deep breath to savor it as Ravi crossed to her and reached out to open the belt at the front of her robe.

She moved her hands to his.

"Before you do that, I wanted to have a word with you about this bathing suit, or should I say lack of it, that you picked out for me."

Ravi let a smile form on his lips.

"What... you don't like the color?"

Andrea frowned and kicked him lightly in the shins with her bare foot...

"It's not the color that's the problem, and you know it. It's a beautiful shade of blue, but I do think that I might as well be wearing nothing at all in view of the miniscule areas of my body that this suit almost manages to cover."

Ravi fixed his eyes on hers and pulled the belt open in one swift motion.

Her robe gaped slightly down the front and he dropped his eyes.

"Well, I thought you weren't interested in making any more decisions today, but if you feel that you might as well be wearing nothing, I certainly won't argue."

He tilted his face toward hers unhurriedly and waited for her to move up against him to complete the kiss.

It seemed a long time before he felt her arms slip around his sides to pull him closer against her. His tongue began to investigate, probing ever so gently into the interior recesses of her mouth.

When he lifted his lips from hers he stepped back and used his hands to gently push her robe off her shoulders.

"Tell you what, since you seem to be considering going back to making decisions again, how about you decide on whether or not you want to play 'you show me yours and I'll show you mine' with me. I've never considered wearing bathing suits in a hot tub as being very cool."

Andrea tossed her long hair back and smiled up at him.

"Could this be considered 'applying pressure', do you think?"

Ravi shook his head.

"No. I'm not being one damn bit demanding...it's only a suggestion."

Andrea pressed her lower body firmly against his and began to rotate her hips slowly.

"I wasn't talking about what you were saying...I was

talking about this."

She increased the pressure of her body against his a little as she moved and he let out a deep groan as his eyes widened in arousal.

"Well, I am only human you know."

She tilted her head back and stood up on her toes to kiss him lightly on the lips. He felt her fingertips slide down and inside the front edges of his robe and push it off his shoulders, then he felt a deliciously tingling sensation as they began to move slowly down his sides and into the waistband of his trunks.

"Okay, I'll play your game, but I'm not going first."

Despite the very noticeable bulge in the crotch that was providing quite a formidable barrier to any downward movement she was able to shove his trunks down to his knees in one smooth move. They lingered there for a moment, and then Ravi bent slightly to push them past his knees and down to his ankles.

Andrea moved her hands behind her back and then swung the bikini top up over her head and dropped it. Ravi was stepping out of his bathing suit as she bent forward slightly to push her brief bikini bottom down and off.

As she did, she got an eyeful of at least one of the reasons behind Ravi's reputation for being both very confident and very much in demand with women.

She rationalized that it probably wasn't the only reason, but she thought it just might be one of the bigger ones.

* * * * *

Pat completed wrapping the tensor bandage around Barry's ankle and clipped it into place.

"Now, before you go to bed ice it for about twenty minutes, and then rest it for twenty and repeat. Do that until some of the swelling comes down then go to bed. Give me a call in the morning and tell me how it's doing."

Jim came into the living room carrying two ice packs and placed them on the coffee table where Barry could reach them.

The two of them then said goodnight to Barry, and left.

They had only driven a few blocks when Jim spoke.

"You don't think that we might be doing too much too soon, do you?"

Pat glared across at him.

"Little too late to be wondering about that, don't you think?"

Jim was quiet for a few seconds then he shrugged.

"What the hell…if anyone is going to get away with it, we are. They've got all these new fangled training and forensic investigative methods, but that isn't going come out on top when it's preempted by all the knowledge and experience our people have."

The rest of the drive to Jim's house was completed in an uneasy silence.

* * * * *

Andrea was lying on top of him in the tub.

They had both been very content to share nothing more than slow lingering kisses for almost forty-five minutes as their hands roved over each other, in leisurely exploration of new territory.

Both were highly aroused when Ravi pulled himself slowly up out from under her and then took her gently under the armpits and lifted her into a sitting position on the heavily cushioned edge of the Jacuzzi.

Then, facing her, he slowly dropped down in front of her until his knees rested on the bottom of the tub.

As he moved, he kissed first her nose, and then her lips before slowly paying homage to both of Andrea's firm breasts, giving extra special attention to each of her engorged nipples.

Andrea was moaning softly and he heard a sharp intake of air as his lips began to move lower, down over the firmness of her flat belly, his tongue working in small tantalizing circles all the way.

His downward progress began to slow as he shifted his hands to the insides of her knees to gently part her thighs and expose the silky treasure dwelling between them.

Ravi was pleased to find that Andrea too choose to shave that area and he paused for a few seconds to appreciate her artistry with a razor with his eyes before he lowered his mouth to her again.

There could be no doubt in Andrea's mind as to where that deliciously sensuous tongue was headed and, growing impatient, she reached for his head and firmly guided him there.

Her arousal had already built to a feverish pitch by his gentle, sensuous foreplay.

She lasted only a matter of minutes, once Ravi's tongue began to move, working determinedly upward in a slow flicking motion to finally settle directly on his swollen, engorged target and immediately got down to some serious work on it.

Her shrieks of pure pleasure and the hammering shudders that he could feel reverberating throughout her taut body as she climaxed coupled with the powerful tub jet directing a forceful stream of water directly over his stiff member was a powerful enough combination to bring Ravi over the edge with her.

His body tensed and his head rolled back as he let out several deep moans of pleasure and exploded into the churning water below.

It took them a long time to come back down to earth, Ravi held her until she stopped shuddering and went limp, then he got to his feet, scooped her up in his arms and stepped out of the tub. He stood her up gently as he reached for a big bath sheet and began to rub her down with loving care.

After her powerful sexual release, the total exhaustion that was a result of the past two days of sleep deprivation hit Andrea like a ton of bricks.

By this point she was completely drained both emotionally and physically.

Ravi recognized the fact and he let her use him for support while he toweled her dry.

Once the towel had done its job, he scooped her up into his arms again, and then took her out and through his bedroom then down the hall and into the room that she had used for her short nap earlier in the day.

He cradled her easily in the crook of his right arm as he pulled back the bedding with his left, then he laid her down gently and covered her.

He paused to look down at her, then reached over and picked up the remote from the bedside table and used it to close the drapes over the expansive wall of glass and the now less intense flashes of lighting that lashed through the darkness beyond.

Andrea hadn't even opened her eyes as he carried her to the room and once in bed she immediately cuddled down and gave a deep sigh of contentment. Ravi smiled as he watched her, and then crossed the room to the doorway.

He switched off the bedroom light and closed the door behind him without looking back.

CHAPTER TWENTY-SIX

A sharp pain shot through his ankle each time he shifted positions in his sleep, ensuring that Barry Newton had a restless night. He finally gave up trying to sleep at six in the morning.

He sat on the edge of his bed and unwrapped his bandaged ankle to look at it, then reached for the TV remote and flicked the set on.

The ankle was still badly swollen, but it didn't look as bad as it had the night before. Satisfied, he glanced up at the TV screen and it immediately held his attention.

Barry stiffened slightly as the news camera zoomed in from the top of the cliff to show the freight train stopped below. He tried to pick out the few remaining pieces of the truck that were situated in various locations just off the track itself, and then hit the remote button to take the mute feature off.

The sound of the unseen anchorwoman's voice filled his small bedroom.

"...hit the remains of the pickup truck which had apparently gone off the roadway above and plunged over three hundred feet before hitting the rocks below, bursting into flame, and coming to rest on the tracks early this morning. Police have not released the name of the deceased occupant of the vehicle, and at the time of this report believe that there was only one person in the truck when the accident occurred.

They also suggest that alcohol, excessive speed and the poor road conditions brought on by last night's heavy round of thunderstorms may well have been contributing factors.

The engine that hit the remains of the truck suffered

little damage and there were no injuries to the crew brought on by the emergency braking of the freight train itself. This incident brings to three the number of accidents recorded this month on that section of the Sea-to-Sky highway, and Whistler residents have once again voiced their displeasure at the slowness with which this treacherous section of the roadway is being upgraded..."

Barry hit the mute button again and laughed before observing to himself.

"Yep...'nother one of them damn accidents all right. Bloody road is a deathtrap"

He ignored the flickering TV screen and looked back down at his ankle, his thoughts moving to other things.

He hoped he had a couple more ice packs in the freezer. If not, he'd just have to wrap up some ice cubes in a plastic bag and towel and use that until his thawed ones from the night before had a chance to refreeze.

He chuckled to himself as he remembered Pat's remark from the night before, and he mutter to himself as he pushed up off the bed carefully and hobbled across the room and into the hallway, heading for the bathroom to shower.

"Ya...I should call him now. I'm sure that he would appreciate that."

* * * * *

Ravi awoke, stretched and raised his arms up to cup his hands under his head and raise it slightly off the pillow.

Normally when he woke in the morning, he was immediately active, getting straight out of bed and starting into his routine, but flashbacks of the night before filled his mind this morning and he found himself smiling as he stretched and took a few minutes to relive the excitement of it. He glanced over at the clock.

It was only six thirty, which meant he'd only gotten

about four hours sleep, and yet he felt complexly rested. He considered looking in on Andrea, but aware of how exhausted she had been when he put her to bed, he was sure that she would sleep for some time yet.

He rolled out of bed and pulled on his robe before grabbing a clean towel from the stack in the bathroom and heading for the elevator.

A few minutes later he was moving across the heated garage to open the door that lead to the room containing the lap pool. Once inside he draped the towel over one of the lounge chairs by the door and took off his robe, which he hung on one of the hooks affixed to the wall behind the chair.

He stretched his lithe body then dove into the pool and began to swim.

* * * * *

Two uniformed R.C.M.P. traffic members were standing and talking behind yellow tape at the top of the cliff, overlooking the still stationary freight train below, when a supervisory SUV rolled up and a Sergeant got out and crossed over toward them. They turned to face him as he stopped on the outside of the tape.

"You guys almost done here? We got a shitload of calls back-logged, Sunday and all."

The older of the two Constables responded.

"Ya...just the report to do and that shouldn't take long. Not much to tell. Hit the corner too fast and lost control, left plenty of rubber on the road trying to save it, but slewed sideways and then went straight through the barrier. He simply ran out of road, short and sweet."

"Identify him yet?"

The second Constable shook his head.

"Not at positive yet...ran the plate and it's registered to a Fred Kowalski. We've collected what was left of the body, but there wasn't a lot and what there was, is burned to a crisp. Doc figures he might be able to use teeth, but guesses that it will probably require a DNA match to insure positive identification. There is also an outside chance that they may be able to lift some prints from a vodka bottle that was found mixed up with some of the wreckage. Not likely that it was in the truck when it went over and somehow managed to make it through the ordeal unscathed. It was probably dropped down by the tracks awhile back, long before accident, but it could have been in the truck when it went over and if so we might get a break there."

* * * * *

A bleary-eyed Kevin, his editor, and the cameraman who had been assigned to the Fraser take-down scene were gathered around the small boardroom table situated at one end of the editor's office.

Coffee mugs were interspaced between the two articles Kevin had brought with him and the photos of the house in North Vancouver.

They were on their third pot of coffee for the morning, and no one had as yet commented on the fact that Kevin had liberally fortified each of his refills with a shot from the bottle of rye that he had brought with him and whose remains rested on the floor beside his chair.

Contained in a folder sitting on the empty chair beside Kevin were the five additional articles that he had roughed-in and that would be the basis for the stories which would be used as daily follow-up pieces on the larger story.

This gave his editor an understanding of how the story would flow and guaranteed that he would have at least six days of coverage in the initial stages and ready for the national side of the situation.

The Fraser piece would run front-page on Monday morning and it would contain several tie-ins with the overall story, the first installment of which would also be a front page participant on the first day. After that, its positioning would depend on what kind of public reaction the day before had generated.

* * * * *

Andrea stretched lazily in the big bed, and then rolled over onto her back.

The room was dark and she luxuriated in the feel of the comfortable bed for a few minutes staring blankly upward at the dimness of the ceiling as she let her mind drift back over the Jacuzzi experience of the night before.

It had been the most intense sexual encounter that she had ever experienced. She had never been more exquisitely and completely satisfied by any of her previous lovers.

She could still feel the remnants of the warm glow of it coursing through her body as she took the time to mentally relive it with relish.

She pulled the bedclothes tightly around herself, then letting out a soft sigh, closed her eyes and smiled.

She needed a shower, but she felt completely relaxed for the first time in days and strangely secure. She wanted to savor the moment, and was in no hurry to let it pass.

* * * * *

Barry's phone rang at half-past nine, Pat was on the other end. Much of the bluster had gone out of Barry after a night of pain and little sleep, and he was no longer using rose-colored glasses to minimize the seriousness of the injury when Pat asked him how it was.

After a short exchange it was clear to both of them that Barry would have to remain on the sidelines as an observer of their endeavors for a few weeks until the ankle had healed.

The group was, for its own protection, a small one and any time someone was unable to take an active part, their ability to function overall was somewhat hampered.

The experience and expertise that each man provided to the group was as individual and specialized as the man himself and it was their ability to cover the varied causes of death as experts that made each of their targets sure and easy prey, without risk that their deaths might be recognized for the murders they were.

* * * * *

Ravi dumped his damp towel into the laundry chute in his bathroom then shrugged out of his robe and hung it up on the hook on the back of the door before moving back into his bedroom and selecting a pair of sweatpants from the walk-in closet.

He pulled them on and paused for a second, considering on whether to check on Andrea to see if she was up, but decided against it and went back through the bathroom to the exercise area on the opposite side.

Thinking of Andrea brought a smile to his face and he let his mind move back over the time that he had spent with her on the previous day as he started his normal daily exercise regimen, almost robotically.

As he worked out he wondered how he would react when he saw her again this morning.

By the time that he had gone to bed the night before, he had recognized that he was no longer uneasy about the strength of his feelings for her. It wasn't that he had nailed down exactly what it was about her that made her different from the other women that he was been attracted to, that was something he had yet to do, but the whole concept seemed less important to him now.

Instead he had somehow come to terms with the extremely strong attraction that he felt and was beginning to be comfortable with it and subsequently comfortable with her.

Would their overnight separation affect the chemistry he felt for her? Would he still feel the same way as he had when he went to sleep the night before?

He speculated on how she would feel about the intense sexual contact that had taken place before he had put her to bed. There was a very strong and mutual animal attraction between them; the hot tub session had left no doubt about that in his mind. The question was how she was going to deal with that fact. Did she feel more, as he did, than just raw lust? Would she just take it as a great one-night stand? Was she going to be interested in more than that?

He was a little surprised that he gave a damn one way or another. That was something new for him, and yet he no longer lacked the confidence at being able to deal with that type of scenario.

It had become too damned important to him to broaden the relationship, and he had no intention of letting it go that route without a fight.

He wanted more than just good sex from this particular girl, a lot more.

He was glad that he had not slept with her the night before, although the thought had certainly occurred to him at the time.

The fact that he had not woken up beside her this morning had given him a chance to make a sober and honest evaluation of how he felt before he found himself face-to-face with her again.

He had no way of knowing how she was going to react when they did meet again, but he was thankful that, by not taking her into his bed, he had provided both himself and Andrea a cooling-off period. It had given them time to come to terms with how they felt about each other without the obvious complication of awakening beside each other in the same bed.

He was secure now with his feeling about her and wanted the chance to develop a deeper relationship. He knew that at least, from his point of view, the sex part of it was no longer the driving force behind the attraction.

* * * * *

After speaking with Barry, Pat had a left a message for Jim to call him. The call came through about fifteen minutes later.

"Sorry I missed your call, I was outside having a smoke."

Pat wasn't surprised but let it pass.

"I talked to Barry and I was right, the ankle is badly sprained. We aren't going to be able to count on him for at least a couple of weeks. I just wanted to touch base with you to confirm that we have nothing that I might not know about planned that will require him over that time frame."

There was a pause and then Jim answered.

"No. Not unless something urgent presents itself, which is something that seems to be happening a lot lately."

Pat laughed.

"Yes, I know what you mean. Okay, I just wanted to make sure in case we had to find someone to fill in for him in a pinch. Shifting Mike and Phil around and now with Barry laid up; things could get a bit sticky."

* * * * *

By the time she had finished her shower, Andrea had conflicting thoughts about where she was heading with Ravi.

Despite the fact that she had no regrets about what had happened in the hot tub, she was displeased that she had allowed it to get to that stage so quickly in their relationship.

She had been slightly attracted to him from the first time

they met, but had thought she had recognized that attraction as the same sort she had had before, purely physical in nature. In the past, these had rarely led to anything more than short term sexual contact.

That part she understood. What she didn't quite understand was the other feelings that had been building up over the past day.

She had found that she enjoyed his company, that he made her laugh often and continually impressed her with his intelligence, confidence and unbridled enjoyment of life.

And yes, she was impressed with his lifestyle; it was hard not to be.

What she felt for him at this point was a great deal more than just sexual attraction. What she didn't want at this point was to ruin the chance of developing a burgeoning long-term relationship by allowing it be overshadowed by a spontaneous race to satisfy a mutual lust.

She wanted more than just the sex part of it from him at this point. She liked being around this man, and that made her feel vulnerable. She wanted to explore the possibility of a solid and lasting relationship with him. Did he felt the same or was simply in it for the sex?

The more she thought about it the more she wondered if she was envisioning more for their relationship than he was prepared to offer. Had she read the signals right or was she in for a let down? She was a little apprehensive to say the least…this was all happening far faster than it should have been, and although it was admittedly very exciting and stimulating, it was also triggering an emotional overload for her.

As she put on the negligee that had been at the bottom of the bed and then pulled her robe on, she realized, for the first time since getting up, that she had thought of nothing but Ravi since she opened her eyes that morning. That did nothing to reduce her anxiety at the thought of seeing him again.

For the second time since getting up she considered doing her makeup, but decided against it.

She wanted to be as honest with him as she could from this point on; makeup seemed a form of window dressing somehow. She wasn't sure why, but it was important to her that Ravi like her for herself, not for whatever adornment or plumage that she could manage. She wanted to ensure that things were as simple and basic as she could make them before she exited the bedroom.

As she left the room and moved down the hallway she heard the metal clang of shifting weights coming from the direction of the master bedroom. She took a deep breath before moving in the direction of the sound.

CHAPTER TWENTY-SEVEN

Ravi was stretched out on his back on the weight bench when Andrea knocked softly on the door frame then entered the exercise room. He lifted the bar back up and let it settle into its rack, then rolled forward into a sitting position.

A thick sheen of sweat covered him and Andrea reacted appreciatively to the sight of the glistening droplets adhering to the dark expanse of hair that covered his toned chest and solid six-pack abdomen.

His sweat pants had absorbed their share of moisture as he'd worked out and were clinging to his muscular thighs and legs tightly, leaving little to the imagination.

As Ravi waited for his slightly labored breathing to settle back to normal, he let his eyes rove from her damp hair to her bare toes then he stood up to face her. He was instantly aroused mentally and he felt the inevitable physical reaction commence.

He shifted his eyes away from her before her affect upon him could become obvious to her as well.

"Good morning, princess. How did you sleep?"

Andrea raised her eyes up to meet his and watched as he stood, picked up a towel from the rack and used one end of it to cover the front of his body and his growing erection while using the other end to wipe the sweat from his face and chest.

"Very well, thank you."

Ravi turned away and tossed the towel into the laundry chute while swiveling his head around to look at her over his left shoulder.

"You must be hungry. Just let me grab a quick shower and I'll see what I can whip up for breakfast.

Why don't you see if you can find some music that you

like? There's a pretty good selection in the entertainment centre in the living room. You'll find the remote on the coffee table, press the green button and it will open the panel for you. I won't be long."

Andrea nodded, and gave his rear view one last appraising glance before she left the room.

* * * * *

Kevin sat down at his laptop as soon as he got home and poured himself a drink. He was tired and knew he should be catching up on his sleep, but this story was really coming into focus for him now and his mind was full of ideas about how to flesh it out and increase its impact.

It had been a long time since he'd felt this way about a piece and past experience told him that he would have to get it down while the thoughts were fresh in his mind or he would find himself cursing himself later.

As he worked, he began to seriously regret that it was a Sunday and impossible for him to check on various points that needed clarification.

He started to make a list of questions on the scratch pad next to his laptop, carefully noting beside each the specific individual he needed to contact on each point, come the morning.

* * * * *

Ravi had been as hard as a rock when he entered the shower. After adjusting the temperature to his satisfaction he soaped himself up and immediately began to stroke himself to relieve the tension that had built up in his gently aching balls.

Finding himself aroused when he woke up in the morning was nothing new to him and he often satisfied the need while having his morning shower, but the intensity of his pressing desire brought on by seeing her for only a few moments did surprise him a little.

He didn't think that it would be particularly intelligent to have to spend breakfast with Andrea with a hard-on that wouldn't quit, especially since it was now his aim to impress her with a desire to let their relationship expand into something more than just sex.

He certainly didn't want to come off to her as some kind of sex maniac with a one track mind. He did what he needed to do to settle things down then scrubbed clean and stepped out of the shower and began drying himself.

* * * * *

Phil awoke a little groggy and not well rested by any means, but at least the earlier bouts of coughing had seemed to have passed and he was thankful for that.

He showered, dressed and headed into the kitchen, but once there found himself staring blankly into the open fridge. He knew he should be hungry but nothing seemed to appeal and he finally gave up, shut the door and settled for coffee.

As he went about making it he realized that he hadn't been much interested in food of late which was probably why he was losing weight. In the back of his mind he knew that it was probably part of the whole lung cancer scenario and that he should probably be forcing himself to eat if only to keep his strength up.

Despite that fact, he still settled for just coffee.

* * * * *

When he had finished drying himself, Ravi returned the bath sheet to its hook then, naked, crossed the room, entered his bedroom and went into the closet.

He began the process of selecting clean clothes and then,

remembering that Andrea had no clean clothes to wear, reasoned that she would be more comfortable about the situation if they were both in robes. He went back into the bathroom and took his robe off the hook on the back of the door and put it on.

When he entered the living room, she was standing in front of the large entertainment centre that had been revealed when she had opened the panel that concealed it from view.

She had a CD case in one hand and the remote in the other and when she heard him come in she turned and held them out to him.

"I'm afraid that this is a little too complicated for me."

Ravi chuckled and relieved her of both. Within a few seconds the soft strains of a classic instrumental filled the room.

It fit the mood and he gave her a thumbs-up and smiled, then he pressed two buttons on the remote and the lights went out as the curtains covering the glass wall slid silently open to allow in the natural light of an overcast day.

Ravi grinned, bowed and waved her in the direction of the next room.

"Let's see what we can find in the kitchen, shall we?"

She led the way and Ravi watched her move as he followed.

"I eat a pretty light breakfast; what about you?"

She looked at him across the island which was in the centre of the kitchen.

"What would you usually have?"

He shrugged and crossed to the massive two door stainless-steel combination freezer and fridge and opened the right door.

"Well, probably fruit and yogurt, and coffee, of course."

Andrea could see that the fridge was well stocked and when he lifted a large bowl of fruit salad for her inspection, she smiled and nodded enthusiastically.

"Sounds wonderful! I'll make the coffee; where do you keep it?"

Ravi placed the bowl on the large island then opened one of the cupboards behind her and pulled out a canister and filters, which he then placed beside the coffee maker on the counter. Having done that, he took the yogurt from the fridge and set it beside the bowl, then added cutlery and dishes before pulling out two of the upholstered stools from beneath the island.

"Okay if we eat in here. Closer to everything"

Andrea, who had by now figured out how to operate the coffee machine, was adding water as her first step in the process of getting the brew underway.

"Sounds good."

They worked silently, each with their own tasks and moments later they were sitting side by side, enjoying their food.

Any apprehension that they had individually felt at facing the morning together had quickly melted away. Neither of them felt a need to talk as they ate, other than to comment on how well the combined fruits complemented each other.

There was no awkwardness. It was as though sitting and eating breakfast together in matching robes was the most natural thing in the world.

* * * * *

Chris, as usual on a Sunday, was ensconced comfortably in his Lazy-boy in front of the TV watching a football game when the phone rang.

As Janet, who normally answered the phone when he was into a game, was out doing some shopping with a friend, he picked it up on the third ring.

"Chris, Ken Fisher. I hate to bother you at home on a Sunday..."

Chris, who was always on call for any new IHIT case, had expected just that. He was relieved to find out that the call originated from Fisher, who at one time had been Chris's partner on the street and was an ex -VPF Inspector who had moved into the position of Deputy Chief in Delta. This call would obviously have nothing to do with a new case that might require immediate action on his part.

He pushed the mute button on the remote but let his eyes follow the play on the screen as Fisher continued.

"There is something I'd like to bounce off you."

Chris put the remote down and leaned back into the chair.

"Bounce away."

I don't know whether you know it or not, but Ravi Sharma wrote the Sergeant's exam last month. Anyway, he's passed, and the selection board has placed him on the shortlist for one of the two positions that are open. He's really junior but he's got a very impressive educational background and although he's only had limited experience on the street, he's preformed way over standard out there too. Added to the experience he's getting with IHIT, he seems pretty likely to be picked for one of the positions. Problem is that if he accepts it, the boss will want him to come back out here and provide you with a new Detective as a replacement."

He paused for a breath.

" When I spoke with Ravi after his appearance before the board he made it quite clear to me that he was enjoying working with you very much and I'm concerned that he might pass up promotion if it means that he has to come back here in order to take it. I don't know if you are as enamored with him as he is with being there with you. But if you are, I was wondering if you might consider giving my Chief a call and letting him know that. The Chief is pleased to have one of our guys as part of the IHIT team and a call from you might be enough to convince him that Ravi should be promoted in place with you at IHIT; that is, if you could use another sergeant and think that Ravi is ready to take on some additional responsibility?"

Fisher paused, obviously expecting some feedback.

Chris closed his eyes for a second and let the suggestion rattle around in his mind before responding.

"Well, I'd be lying if I said he wasn't a damn good cop and one of IHIT's best assets, and I am short a Sergeant at the moment. It would be a hell of a waste to see him pass up the opportunity for promotion if it can be avoided, and I can replace a Detective Constable a hell of a lot easier than I can a Sergeant... besides my driver is supposed to be a Sergeant anyway. Tell you what, you let me know when he's been confirmed for one of the openings, and I'll give your Chief a call and see what I can do."

* * * * *

Once they had finished eating, Andrea helped Ravi clear away the dishes and rinsed them in the sink before handing them to him to load into the dishwasher. That done, she took their mugs over to the coffee maker and poured fresh cups as Ravi returned the unused fruit salad and yogurt to the fridge then used the dish cloth to wipe down the island. He then rinsed out the cloth and hung it to dry.

"Let's take those into the living room. We'll be more comfortable in there."

Andrea followed him out. Ravi crossed to sit on a big couch across from the fireplace. He bent down to lift the lid on a silver box that rested in the centre of the coffee table, removed a pair of coasters from the box and placed them on the coffee table in front of the couch then sat down. He pointedly patted the soft leather beside him as she placed the two mugs that she had been carrying on the coasters.

She studied him for a second before she responded to his

obvious invitation to sit beside him.   Ravi gave her his best smile and raised his hands in the air.

"I'll be good."

Andrea laughed.

"You proved that last night, and don't you dare say 'scouts honor'; that didn't seem to help much then."

He joined her laughter and patted the couch beside him again.

"No really, I just want to talk and what happened last night is as good a place as any to start."

Andrea dropped down onto the couch beside him, curling her feet up under her and wrapping the robe around them in one smooth motion.   She reached for her mug and took a sip before turning to face him.

"Yes, we do need to talk, I think. This past twenty-four hours or so seems to be a bit of a blur.   I don't want you to think that it was in any way routine for me to act the way I did last night...I don't normally melt and become putty in a man's hands like that."

Ravi took her hand and raised it to his lips to kiss it softly then held it in his, letting it rest against his leg.

"I didn't think you did, and I'd like to be able to say that nothing like that has ever happened to me before, but I wouldn't be being honest if I did. I've had lots of quickies on the spur of the moment, some of them in the oddest places, but I can say that I've never felt that strong an attraction for any woman in my life and I would have loved to have it last forever."

His eyes locked with hers as he continued.

"I don't regret what happened but if I had to do it over again. I would probably have waited. I want you to become a more permanent fixture in my life, and jumping into sex that quickly probably wasn't the best way to demonstrate that to you. But at the time it seemed so natural that I doubt that I could have resisted the opportunity if I had wanted to. I think you have somehow bewitched me completely, princess."

He seemed genuine. She thought for a second.

"Why didn't you put my negligee on when you put me to bed?"

Ravi was a little taken aback by the question. He managed a nervous laugh.

"Well to be truthful, I peeked in on you when you were napping yesterday, just to see if you were okay and you had pushed the covers down a little and I couldn't help but notice that you were naked. I concluded that you preferred to sleep nude."

Andrea laughed and shook her head slowly.

"I thought that maybe you were in a hurry to get out of there in case you changed your mind about me sleeping by myself. After all, the hot tub sex was definitely one sided...not that I'm complaining by the way."

Ravi laughed.

"Well, there was that...but to be honest, the Jacuzzi sex wasn't as one-sided as you might think. Going down on a girl, has, quite frankly; always been an enjoyable means to an end for me, and nothing more.

However, in your case, I found the whole experience of feeling your body racked with shudders of obvious and intense ecstasy as hot as hell and personally, very satisfying. All of a sudden it was no longer a means to an end but became a unique and complete sexual experience in itself."

His eyes moved to hold hers and he smiled.

"With you, just enjoying that I was responsible for bringing pleasure became paramount. I found it so hot that it brought on an involuntary explosion of my own. Believe it or not, last night's Jacuzzi was one of the most unique and satisfying sexual experiences that I've ever had."

Andrea laughed and squeezed his hand.

Ravi leaned forward slowly and touched her lips with his. He kissed her softly, but briefly, and then leaned back as his features took on a more serious composure.

"No shit, girl. It was astounding, without a word of a lie."

He let his words sink in for a second.

"So how would you like to spend your day? I should probably take the unmarked car back to the office and pick up the Hummer at some point and, if you like, I can take you home when I do. Other than that I've got nothing on my plate. Now that you're back to normal and ready to make your own decisions, I'm at your service - you in a hurry to get home?"

Andrea shrugged.

"I'm in no hurry; but I have no clean clothes to wear."

He smiled, pleased that she wanted to stay.

"No problem, you can take your pick from my sister's stuff."

This time it was Andrea who leaned forward for the kiss, and it contained a good deal more passion than the one he had offered her earlier.

When their lips parted she took a deep breath, and despite the fact that he had shifted his position slightly, she had not missed the pressure of his growing erection.

Without embarrassment, she glanced down at the considerable tent that had formed in his robe and gave a little shrug.

"I was kind of hoping we could just hang out here... I still think that I owe you something for last night, even if you seem to think that it wasn't all that one-sided. You did say that you were 'at my service' didn't you?"

Ravi had to admit that he'd said exactly that... and he had always prided himself on being a man of his word.

His eyes followed her as she stood up and undid the belt of her robe then turned to face him as she took it off and let it drop to the floor.

The sight of the brief and sheer negligee that was now all

that covered her immediately caused the tent in the front of Ravi's robe to lurch upward and expand.

Andrea studied its increased volume with anticipation as she dropped to her knees on the plush carpet in front of him. Her hands busied themselves with the tie of his robe and then she moved them down to rest on his legs, just above the knees; for a second before she spread them apart slowly.

The robe opened down the front when his legs moved and as it did, Andrea reached for him. Ravi let out a deep guttural groan and his eyes closed as she began to fondle him.

"Wow... you are a very big boy. I hope I can handle this."

Ravi hoped so too.

His head rolled back against the top of the couch and his hips lifted slightly off the soft leather in an involuntary response to the sensation that filled him as Andrea bent her head.

CHAPTER TWENTY-EIGHT

Ravi's groans of pleasure, now interspaced with her softly muffled moans, had become deeper and more labored as he moved his hand to her shoulder and caressed it briefly before moving it to cup the back of her head and begin to gently guide Andrea as she experimented with her ability to handle his impressive size.

Andrea moved her hands back to him, one firmly holding the base of his shaft while the other gently cupped and massaged the now blissfully aching contents of his constricting sack.

Ravi had had more than enough blowjobs to be able to read by her actions that Andrea was unquestionably enjoying what she was doing and sharing in his pleasure.

He opened his eyes and looked down to watch her work on him, something that instantly increased the growing sensations of pleasure that he was experiencing.

Sensing that she felt no urgency or desire to end it quickly pleased him and caused him to appreciate and reflect upon her eagerness to please him.

It filled him with enveloping sexually charged warmth that he had rarely experienced before while having sex and intensified his enjoyment.

He lost himself completely in the exquisite sensations that were radiating out from his groin and moving in sharp, pleasure filled spasms throughout his body.

His head rolled back against the top of the couch and he closed his eyes again. He closed his mind to the outside world and concentrated solely on relishing the overwhelming enjoyment of each new pass of her eagerly swirling and surprisingly talented tongue.

* * * * *

The two Constables who had investigated the accident on the highway earlier in the day were in the detachment working on reports when the Sergeant came into the room. He held up a sheet of paper and smiled.

"They got prints off that Vodka bottle. We can now confirm that your victim was one Frederick Arnold Kowalski and you should see the record on this bastard…likes little boys, it seems."

He handed the sheet of paper to the older Constable, who began to read.

"Just released a short while ago. Jesus, would you look at this record. Multiple convictions for sexual assault on boys…what in God's name are these people at Corrections high on that they allow an animal like him back out onto the streets to do it again?"

The sergeant shook his head and shrugged.

"Served his full sentence according to the printout of his record, so they didn't have much choice. Anyway, thanks to his little trip over the cliff he won't be having another opportunity to screw up some poor kid's life."

The younger Constable looked up from the report he had been punching into the computer keyboard and laughed.

"Yes, an accident like that is hell of a way to go I wouldn't wish it upon anyone, but in this case, all things considered, I'd consider it as long overdue payback."

* * * * *

Andrea felt Ravi's muscular body begin to tense.

His hand, which had been urging her further and further downward on each pass, left the back of her head and she opened her passion glazed eyes to look up at his contorted features as he huskily struggled to get the words out.

"Holy fuck, princess…I'm going to explode…"

He had barely managed to get the warning out before the building convulsions of his body made it visually apparent to her that he was about to climax.

Andrea didn't have much time to make her decision. For the first time in her life she didn't back off.

Instead she took him into her mouth as deeply as she could and as he heaved up off the couch with a tremendous groan her soft moan intensified.

The instant that Ravi's body reached the pinnacle of its upward arch, he reached for the back of her head again with both hands and held it firmly as he slid deep into her throat and crested.

Andrea's hands moved under him to cup his muscular buttocks as they began to buck and she hauled him tightly up to her.

To Ravi it seemed to go on forever, but finally he was completely drained. He collapsed back down onto the couch, covered in sweat, exhausted and struggling to regain his breath.

* * * * *

Kevin dropped his pen onto the pad that now had a full two pages of notes and then reached for his burning cigarette and took a final drag before putting it out in the overflowing ashtray.

He drained the remnants of his glass and leaned back in his chair as he stretched and stifled a yawn.

He was finally satisfied that he had drained his mind of all it could offer and decided to call it a night and climb into bed. He was excited at the prospects of the day to come and now that he had satiated the familiar but irksome demand that he get everything he could down onto paper before he called it quits, he wanted to be fresh in the morning and was ready to climb into the sack.

* * * * *

Despite the fact that he had masturbated just prior to joining her in the living room, to say that it had been good for Ravi would have been the world's biggest understatement. He struggled to catch his breath, so he could tell her how he felt.

"Oh my God, baby, that was outstanding. Jesus you've drained me in more ways than one, I'm wiped out."

As Andrea stood, he used the last of his strength to reach up to her and pull her down into his lap. His lips found hers and held them for a long time.

When they finally came up for air she beamed down at him and smiled.

Ravi opened his eyes and took a couple of shallow breaths.

"God...I'm still shaking like a leaf. I'm not sure if I can even move."

He didn't miss the twinkle in her eye as Andrea tossed her long hair and reached for his limp right hand which she then moved between her legs and pressed tightly against herself.

She began to rotate his hand slowly. Her eyes closed and she moaned softly, letting the delicious sensation of his now gently stroking fingers fill her for a few seconds.

"I was kind of hoping that we might manage to move to the next level...after all, we're even now and I'm sure you can feel just how ready I am"

Ravi smiled up at her and let a single finger slide gently inside. It had no difficulty making it all the way home. He began to stroke slowly and was immediately rewarded with a deep moan of delight.

"Just give me a few minutes, princess, and I'll see what I can do about that"

Andrea reached for his still fully erect cock and encircled

it with both hands, one above the other, and then squeezed none too gently.

Ravi's head rolled back slightly and he groaned.

"Easy, princess. That's a pretty sensitive piece of equipment at the moment...it may take a bit before I can manage a repeat performance."

Instead of answering him she stood up and, still holding him firmly with her right hand pulled him up off the couch and started to lead him out of the room and down the hallway toward his bedroom.

"Oh I think that I can manage to find a way to get some more out of this big guy."

Ravi had feigned a halfhearted resistance up to this point, but what Andrea's hand held in a firm grip told her that it was nothing more than a game at this point. As if to confirm her tactile assessment, Ravi grinned broadly and slapped her playfully on her well-formed ass as he thrust his hips firmly ahead and Andrea picked up the pace perceivably.

"I've been told before that I've been led around by the nose on several occasions in my life, but I've got to admit that this is a first for me."

Andrea laughed and squeezed playfully.

"And one heck of a lot more interesting, I'm sure."

* * * * *

They had decided to all meet at Pat's place to go over the preparation for the planned evening's event, as his was the closest residence to their final destination.

Larry Tenant, who was the only one who was not already familiar with the scenario, was the last to arrive, joining them a few minutes after five in the evening.

By that time the others had prepared everything that they would need to complete the event and all that was left to accomplish, was to bring Larry up to speed on the part that he was to play in the scenario.

Each of them had a lifetime of experience in the planning and coordinated execution of complex police operations behind them and they treated the current situation in a calm and organized manner.

There was a touch of excitement and anticipation to be sure, but not even a hint of hesitation about getting the job done.

* * * * *

It was just after seven when Ravi, who was gently stroking Andrea's back and firm buttocks with both hands, and was spread-eagled below her on his back in the centre of the rumpled and sweat soaked king-sized bed, glanced over at the clock.

Andrea, who had collapsed on top of him after reaching the last of her orgasms, was gently nuzzling his neck with her tongue, moving it in small circles to pick up droplets of perspiration.

Each gentle, moist stab sent little shivers through his body and he let out a soft moan as Andrea clenched her muscles around his still deeply embedded organ one last time.

Her entire frame heaved rhythmically as she worked at catching her breath.

Both exhausted and completely satiated for the moment, they drifted off to sleep in that position.

* * * * *

Larry Tenant had picked up Phil and Pat in the lane at the rear of the house within seconds of their call and they were just entering the intersection containing the phone booths they had intended to use to report the fire if it became necessary, when they heard old Jimmy come on the air and call it in.

Larry looked over at Phil, who was sitting in the passenger seat, and grinned as he gunned the car through the intersection.

Four blocks later they met the first of the fire rigs coming at them from the opposite direction. Tenant graciously pulled his unmarked unit over to the curb and stopped as they screamed past, while being overtaken rapidly by an ambulance with all its emergency equipment operating.

* * * * *

Ravi opened his eyes and remained as motionless as he could as he turned his head to glance at the clock on the bedside table.

It read nine-fifteen. He let his head roll back and smiled as he looked down at Andrea's head, nestled in the centre of his chest.

Her long dark hair, slightly matted from their earlier exertions, framed her face and she was breathing deeply and contentedly as she slept.

He couldn't resist lifting his hands and letting them gently rove over her naked back and down to cup the cheeks of her magnificently formed ass.

Andrea let out soft sigh and opened her eyes as she shifted her head to look up at him.

"Mmmmm…that feels very nice."

Ravi smiled and released then re-cupped the now clenching mounds firmly in his palms and pulled her tightly against him.

"Yes, they do. But, I'm afraid its time for us to get the car back and get you home. If not, we might have a rather tough time explaining our arrival together at work in the morning."

Andrea gently rubbed her cheek against the mat of dark

hair covering his chest and she let her lips encircle one of his nipples and darted at it with her tongue briefly.

"It might be worth it."

Ravi laughed and rolled over; taking her with him, then stretched his arms out and raised himself slightly to look down at her. As he did, he slipped out of her. She grimaced and moaned softly as she grasped his ass trying to pull him back inside but it was too late and Ravi grinned broadly.

"I'm pretty sure that we are in agreement about that right now, but in the bright light of morning when we got the office, I think that we might be having some second thoughts about that."

Andrea gave his muscular ass cheeks a squeeze and frowned.

"I suppose you're right."

* * * * *

The grey unmarked police unit containing four members of the VPF 'Gang Task Force' slipped out from its parking spot and dropped in at a discrete distance behind the silver Mercedes SUV.

Its headlights didn't come on until the Mercedes had rounded the corner and briefly disappeared from view.

The cop in the passenger seat of the car keyed the mike that was fixed to the collar of his bullet-proof vest and made a brief broadcast.

"They are on the move, west on Broadway."

Each of the two other GTF units working that night acknowledged the message and quickly moved into position on roads that allowed them to parallel the SUV's progress.

* * * * *

Pat sat in his living room just before ten o'clock, waiting

impatiently for the late night news broadcast to commence. He raised the bottle of Perrier to his mouth and took a swig as the familiar face of the female news anchor appeared on the screen.

The fire was the lead story. Pictures of the scene filled the screen as he listened to her voice in the background. The fires crews were in the mop up stages at this point and a pall of thick smoke still hovered around what remained of the house.

"...not know yet what caused the fire, but have confirmed that it started in the basement laundry room of the house..."

Pat turned up the sound slightly and leaned back into his chair still cradling the bottle of Perrier in his hand as he watched the screen intently.

The picture had changed and was now showing a reporter speaking to a uniformed Assistant Fire Chief who was standing in front of a fire engine that still had its emergency lights flashing.

"We understand that a body has been found in the basement area near where the fire apparently started. Are there any other people unaccounted for?"

CHAPTER TWENTY-NINE

Ravi drove the unmarked unit out of the underground parking area of his building and pulled easily into the relatively light Sunday night traffic. He was driving with his left hand only, hesitant to release Andrea's hand from the warm grasp of the other hand.

They were still feeling the warm fuzzy remnants of the pleasure that they had shared earlier in the shower when he had succumbed to her urgings and taken her yet again, none too gently, entering her from behind and hammering her body powerfully against the glass shower enclosure door until they had reached an exciting simultaneous climax.

They were both very relaxed and found no need to talk as they simply lost themselves to the silent enjoyment of each other's company.

The intermittent broadcasts coming over the police radio were the only sounds filling the car.

* * * * *

The three occupants of the Mercedes SUV, all currently out on bail on weapons charges, were well know to the GTF members shadowing them, and information provided via phone taps had strongly indicated the occupants of the vehicle were on their way to carry out a hit on a rival gang leader.

That the gang members in the Mercedes would be heavily armed was a given, and each member of the GTF was suited up with vests and carrying automatic rifles.

They had been waiting for an opportunity like this for months; adrenalin surges brought on by the excitement and anticipation filled the occupants of all three of units that were involved in the tail of the Mercedes.

If the intelligence was correct, they expected to be travelling across Vancouver and into Burnaby before the SUV reached its target, and they were playing the surveillance carefully, rotating the tailing unit every few blocks by radio in the hopes of escaping notice of its occupants.

* * * * *

Pat waited until the anchor had shifted to the next story before he reached for the remote and turned the TV off.

So far, so good; it had gone to plan.

He knew that the investigative team of fire and police personnel would work through the scene of the fire overnight and wouldn't come up with any more information for the public until afternoon the next day, at the earliest.

While the results of that investigation would either confirm the death as accidental or not, from what he had seen so far, Pat had no reason to expect anything other than the outcome they had planned.

It had been a busy weekend and he was tired. It was time for bed.

* * * * *

It was ten twenty-five when Ravi pulled the unmarked unit into the curb in front of the well kept house that Andrea had directed him to. She leaned across and her lips found his. They kissed softly for a few seconds then the embrace began to grow more passionate.

Andrea's hand had found his growing member through his pants and Ravi pushed her away gently and let out a guttural moan.

"God, Princess. Keep that up and I'll drive you back to my place."

Andrea gave him gave him a final squeeze, smiled and

kissed him again lightly, then turned and opened her door.

Ravi watched her as she closed the door and moved up the walkway toward the front step, appreciatively taking in the swinging hips and well-outlined ass in the snug fit of his sister's pantsuit that Andrea had chosen to wear home.

He waited until the door closed behind her then paused for a few seconds to relive the bliss of the past several hours before he put the car into gear and began to head back to the office to pick up the Hummer.

He spoke out loud to himself as he automatically reached to increase the volume of the police radio slightly.

"This girl is a keeper, Ravi old boy…please God, if you exist, help me not fuck this one up."

* * * * *

The Mercedes pulled into the curb in the affluent Burnaby neighborhood and switched its lights off. The GTF vehicle tailing had anticipated the move and, its lights already extinguished, slipped silently into the curb a half block behind the SUV.

The passenger in the police unit keyed his mike and advised the other two units to move into position on opposite ends of the block. The waiting began.

At ten forty-two the headlights of a black Lincoln Navigator turned onto the block and proceeded toward the primary GTF police unit.

You could cut the tension in the air with a knife, as the four occupants of the vehicle locked their eyes on the progress of the vehicle, and as it passed the Mercedes there was a brief flicker of light as the passenger and rear doors of the SUV opened briefly to allow all but the driver to exit the vehicle.

The Navigator turned into the driveway of a house on the right and the overhead door on the garage began to lift, sending a burst of light out onto the driveway.

The outline of two darkly dressed and balaclava-wearing figures were clearly illuminated by the light, and in reaction the police unit launched itself out from the curb with a screech of rubber and rapidly closed the distance to the Navigator. The cop in the passenger seat began to broadcast.

Either unaware of the moving police car or too concentrated on the job at hand, the two figures raised their automatic weapons and began to rake the Navigator with automatic fire, concentrating on the shadowy outline of the driver that could barely be made out behind the dark tinted glass of the driver's door.

The quiet neighborhood was filled with automatic weapon fire as the four cops burst free from the confines of the police car screaming 'Police' before opening up on the two shooters with their own weapons.

The Mercedes' lights came on and it pulled from the curb and shot past the end of the driveway and around the still running, open-doored police unit that had so recently dislodged its four occupants.

While this was happening, the remaining two GTF cruisers raced toward the driveway. The driver of the Mercedes spotted one of the units coming down the block towards him with its emergency equipment operating. The SUV lurched to the right and careened over the curb onto the sidewalk, managing to evade the police car before hitting the road again and taking a sharp right turn.

The GTF vehicle screeched to a stop and began to burn a one hundred and eighty degree turn in the tight confines of street as the cop in the passenger seat switched the channel on his radio and began to broadcast.

Ravi was about twelve blocks away when the call for assistance and a description of the Mercedes came in. He reacted instantly, hammering his foot down onto the accelerator and taking a sharp left at the next corner.

He had driven only three blocks when he spotted the

Mercedes coming toward him at high speed.

He hit his equipment and his unmarked unit lit up like a Christmas tree and the siren screamed. As he brought it to a rubber-burning stop crossway in the road, his bullet proof vest slipped off the rear seat onto the floor.

The driver of the SUV used one hand to press the switch for the power window and floored the potent vehicle as he clutched the wheel tightly in his other hand.

Window down, he used his now free left hand to reach across for the 'Mac 10' machine pistol lying on the passenger seat.

The gun was a favored weapon among gang members, being both small and light, and, when machined to full automatic as this one had been, rained lead when activated.

He shifted the gun outside the window and steadied the barrel on his driver's side mirror before pulling the trigger as he closed on the police unit.

A hail of bullets raked the windshield of the Crown Vic as the Mercedes hit it squarely on the right front fender.

Ravi's mind registered the sound of the automatic fire over the roar of the SUV's engine a split second before his windshield shattered under the impact of multiple bullets, but by that point it was much too late for him to react.

* * * * *

Andrea was just climbing into her bed when the two vehicles impacted and erupted into a massive fireball.

CHAPTER THIRTY

Three rounds had entered Ravi's chest but were not instantly fatal. The two that caught him in the face were.

He died shortly after midnight.

The driver of the Mercedes, who had not been wearing a seat belt, was ejected out over the top of the inflating air bag and through the windshield of the SUV on impact. The result was a nearly complete decapitation, and by the time he landed in a crumpled mass onto the buckled hood of the Crown Vic, he too was dead.

The first marked Burnaby R.C.M.P. unit that reached the scene of the collision had been diverted from the emergency response to the scene of the frantically reported gang shooting and VPF GTF incident.

It took several minutes for it to reach the scene of the burning vehicles, and the young constable behind the wheel was in no way prepared for what she found when she finally arrived.

Her voice was shaking with emotion as she reported the incident to her dispatcher. The quiet night air soon filled with the screaming sirens of the emergency vehicles responding to her frantic calls for help.

Although she recognized the Crown Vic as a police unit, she had no way of knowing what exactly had taken place and it wasn't until over an hour later that her supervisor was able to garner the fact by running the license plate, which in turn led to the VPF and allowed him start to make enquires as to whom had been operating it.

As Ravi had not been the member to sign the vehicle out originally, it wasn't until nearly one-thirty in the morning that Chris got the call from the IHIT duty Sergeant, Gordon Clark, and by that time most on duty members of the VPF were aware of what had transpired.

Chris had a hard time accepting the news.

Clark had to patiently go over it three times before Chris responded. When he did his voice was choked with emotion and the Sergeant could barely understand him.

"Meet me at the scene; I'm leaving now. Sergeant, I want you to see to it that a full complement of our team is there when I arrive. I don't want him surrounded by strangers...is that clear?"

It was an order, not a request, and although Clark knew full well that there would be little real purpose in IHIT's attending at the scene, he knew just as surely that he'd better ensure that the order was carried out.

After he hung up Chris sat on the edge of the bed staring at the phone blankly until he felt Janet's anxious hand on his arm.

He gave a helpless sigh and turned to face her and the deeply etched grief registered in his features deepened her concern.

She had not seen this type of reaction from him in years and it frightened her...it was as if he had instantly aged by ten years.

"What is it...what's happened?"

* * * * *

Sergeant Clark dialed frantically for fifteen minutes and finally satisfied that he'd reached everyone he could, he returned the now sweat-coated hand unit of the phone to its cradle and quickly grabbed his coat off the hook by the door and headed down to the IHIT garage to get a car.

He knew that Chris was closer to the accident scene than he was and although he had awaked his boss from an obviously sound sleep might have a slight edge on him. He was going to do everything in his power to arrive there before Chris did.

* * * * *

Chris managed to make it two blocks before his eyes begin to fill blurring his vision.

He pulled his unmarked unit over to the curb and shoved it into park and remained there for several minutes before he was able to shed enough of the emotional pain to get himself under control enough to drive.

Violent death was even more commonplace to Chris than it was to most cops who, like him had over time steeled themselves to take it in stride, but the death of a cop always hit hard and when it happened to someone you worked closely with, that police bond of 'us against them' came into play and it took a tremendous emotional toll.

Over the past year Chris had probably spent more waking hours with Ravi than he had with Janet.

He had been his mentor and, within the confines of the police structure, his friend and almost surrogate father.

Ravi's death had hit Chris very hard. He needed a few minutes alone to begin to deal with it.

* * * * *

Kevin was roused out of a very deep sleep by the ringing of the phone.

It took three rings before his mind was finally able to grasp the meaning of the sound and struggle to rise into a sitting position on his bed.

Ten minutes later the little rusty yellow Bug crawled out of its underground parking spot and, with a single dark blue belch of oily smoke, made it onto the street and headed for Burnaby.

Kevin had his scanner on, but the police radio was strangely quiet. He gave it a couple of bashes to satisfy himself that it was still working as he shoved a cigarette into his mouth and fired it up.

* * * * *

Phil was suffering through another coughing fit. It seemed like an uphill battle, but he was less panicked by this round and he effectively used water and tissues to bring it under control. Cecil had a leapt off the bed when the bout commenced but by this point seemed to be accepting the sessions as inevitable, and he soon returned to the side of the bed where Phil was sitting as he slowly regained his breathing, and peered up at him.

When he felt able to walk Phil stood up, grabbed one of his pillows and a blanket off the bed and made his way into the living room. He dumped the articles onto his Lazy- boy and then went into the kitchen and poured a drink. Taking a good slug as he returned to the living room, he then extended the chair and dropped into it resting his head against the pillow and wrapping himself in the blanket.

He figured that he had a better chance at sleep sitting up, even though he knew he would find it hard to get used to.

Cecil watched the preparations with great interest and Phil was sure that the cat thought that he was crazy. He was pleased when Cecil seemed to accept the move and jumped up onto the couch beside him and curled into a ball.

* * * * *

Sergeant Clark was pleased to note that he didn't spot Chris's silver Crown Vic at the scene when he arrived. Due to the array of emergency vehicles cramming the street, it had taken him a few minutes to be sure it hadn't arrived ahead of him.

He was also pleased to see that the marked IHIT crime scene unit and several members of the IHIT team were also on site. They were all huddled together in a tight group slightly away from the rest of the emergency crews that were converged on the two vehicles involved.

Clark knew that he would find them this way; emotionally charged and unsure of what was expected of them.

He crossed to them and began to bark orders.

"Forensics, get your asses over there and take charge of this crime scene. If you get any flack from the Mounties, send them to me. The rest of you come with me."

They responded as one, and by the time Chris arrived ten minutes later there was no doubt as to who was in control of the area behind the yellow tape.

Knowing that the entire incident had been a VPF operation and that it had been a VPF member who had died in the unmarked unit, there had not been any hesitation on the part of the Burnaby officers to relinquish their territory once Winters had identified himself as IHIT.

The fire crews were finished and returning their equipment to their vehicles in preparation for leaving the scene, and most of the R.C.M.P uniforms were on the outside of the yellow tape that surrounded the burned out and cooling wrecks by the time Chris arrived.

He noted with satisfaction, that the area inside the yellow tape was very definitely dominated by reflective IHIT jackets, but a look of concern came over his features when he was able to pick out only two of the white clad members of his forensic team near the vehicles.

He spotted Sergeant Clark and dipped under the yellow tape to cross towards him. The Sergeant, who had been speaking with one of the white clad members of the team, noticed the look on Chris's face as he approached and stopped speaking mid-sentence turning to face him.

Chris addressed him immediately that he was in range.

"Is this all the forensic people you could raise?"

Gordy Clark hesitated for a second, realizing that Chris was unaware of the incident several blocks away involving the gang members and the GTF units that required IHIT members, especially forensics, at that scene. He took Chris aside and brought him up to date with what had transpired there and how it had led to the separate incident involving Ravi.

Chris took a couple of seconds to digest the information, and then nodded.

"Raise Jeff Winters and ask him to see me here as soon as he can. Tell him to leave the other three forensic staff to finish up there."

Clark was already reaching for his cell, as Chris continued.

"What the hell was Ravi doing here, anyway? He wasn't on call this weekend...I know he worked Saturday, but we finished up and he went off duty. What the hell was he doing here involved with GTF?"

Sergeant Clark shrugged.

"I don't know Boss; I've been trying to figure that out ever since I got the call."

* * * * *

Staff Sergeant Winters was supervising the loading of the Lincoln Navigator onto a flatbed tow truck when his cell rang.

The bodies of the three gang members had already been loaded into the Coroners' van and were on the way in to await the autopsy that would take place in the morning.

He nodded toward the IHIT exhibit man R.C.M.P. Corporal Kosky, who was standing across from him, before he answered the phone.

"Keep an eye on things, Craig."

Once he had received a returned nod of acknowledgement, he took the call.

"Winters."

He recognized Clark's voice immediately and stepped a few feet away from the tow truck, whose engine had risen in pitch as the winch began to haul the Navigator up the slope of its tilted rear deck.

"Jeff, the Boss would like to see you here as soon as possible. Can you leave there now?"

Winters considered for a second, letting his gaze move over the confines of the yellow taped crime scene before responding.

"Yes, Corporal Kosky can finish up here...where is it exactly, that you want me?"

"Ravi was the guy who stopped the SUV that fled your scene, and I'm afraid he got himself killed doing it."

Winters cut him off.

"Jesus Christ! Ravi...how the hell?   Yes...yes of course, I'll be right over. Where the hell are you located?"

* * * * *

Ravi's sister, Anahita Sharma, affectionately known to friends and family as 'Ana', adjusted her first class seat into the upright position and reached across to fasten her seatbelt as the flaps dropped on the Airbus in preparation for its scheduled landing at Vancouver International Airport.

It had been a long trip, but she had been able to nap and she was looking forward to getting home. She didn't feel at all tired.

* * * * *

When Jeff Winters reached the location of the second crime scene, a second coroner's van was pulling up. The ambulances had left, as had all but one of the fire rigs.

He had no more than exited his car when Chris, with Gordy in tow, approached him.

"Jeff, I want you to take over here. Gordy can bring you up to date on what we have so far."

Almost as an afterthought he continued.

"...You don't know how in hell Ravi managed to get himself involved in this in the first place, do you?"

Winters looked from Chris to Sergeant Clark, then back at Chris.

"Well, I know that he was going to take Andrea home, and although that was on Saturday night, I know that she lives close by. I'd be guessing at this point, but he may have been dropping her off when this went down, and if he was driving one of our unmarked units, he may have heard the call for assistance. Just at the wrong place and time, maybe."

A look of disbelief filled Chris's face and it was mirrored by the look on Clark's.

Chris's shoulders slumped before he spoke.

"Son-of-a-bitch! Do you think that they have been together since Saturday night? I sensed something between them, but she's only been with us for a few weeks. I had no idea anything serious had developed between them."

Winters nodded.

"I'm no expert but even I noticed that there were some pretty strong vibes between them when I saw them last."

Chris shook his head slowly.

"Fuck...talk about bad timing."

* * * * *

Kevin found the flood lit GTF crime scene protected by yellow tape and manned by two R.C.M.P. members. He could make out some forensic members working, and spotted Corporal John Bernier speaking with one of the uniformed R.C.M.P Constables.

As soon as he had parked his Volkswagen he made straight for Bernier.

CHAPTER THIRTY-ONE

Ana cleared customs quickly and spotted her waiting mother as soon as she had left the secured area and entered the main concourse of the airport.

They embraced warmly and were just beginning to talk when her father, baggage trolley in tow, joined them.

There were more hugs and then, deeply engrossed in animated conversation, the three of them headed for the exit and the trip home.

* * * * *

Satisfied that he had done all he could where he was, and that the crime scene was in good hands, Chris turned to Sergeant Clark, who had been hovering around nearby ever since Winters had arrived.

"Okay, we're done here. Let's give the other scene a quick check and then I've got some notifications to make."

Gordy Clark nodded.

"Okay, Boss. Look, I can look after the notifications…you don't have to do it."

Chris, who had made more than his fair share of death notifications over his career, and was certainly not looking forward to having to make these specific notifications; cut the other man off mid-sentence.

"Oh yes I do, Sergeant…Oh yes, I do."

* * * * *

Kevin had waited patiently at a distance as Corporal Bernier finished speaking with the uniformed R.C.M.P.

member just outside the yellow crime scene tape.

He had his camera slung around his neck and very much wanted to take a few shots of what was left of the activity within the crime scene while there was still something to shoot, but he knew better than to do so until someone in authority had cleared it.

He didn't approach the Corporal until the Mountie had moved away from him. Although he didn't know Bernier nearly as well as he did Chris, he had met with him several times in his capacity as press liaison office for IHIT.

Bernier turned to him as he approached, and studied Kevin briefly before he spoke.

"Go ahead and take some shots if you want, but I've got nothing for you at this point."

Kevin started to open his mouth, but the Corporal cut him off in no uncertain terms.

"I mean it Connolly. I've got nothing for you, period."

Bernier turned his back on Kevin, slipped under the protective tape and approached one of the forensic members.

Kevin was surprised to say the least. It was a strange way for the IHIT spokesman, its prime PR man, to act with a reporter. It gave Kevin pause; he sensed that there was 'something more than met the eye' going on.

His first instinct was to start digging, but Bernier's attitude had really been quite chilling and Kevin decided that this was neither the place nor the time to push the matter.

He snapped a few halfhearted pictures of the scene with its multitude of numbered yellow markers then turned around and started back toward his car. He had just pulled the door open when Chris's car with Gordy behind the wheel pulled up to the curb.

Kevin paused, the door still open and watched as Chris and the Sergeant got out of the car. He closed the door again and headed toward them, but Detective Sergeant Gordon Clark intercepted him with a look that easily matched the coldness of the earlier one that he had received from Bernier, shaking his head.

Kevin didn't miss the message. He pulled the door of the Volkswagen open and climbed into the driver's seat.

He spoke out loud to himself as he pulled the door closed behind him.

"Christ, something is very wrong here."

* * * * *

Mike woke and sat bolt upright. He threw the covers off his sweat-soaked bed and swung his legs out to sit on the edge as he raised his hands to the sides of his head and rubbed his temples.

It was the same recurring nightmare. The body lurching over the cliff and slipping into the darkness...and the screaming, always the screaming...

It was two hours and three drinks later before he tried to sleep again.

* * * * *

Ana had parted company with her parents at the door of her apartment and was beginning to open the first of her suitcases that she had dumped unceremoniously onto her bed, when she noticed the note taped to the shade of the lamp that sat on the end table on the left side of her bed.

She let the lid of the suitcase drop back down and went over to get it.

She and Ravi had always been very close and they often left notes for each other, so she was not surprised to find it, but she was surprised at the length of it as she pulled it off and opened the four pages of neat script.

She sat down on the edge of her bed and began to read.

'Hi sis, welcome back. Sorry that I wasn't at the airport to

meet you with Mom and Dad but I'm sure that you will understand and forgive me when I tell you why. You remember that stunning girl, Andrea, that I told you about; the latest addition to our forensics team? Well the two of us got kind of got thrown together work-wise over the last few days and one thing led to another. I ended up taking her home and Christ, Ana, she's one fantastic girl. I'm so bloody wound up over her that I've got to tell someone about it and who better than you, baby sister. Keep up the tradition of no secrets between us, you know.'

Ana smiled and put down the letter long enough to dig a pillow out from under the bedspread. She shoved it against the headboard, then kicked off her shoes and leaned back against it before she retrieved the letter and continued reading.

'I'LL BE THE FIRST TO ADMIT THAT THERE IS WITHOUT DOUBT A HINT OF LUST INVOLVED, BUT I DEFINITELY THINK I'M IN LOVE! No shit sis, I've never felt like this before."

Ana flipped over to the second page and the smile on her face broadened as she read on.

She and Ravi had always used each other as trusted sounding boards when it came to their interactions with members of the opposite sex and she was not overly surprised to find that he had spent a good portion of the remainder of the letter in outlining the activities that he and Andrea had enjoyed together before he had left to take her home the night before.

Ravi omitted little detail and she found herself flushing slightly at the sexual liaisons that he eagerly related and which took up a fair part of the rest of the letter. That these frank descriptions were so filled with a sense of deep affection was immediately apparent to her. As such they did not shock her, but instead, only served to fortify the warm, loving feelings that Ana had always shared with Ravi since they were kids.

She read on with great interest and laughed out loud at

the part about the clothing that Ravi had borrowed from Ana's apartment in an attempt to keep Andrea around for as long as he could.

The letter ended in capitals.

'LOVE YOU SIS...CAN'T WAIT TO INTRODUCE YOU TO YOUR, IF I HAVE MY WAY, FUTURE SISTER-IN-LAW'

It was signed, as all his notes to her had always been, with only two words.

'Big Brother'.

* * * * *

Chris and Sergeant Clark stopped off at the deserted IHIT office briefly to retrieve the 'next of kin information' on Ravi plus, in consideration of the fact that she and Ravi had apparently become very close, Andrea's home address, then they had piled back into Chris's car and headed into the west end of Vancouver.

* * * * *

The two men, one wearing fire department dress and the other in dark coveralls, stood talking quietly on the lawn in front of the burned out shell of the house.

They had worked together several times before and were comfortable with each other, having over time garnered a mutual respect for the other's abilities.

The shorter of the two was a police arson investigator and it was he who was speaking.

"Okay, I'll meet you back here at nine and go over it one more time in the daylight, but we are in agreement that so far it looks like the fire started in the dryer and was accidental."

The fire department arson investigator nodded.

* * * * *

Kevin had returned to bed almost as soon as he'd gotten back to his apartment, but he was having trouble getting back to sleep.

He couldn't for the life of him, figure out what could have been so wrong about the gang shoot-out with police that would justify the reaction that he had gotten from the police at the scene.

It bothered him for a couple of reasons.

Firstly it was just his nature to have to find out exactly what had gone wrong, and secondly, whatever it was it would likely break in the morning and if it was very big, it might blow his stories off the front page.

Not a good thought.

His cell phone rang and he reached over to answer it. It was Chris, and the message was short and sweet.

"Sorry about earlier. We lost one of our own tonight and I'm keeping the damper on this for as long as I can. If I get a sniff of anyone else picking it up, I'll give you a call and fill you in, but for the time being I'm sitting on it."

* * * *

It was shortly before three in the morning when Sergeant Clark pulled the silver Crown Vic into the driveway of the impressive high-rise and the two men got out and crossed to the entranceway.

Chris read through the list of names behind the sheet of Plexiglas to the right of the door and when he didn't find what he was looking for, he asked the Sergeant.

"What apartment number was it?"

Gordy opened his notebook and checked.

"1601"

Chris nodded, took a deep breath and pressed the button beside that number. He listened to the buzzer ringing for a few seconds and when he got no answer pressed it again, holding it longer. Several seconds later, his effort was rewarded with a voice at the other end.

"Yes?"

Chris closed his eyes before speaking.

"Mr. Sharma, this is Inspector Chris Chambers of the Vancouver Police. I wonder if I could speak to you, please."

There was a pregnant pause, and Chris unconsciously gritted his teeth as he waited for the response.

"Yes Inspector. Certainly."

The buzzer sounded again and Chris reached for the door and pulled it open with a heavy heart.

* * * * *

Kevin was sitting on the edge of his bed. He was still holding the cell phone in his hand. He set it down gently on the top of the bedside table and reached for a cigarette.

Now he understood why he had gotten the cold shoulder earlier.

This was going to be a front page story when it broke, no doubt about that, but it wasn't going to hit until after the Monday morning paper and that meant that the launch of his stories would be unaffected by it when it broke.

He would probably get less play on the next story in the series that was scheduled to come out on the following day, but he could perhaps tie that story in with his own in some way.

He found himself wondering which member of the IHIT team had been killed and why IHIT was involved in the gang thing at the time of the take-down. Usually IHIT only took over such investigations after someone had been killed and didn't take part in the confrontation at all.

* * * * *

When he opened the apartment door for them Ravi's father was still dressed in the casual clothing that he'd worn to the airport to pick up Ana.

A very expensively dressed, statuesquely beautiful woman in her late forties or early fifties stood just behind him.

Chris was a little surprised to find that she was Caucasian. He also understood where Ravi had gotten his good looks as he shook hands with Ravi's big and still ruggedly handsome father.

Chris could read the concern that was clearly written in there faces and he knew that they were thinking the worst.

There was only one way to do this; he took a deep breath and did it.

"Mr. and Mrs. Sharma, I can't tell you how sorry I am to have to tell you this, but Ravi was killed in the line of duty tonight."

* * * * *

Andrea slipped into her own bed, and despite the lateness of the hour she had found herself unable to sleep.

She tossed and turned and finally flipped over on her back and stared blankly up at the ceiling.

She mentally relived the weekend she had shared with Ravi. She was trying to understand how she could feel as strongly as she did for him despite the short period of time she had known him.

It took her over two hours to manage to find sleep.

* * * * *

Ana had refolded Ravi's letter and placed it into the top drawer of the night table. She was almost finished with her unpacking when her phone rang.

The strain of the long flight was beginning to set in and she swore softly before she picked it up.

It was her father.

"Ana honey…can you come up please."

Her father's voice was stilted and very precise. She knew something was wrong immediately.

"Sure dad…I'll be right up."

Moments later she was knocking on the door of her parents' apartment.

It was Sergeant Clark who opened the door for her, and when she entered and looked over toward her parents who were embracing on the couch across from a man she recognized as Inspector Chris Chambers, she went limp.

Ravi had previously introduced her to his boss when she had accompanied him to an IHIT Christmas party.

The color drained out of Ana's face as she realized that her mother was sobbing softly.

Chris stood and turned to face her.

"Oh my God…it's Ravi isn't it? Something bad has happened to Ravi. Oh God no…please, not Ravi"

* * * * *

Before leaving, Chris handed Ana one of his cards after writing his direct number down on the back of it. He told them that he wanted them to contact him any time they wanted to, and he meant it.

It was almost four in the morning when Chris and the sergeant left the high-rise and got back into the Crown Vic.

Once inside Chris looked at his watch and then swiveled to speak to Clark who was waiting for direction.

"I don't think that there is much chance of Andrea hearing about this before she comes in to work in the morning. What do you think the chances of that happening are? I sure as hell wouldn't want her to hear about it from anyone but us."

The other man considered the question for a few moments before he responded.

"Not very likely, she's so new that it isn't probable she will hear about it from anyone who was at the scene tonight and she sure as hell won't hear about it from the press, at least not before some time late in the day tomorrow."

Chris nodded.

"Okay, let's let her sleep and I'll tell her in the morning. I'm sure that it probably isn't necessary, but you know as well as I do how fast this will get around, so before you call it a night I want you to get hold of everyone in the team who knows what happened and make it clear to them that none of them is to say anything to Andrea or anyone else until I've been able to see her in the morning."

CHAPTER THIRTY-TWO

Andrea's alarm went off at seven-thirty.

She felt rested and relaxed despite the fact that it had taken her so long to get to sleep after Ravi had dropped her off. She realized now, that it was precisely because she had felt driven to spend the first two hours in bed analyzing her feelings that her assessment of the strange situation was now complete.

She was no longer questioning how she felt about Ravi nor was she unsure of whether or not she wanted to develop a deeper relationship with him.

She knew, that this was the man she wanted to marry and have children with, and based on his responses to her, she was confident that despite the fact that they had only known each other for a short time, it was a shared goal for both of them.

She smiled and bounced out of bed, eager to start her day and anxious to get to work and see Ravi.

* * * * *

Chris had managed only three hours of sleep before his alarm sounded.

He reached over to shut it off quickly on the off chance that Janet, who as usual had waited up for him and had listened supportively when he related the unfortunate events that had filled his night and helped him to deal with it by offering what comfort and support she could, might not hear it.

He was not surprised when she sat up on her side of the bed, stretched briefly and then kissed him on the back of the neck.

"You okay?"

Chris turned and returned the kiss with a peck of his own on her lips.

"Yes, I think so. It's going to take a little time but I'm beginning to deal with it. Thanks for listening last night."

* * * * *

It was Andrea's day to drive and because she had left the house early due to her eagerness to begin her day she had to wait a few minutes for her car-pooling buddy, forensic handwriting and document specialist Tim Wong, when she reached his apartment block.

As impatient as she was to get into the office, Andrea was in far too good a mood to allow the delay to bother her and she hummed softly to herself until Tim, still struggling into his jacket and carrying his brief case, exited the building and started toward her car.

Andrea and Tim had only begun car-pooling to and from work two weeks ago but she had found Tim, who was openly gay, to be very good company.

He harbored a sense of humor as strange as hers, and as silly as it sounded, in such a short period of time she quickly realized that he had become a friend to her.

The fact that they had both studied at M.I.T. at very young ages gave them common ground and memories and they felt a familiar comfort in each other's company. They had hit it off from the start, and surprisingly to both of them quickly found that they shared many interests and a general outlook on life.

Tim had registered the signs as she rapidly pulled away from the curb and began to drive. He studied her face frankly for a few seconds.

"Hmmm... aren't we chipper this morning? It could be a lazy weekend with lots of sleep and possibly some new and very expensive makeup, but I'll put my money on a wild weekend with some special man."

Surprised, Andrea laughed heartily and glanced over at him.

"Is it that obvious?"

Tim grinned across at her.

"Oh yes...I'm afraid so honey. You are simply glowing all over. Want to share?"

Andrea smiled broadly, flushed and shook her head.

"No...I don't think so. Not just yet."

* * * * *

Janet was just putting breakfast onto the table as Chris came down the hallway from their bedroom and he gave her a smile as he passed her and headed to the front door to retrieve the morning paper from the front steps.

As was his habit, he glanced at the front page as he closed the door behind him and started back for the kitchen.

When he entered the room, he crossed to where Janet was just sitting down.

"Oh, you are going to love this."

Janet took a sip from her coffee and looked up at him inquiringly.

Chris said nothing as he followed his morning ritual of separating the paper into sections and after he had deposited the sports section to the right of his own plate, he handed her the remainder of the paper.

"Front page...under the 'Why Our Streets Aren't Safe' headline."

* * * * *

Kevin hadn't bothered to go to bed when he got home. He was anxious to see how the morning paper would look and to attempt to gauge the probable public impact his articles would have.

In order to deal with his list of follow-up questions, he had several people to contact after nine but he knew that he would be able to crash later in the morning and had been idling away the hours as he awaited the arrival of the paper with several, generously fortified cups of coffee.

When he heard the plunk of the paper hitting the tiled corridor in front of his apartment door, he hurried to retrieve it.

* * * * *

A flicker of excitement rippled through Andrea as she passed Ravi's Hummer in the underground IHIT parking garage then slipped her car into one of several, still unoccupied spaces.

She registered, that for a Monday morning, the garage was surprisingly empty of vehicles but didn't give it a second thought as she and Tim left the garage and moved down the hall toward the lab.

* * * * *

When Janet, who had made no comment until she had finished reading all of the front page articles under Kevin's by-line, finally looked up she held the paper across the table to Chris.

"You should read this…I can't believe it. I mean, I knew it was bad, but this is absolutely crazy."

Chris, who had read little more than the headline on the page before he had given it to her, took it from her and began to read.

A few minutes later he put it down and raised his eyes to look across at her. She had been quietly sipping coffee as she watched him read.

"You're right. Even I had no idea how many of these bastards were out there. A lot of people are going to very upset about this and I certainly hope that the proverbial 'shit' is going to hit the politicians' fans as a result of it; however, I won't hold my breath while I wait for that to happen"

He glanced at his watch then raised his mug to his lips as he stood up.

"Shit…I'm running late."

* * * * *

Phil was up early.

Sleeping in the chair had been uncomfortable at first but it had helped with the coughing and he'd stuck it out. He felt reasonably rested by morning

His energy level had increased and he had taken the time to enjoy a sparse but none the less sensible breakfast and was now in the process of giving his home a long overdue cleaning.

He had left a phone message for Marshall to let him know that he would be in to see him at seven that evening and, as he cleaned, was occupied with running scenarios through his mind about how he could best manage to ensure that Mike Stanovich became his successor at 'HROT'.

The events of the day before had been very satisfying to him and he had been pleased to find that his generally improved outlook on life had not been lessened by it, but had in fact, been improved.

* * * * *

Chris nodded to LaRue as he paused at the doorway of the Staff Sergeant's office.

He had instantly picked up on the man's somber expression and was sure that LaRue was aware of what had transpired. He was relieved that he would not have to explain it to his subordinate.

"Morning, Don. I'd like to see Staff Sergeant Winters and Andrea Henderson in my office in fifteen minutes, and I want a meeting of the complete squad, with the exception on Andrea and Winters, in the conference room for nine-thirty."

Leaving the words hanging in the air, he then purposefully crossed the reception area and went into his office, closing the door firmly behind him.

His office door was rarely closed but whenever it was, it was a clear indication to the rest of his staff that he did not want to be disturbed.

As soon as he had hung up his jacket, he dropped into his comfortable office chair and reached for the phone.

His first call was to the Delta Deputy Chief who had, over the weekend, called him to discuss Ravi's possibility of promotion.

* * * * *

Ana wasn't sure how long she had remained with her parents, sharing in their mutual grief, before she had finally returned to her apartment and gone to bed.

At some point during the night she had left her parents long enough to pick up Ravi's last note to her and bring it up to them.

Although it contained things that he would never discussed with them, she felt it was important that they know about its contents, even if she knew that she could not share all the facts that it contained with them because that would betray the very special relationship that she had enjoyed with her brother. She considered it important that they at least understand the basic message it contained about the depth of Ravi's feelings for Andrea.

Her sleep had been restless and filled with bouts of heavy crying. She had finally given up and gone to take a shower.

She remained there for a long time, letting the hot water warm her body that felt limp and chilled, and her tears flowed freely to mingle with the water as it rolled over her. She blankly watched it fill the drain below her.

Between sobs she was repeating Ravi's name over and over to herself.

It was shortly before nine when she entered Ravi's apartment, holding his last note to her neatly folded in her left hand.

She couldn't remember getting it out of the drawer, nor was she sure why she had brought it with her, but she felt that it was important to do so.

Once inside she closed the door and felt her shoulders slump as she leaned back against it closed her eyes and began to sob. She breathed in his smell which was for her, because she knew it so well, readily apparent in the room.

His scent brought to mind a thousand memories of him.

She was still in this position when she felt a gentle pressure on her back as someone tried to open the door.

She stepped away to allow it to open fully and turned to find her parents standing there.

Her first reaction was to attempt to choke back her tears and pull herself erect. They moved forward and hugged her.

* * * * *

Chris had expected Andrea to react strongly to Ravi's death, even somewhere along the lines of the grief expressed by the boy's parents and sister, but he had been in no way prepared for her to suffer a complete emotional meltdown in front of his eyes.

She was inconsolable.

His plan to include Winters, who he knew was a father figure to the young forensic team members, in the meeting with Andrea immediately began to bear fruit as the outwardly curmudgeonly Staff Sergeant enveloped Andrea's shattered form in a firm but gentle bear hug.

Neither man spoke as they let her pour out her initial grief.

* * * * *

No one was sure who had initiated it, but Ana and her parents, tightly holding hands, had begun to move through the apartment room by room.

When they reached Ravi's bedroom they paused as one, just inside the door.

Ana's nostrils reacted instantly and she froze as she took the scent in.

While the familiar smell of Ravi was still apparent there was a stronger overriding scent now.

She had no way of knowing if either of her parents had noticed it, but it didn't take long for her to recognize it for what it was; the thick, lingering and musky odor that always followed a long session of hot and fulfilling sex.

The smell itself was quickly authenticated for her by the articles of clothing that had been left around the bed and the rumpled disaster of the bed coverings themselves.

What surprised all three of them even more was the fact that the room was untidy.

Each of them knew only too well that Ravi had a thing about neatness and would have never have left the room as it was unless his mind was elsewhere.

All of them knew that for Ravi to have left the room in its present condition meant that for whatever reason, he hadn't even registered the circumstances of his surroundings at the time.

No one said anything as they took in the room. Ana's gaze picked out the unceremoniously discarded pile of used condoms that was sitting on the night table to the left side of the bed and she, despite her somber mood, found herself smiling.

She said the words out loud and both her parents looked at her in surprise as she did it.

"Good for you big brother...bloody good for you."

Her parents followed her gaze to the condoms on the night table, and as they suddenly understood what had prompted her comment, all three of them, despite eyes clouded with tears, began to laugh in unison. When they finished Ana's mother took their hands.

"I've just had a thought. I'm not sure if it's a sensible one, and I'm not sure that it's even reasonable, but I think we need to have a family conference and discuss it."

At her urging they followed her back into the living room and sat down.

Once they were settled Ana's mother took a deep breath and stood up again, nervously she walked slowly about the room and told them her idea.

* * * * *

When Chris had remained in his office long enough to feel sure that Winters had things under control, he got up and headed for the conference room.

The somber conversation dropped to a hush the second he opened the door and he steeled himself as he took the chair at the head of the table.

"I know that all of you are struggling to understand the events of last night and I also know that all of us will have to deal with that in our own way. I'm not here to tell you that you have to put your grief aside and get on with your jobs, but I am here to tell you that we all have our jobs to do and that our doing them well despite our grief, is something that Ravi would have expected from us. I don't demand that you be unaffected by this as you get back into your normal routines, but I do know that getting to that point is a big part of fulfilling the grieving process and that it's a place each of us needs to reach as soon as we are able. I don't want anyone in this room to think that I, or any other member of the team will think any the less of you because you demonstrate your grief openly, but I also want all of you not to forget that Ravi was very proud to be part of our team and that he wouldn't want his death to affect how we do our jobs."

* * * * *

Ana was speechless for a few seconds after her mother had finished outlining her idea and returned to her seat.

Finally she turned to look at her father, who was seated beside her. His eyes met hers.

"Its something that I would have never thought of, but I have to admit that as strange as it sounds, I'm for it. I think that we have to make the offer at the very least."

Ana looked from her father to her mother and shook her head slowly.

"I don't know. My God, I can't even imagine what I would say if I found myself in that position and I'm part of an Indian family and very much aware of our culture, including arranged marriages, marriages of convenience and brothers marrying their sister-in-law's when they are widowed. This girl will have none of my background in understanding these things. How could she have?"

Her mother smiled.

"Well, would you be willing to discuss it with her? You are very close in age and she might be more receptive to considering it if it was to come from you, at least initially."

Ana stared blankly out the big window for a long time

before she nodded.

"Yes. I'll give Inspector Chambers a call and see if I can get her number and set up a meeting with her."

CHAPTER THIRTY-THREE

Chris had asked LaRue, John Bernier and his section heads to stay behind when the others left the conference room.

He closed the door when the rest of them had trooped out and then, without sitting, advised the remaining people that he would like them to see him at nine the next morning to perform a complete review of their current cases and impressed upon them that they should do whatever they could to get things back to normal a soon as possible, and were to let him know if there was any member of the team that might need time off or counseling.

That out of the way, he asked LaRue and Bernier to stay for a moment and waited until the section heads were out of the room before he addressed them.

"John, I want you to liaise with uptown about the memorial service. IHIT is a joint force operation and the service is going to be a big one unless I miss my guess. I want to make sure that we get it right. I'll get hold of the family later today to see what their wishes are and warn them up front of what a police memorial service is like and get back to you."

"Don, I'm going to be sidetracked by this for a day or two, so I'm going to rely on you to fill in for me whenever necessary. Some of the team will take this harder than others, and I want you to keep a close eye on each member of them and see to it that they receive any help that they may need to get through this."

* * * * *

Chris had paused to speak briefly with Winters and

Andrea, whom he found quietly drinking tea in a corner of the reception area when he left the conference room.

He was pleased to see that although she was still blotting the odd tear with tissue, Andrea seemed to be over the initial shock.

Chris had only just returned to his office when the phone rang. He dropped into his chair and picked it up and was a little surprised to find Ana on the other end.

"Inspector Chambers, this is Ravi's sister, Ana. I'm coming down to pick up Ravi's car, and I have a favor to ask of you. Would it be possible for me to meet with Andrea while I'm there?"

Chris paused for second to evaluate the request then responded.

"Hang on for a minute, Ms. Sharma. I'm afraid that she's just been told about your brother and I don't know if she is up to seeing you, but I will ask her."

"Thank you Inspector, I'd really appreciate that, and I think it's important, or I wouldn't be asking."

He put the call on hold and went back into the reception area.

Winters was holding a freshly steeped pot of tea in his right hand as his left arm covered Andrea's stooped shoulders. Chris gently directed her back toward his office.

He waited until they were inside and closed the door before he spoke.

"Andrea, do you know Ravi's sister?"

Andrea looked up from her mug, startled, and then she shook her head slowly.

"No. Ravi told me a lot about her and I almost feel like I know her, but we've never met."

Chris nodded.

"She's on the phone. She's coming down to pick up Ravi's car and she's asked if she could meet with you. She seems very anxious about it. What would you like me to tell her?"

Andrea raised her head and her eyes appeared clear, if bloodshot, for the first time since he'd given her the news about Ravi.

"Yes…yes I think I'd like to meet her very much."

* * * * *

The police arson investigator eagerly accepted the offer of a refill from the thermos belonging to his fire department equivalent, and they sat down onto the first level of stairs that led down from the lawn at the front of the burned out shell of the house, onto the sidewalk below.

They had spent an additional hour going over the charred remains of the basement and were comparing notes before they prepared to file their respective final reports on the incident.

When they had finished, it was clear that each would be confirming that the fire had originated with the dryer, and was yet another one, of the far too prevalent, fires of that nature that had claimed human life.

The cause of death was accidental. It was clear to them that their findings would be reflected by the autopsy of the body which would take place two days later.

Case closed.

* * * * *

It was just after eleven and Chris had sent Winters back to the lab.

He was sharing a cup of tea with Andrea, who by this point seemed to be coming to terms with the initial shock of Ravi's death and was beginning to move toward taking the first of many painful steps that would, in time, carry her slowly toward some form of closure.

LaRue entered the office through the open door and glanced over at Chris.

"Ms. Sharma is on the way up."

Chris nodded as Andrea placed her half filled mug onto the corner of his desk and he realized that she was making an effort to lift her shoulders as she took a deep breath.

Moments later LaRue brought a strikingly beautiful woman into the office and both Chris and Andrea stood to meet her.

Ana ignored Chris completely as she unashamedly burst into tears and moved directly across to Andrea then wrapped her arms around her and hugged her tightly.

Chris watched for Andrea's reaction and when her arms at first tentatively and then without constraint enveloped Ana and they both began to rock with sobs of grief, he moved out of the office and closed the door behind him.

About twenty minutes later the two women, with Chris's blessing and after being assured that Tim could make it home on his own without a problem, left the building.

Once they had gone, Chris returned to his office and placed a call to Andrea's parents.

He wasn't particularly surprised to find that they were not aware of Andrea's relationship with Ravi and he did his best to bring them up to speed, explaining that Andrea was spending some time with Ravi's sister and that she seemed to be coping well and was in good hands.

He told them that she would be calling them shortly but suggested that they shouldn't be concerned if it took her a little time to contact them.

He then gave them his direct number, his home and cell numbers, and told them not to hesitate to contact him if they felt the need.

After the call, he took a short break to regroup his thoughts then moved on to his next call.

The phone rang several times before it was answered by

Kevin, whom he had woken up. Chris quickly provided him with the full scoop on the incident that had taken place the evening before.

* * * * *

Andrea noted that Ana was very much like her brother in the way she handled the oversized Hummer. She paid a great deal of attention to her driving, but was in no way intimidated by the size of the vehicle.

Ana concentrated on clearing the underground parking area of the IHIT building before she spoke.

"I know this sounds silly, but I feel like I've known you for ages. There is a letter in my purse. It's a letter that was only meant for my eyes, but I would like you to read it. I think it may help you to understand why I feel the way I do about you."

She glanced over at Andrea and managed a smile.

"Oh...and by the way, Ravi and I didn't have any secrets between us, and I warn you before you read it, that it's very explicit."

She turned her attention back to the road.

"I think you and I need to let down our hair and spend some quality time together, and I know just where we can get it."

Andrea opened the purse sitting on the centre console between them and found the four neatly folded sheets of paper on top. She opened them and began to read and as she did, the Hummer filled with her soft sobs.

Ana reached out her right hand and took Andrea's left and held it firmly.

"Phenomenal guy, that brother of mine."

* * * * *

Pat and Jim were in a back booth of a restaurant that was situated across the street from the clinic where Pat was currently working. They had pushed their empty plates to one side and a copy of the morning paper, front page up, lay between them in the centre of the table.

They stopped talking as the waitress arrived to refill their coffees and pick up their plates. Once she had disappeared back toward the kitchen, Pat continued the conversation.

"Story says it will be a series. That means that it's not only going to put the issue up front for the public, but keep it there for awhile. Question is, what effect is that going to have on our operation, if any?"

Jim raised his mug and took a sip of the freshly brewed contents before he answered.

"Well, one of the reasons that we felt pretty safe doing this was because we knew that both the general public and the cops shared our outlook on this scum. Maybe some of them wouldn't agree that the level to which we are taking it is acceptable, but a lot of them would. If this does anything, I think that it just builds that kind of response up, and strengthens our position."

Pat gave some thought to what Jim had said before answering.

"Okay, we agree on that much, but this is going to draw a lot of attention to the situation of these guys overall and the more that people, including cops and politicians, learn about it the more eyes that are going to be on what happens to them. It puts us under a microscope."

Jim shook his head.

"I don't see it that way...seems to me that it puts them under a microscope, not us. It's just going to serve to build public indignation and increase police apathy to a higher plateau, two things which are just going to make things safer and easier for us."

Pat took another drink from his mug and then set it down on the table.

"Look, we've been very successful so far, not even a twitch of interest from any quarter that our activities might be anything more than what we set them up to look like. We all agreed up front that we could only find ourselves in trouble once we had begun for two reasons. First, if one of our own decided to spill the beans, and second, if some investigator does some sort of statistical evaluation of the overall picture and realizes that one hell of a lot more of these bastards are dropping dead here in the lower mainland than anywhere else in the country. It seems to me that the second of those two will be much more probable with this sort of publicity being flung out for public consumption."

Jim shrugged.

"With this kind of publicity, we'd know the instant anything like that happened and we could simply lay low until it cools down. You know damn well that every story has a shelf life. This isn't going to be front page forever. On the other side of the coin, these stories are going to raise one hell of a public stink and sway even more people over to our way of thinking.

It's not like we leave any evidence of what is really taking place when we deep six one of these pieces of shit, and I hardly think any of us will ever eagerly provide a statement of our guilt for the fun of it.

There is nothing in this paper that should cause us any concern. Even if the police found out exactly what we were doing they'd be hog-tied. Can you imagine any jury in the country finding any of us guilty of murder, once they knew the whole sick story of the revolving door being provided by the legal system for these pricks? Christ, I doubt that a charge against any of us would even be accepted by a Crown Prosecutor, let alone ever reach a jury. We don't leave any evidence behind, certainly never enough of it to form the basis for a charge that would have the slightest chance of sticking. No, this publicity can't hurt us; it can only make what we do easier and safer."

Pat let Jim's words dangle in the air for a few seconds than raised his eyes to meet his.

"You obviously don't see a need for us to rein in our little operation then?"

Jim didn't even hesitate. He shook his head.

"Nope, I say let's get on with it, and the more the merrier. None of us are getting any younger. We have three in the final planning stages now, and I say let's get on with them. I'll bet my left nut that any of the others you talk to will tell you the same thing."

* * * * *

Andrea found herself re-reading several sections of the letter over and over.

She was no longer sobbing but she was still holding Ana's hand firmly in her own.

Absorbed as she was, she hadn't been paying any attention to where they were going and when Ana pulled the Hummer into a parking lot she had absolutely no idea where they were.

Ana put the big vehicle into park and shut it down before she said.

"Ravi gave me a full weekend at this spa as a twenty-first birthday present. It was the best present I ever received. I think he would be very pleased to see the two of us spending some time together here and in consideration of what wrecks both of us are at the moment, we deserve to be pampered a little while we spend some time getting to know each other better and sharing just how much he meant to each of us."

* * * * *

In consideration of the somber mood that filled the building and the fact that despite it everyone was going through the motions of getting on with their jobs Chris, after designating a skeleton emergency crew, told the remainder of them to call it quits at three and sent them all home with the clear admonition that things would have to get back to normal by the next morning.

He made sure that he was the last one out of the building, remaining in his office to be available to anyone who felt that they needed to talk to him, until they had all left.

He was both physically and emotionally drained by the time he pulled out of the underground parking lot and headed home.

He dug out his cell and gave Janet a call to let her know that he was on the way.

* * * * *

Pat had arranged to see Phil at his Burnaby apartment on his way home from the clinic that evening.

He was a little taken aback by Phil's upbeat mood as he opened the apartment door and waved him inside. He seemed to be a good ten years younger than he had when Pat had seen him last; hardly what one would expect to find in a man that had recently been told he didn't have long to live.

His surprise increased as Phil led him into the small living room and waved him into a chair. Pat had been in the apartment several times over the past year and he had found it to be a minor disaster area on every previous occasion.

It was spotless this time.

Obviously Phil was not letting his prognosis get him down, and that pleased Pat.

He provided Phil with the gist of the conversation that he and Jim had had in the restaurant earlier in the day, and was not surprised to find that Phil was in full agreement with the conclusions that Jim had reached.

The conversation moved to other topics as they finished a couple of cups of coffee. It wasn't until Pat was standing at the door ready to leave that he passed Phil the small vial.

He looked directly into Phil's eyes.

"There is enough here to kill a horse and it's both quick and painless. Just put it into some good scotch and toss it back when you're ready."

Relief flooded Phil's face as he pocketed the vial into then reached out to give Pat a bear hug.

"Thanks Pat...I really appreciate your help with this."

* * * * *

Andrea's mind was blissfully blank.

She and Ana were stretched out face down, side by side, on matching thickly padded beds, being massaged by a very well trained team of masseuses.

The sensation was wonderful and although they had talked briefly at the start of the session, by this point, both were lost to the sensations brought about by the hands that were working on them and felt no need to talk.

CHAPTER THIRTY-FOUR

Kevin arrived at Marshall's broom-closet office a few minutes after seven.

As he opened the door and stepped inside the Sergeant looked up from a pile of papers on his desk then leaned back in his chair, raising his hand to indicate the empty chair on the other side of his desk.

"Ah. The man of the hour arrives!"

Kevin dropped down into the chair and pulled out his notebook and pen, placing them on the desk in front of him. Marshal lifted the newspaper off the top of his in-file and waved it in the air between them.

"I must say, my dismal existence has certainly brightened up since this appeared."

A somewhat quizzical expression filled Kevin's face as he smiled across at the other man.

"How is that? I think it's pretty good, but I'm not sure how that relates to your existence?"

Marshall rolled forward in his chair and laughed.

"It seems that it is a very popular story upstairs. I've got one hell of pile of phone messages here from reporters of all areas of the media who seem very eager to talk to me, and who I am staunchly ignoring per our agreement and, suddenly those on high…"

The Sergeant pointedly raised his eyes upwards.

"…seem to have been reminded of the existence of my little operation down here. They want to meet in the morning to see what can be done about expanding it….hell there is even some suggestion that HROT may be moving up to some location in the building that has a window!"

Kevin laughed, and Marshall joined in.

* * * * *

Andrea and Ana, wrapped in matching white fluffy towels, were sitting side by side, alone in the sauna.

After they had gotten themselves acclimatized, Ana started talking. She rambled on for some time, bouncing from place to place through her memories of Ravi. By this point in the evening she felt very much at ease with Andrea.

A sincere and strong bond had begun to form between them and anyone who saw them now, would have taken them for very good friends. Surprisingly, in consideration of the short period that they had known each other, they wouldn't have been far off target.

Ana took a deep breath of the hot moist air then blurted.

"You don't have to answer me if you don't feel comfortable doing it, but I would like to ask you some questions."

Andrea was completely relaxed and feeling very at ease with Ana by this point. She turned slightly to face her and smiled.

"Ask away."

Ana hesitated for a second, trying to arrange what she wanted to say in her mind.

She needed to take it slowly and ensure that what she said didn't come out too suddenly or overwhelm Andrea.

"Ravi's letter made it pretty clear to me how he felt about you. Did you feel the same way about him?"

Andrea pictured the letter in her mind for a second then smiled.

"Yes...I did"

Ana, her expression serious, nodded.

"He was obviously in love with you, and he wanted to marry you. If he'd had the chance to ask you to marry him before he died, what would you have said?"

Andrea responded without hesitation.

"I would have said yes."

"You would have been ready to settle down with him and have his babies?"

Andrea managed a slightly embarrassed smirk.

"I'd have been ready to have his babies with or without marriage."

Ana's features softened instantly and she laughed.

In that instant, the bond that had begun to form between them was cemented.

Ana leaned forward and planted a sisterly kiss on Andrea's cheek.

"Well, in that case...do I have a deal for you! Let's grab a shower and I'll explain it all to you over dinner."

* * * * *

Kevin was just about to leave Marshall's office with an updated list of the country's, at-large, dangerous offenders under his arm when Phil opened the office door.

Marshall introduced the two men and they exchanged pleasantries, then Kevin left.

Once he had closed the door behind him the Sergeant motioned Phil into the chair Kevin had so recently vacated and waited until he was seated before he said.

"Okay Phil, what's on your mind?"

* * * * *

Janet had suggested a walk after they had finished dinner and Chris, liking the idea of fresh air and a chance for him to think along with an opportunity for them to talk without interruption, found the idea appealing and agreed.

They had gone several blocks when his cell rang and it was with some displeasure that he pulled it out and answered.

"Inspector Chambers, its Ben Henderson calling. I'm sorry to disturb you, but my wife and I are getting a little worried about Andrea. We haven't heard from her, you see... and this whole thing has sort of blind-sided us. Frankly both my wife and I are at a loss to understand it. Andrea can't have known this policeman for long, and she's said nothing to us about a new man in her life. We want to get a better understanding of it all and give her what help we can. If the relationship was as serious as you've suggested, and we have no reason to doubt it, I'm sure that Andrea just needs some time to deal with her grief before she feels comfortable enough to calls us, but..."

The displeasure that Chris had felt when the cell had gone off dissipated instantly.

"Don't give it another thought, Mr. Henderson. As I said earlier, she's in good hands, but I'll see if I can reach her and get back to you. What's your number...I'll give her a call and get back to you as soon as I reach her."

* * * * *

Andrea and Ana had finished showering and were getting dressed when Andrea's blackberry sounded. She noted that she had missed two previous calls as she answered it.

"Andrea? It's Chris Chambers. I just had a call from your dad. He and your mother are a little concerned about how you're doing.

Andrea picked up her watch and checked the time.

"Oh my God! I'd lost all track of time...I'll give them a call right away."

Chris could tell from her voice that she was feeling considerably better than she had been earlier.

"Good, you do that...and are you okay, all things considered?"

Andrea took a second to consider the question before she answered it, honestly.

"Yes...yes I am much better. Ana has been seeing to that, and thanks for asking."

* * * * *

Phil explained to Marshall that he was no longer in remission and even though he appeared as healthy as an ox to him, Marshall understood why he no longer wanted to work.

Phil suggested that Mike be his replacement. Marshall was pleased that he could fill the empty slot that easily and readily agreed.

* * * * *

Kevin had stopped for a bite to eat on the way home and was now sitting in front of his laptop entering the updated information, adding new names first and then deleting others.

He was surprised to find he was doing far more deleting than adding when he brought the British Columbia portion of the list up to date. He had done the opposite while adjusting the list for the rest of the country; but it didn't seem to be a particularly significant, just odd, so he didn't give it much thought.

* * * * *

Ana and Andrea turned heads when they entered the nearby restaurant to eat.

Neither of them missed the reaction brought about by their entry. Although they were still very broken up inside, the realization that it wasn't showing on the outside pleased them both and they met each others gaze and laughed.

As expensive and chic as the restaurant was, it was

relatively empty on a Monday evening and they were quickly led to a quiet booth at the back of the room.

Once seated, they were pleased to find that they shared an overwhelming need for a good stiff drink and placed their orders with the hostess.

Ana purposely kept the conversation limited to light small talk until they had ordered and were well into their second drinks, then she set her glass down and paused for a moment. Taking a deep breath, she looked directly into Andrea's eyes.

"Okay, here goes. I want you to promise me that you won't respond to what I'm about to say to you until I'm finished. We've both been through enough for one day, and I think it's very important that you give it some serious thought. Take some time to carefully consider how you really feel about what I'm about to propose before you reach a judgment about it one way or the other."

She paused for a second and then continued.

"I want you to know up front that I like you very much and whatever decision you arrive at will not alter the fact that I want us to be very good friends."

She took Andrea's hand in her own and let the words sink in before she continued.

"My mom, dad and I somehow ended up in Ravi's apartment early this morning. It was after I read them the letter.

She smiled and squeezed Andrea's hand.

"Not all of it, only the parts that I thought they should hear."

Andrea returned the smile and Ana, satisfied that Andrea had understood her meaning, continued.

"Anyway, all of us know only too well how tidy my big brother was, and the sight of the disaster in his bedroom had a pretty deep effect on all of us. We each sensed that the girl who could mean so much to Ravi as to cause him to leave his room in such a state must have been someone very special to him."

The eyes of both women began to mist and Ana paused for a second, giving herself a chance to regain her composure before she went on.

"Ravi was the only son, and both my mom and dad are completely shattered by what's happened. In my dad's culture, having a son to carry on the family name is very important. One of my parent's biggest concerns is that there will be a male heir produced to take over the position as head of the business, and as my uncle has produced only girls, poor Ravi, would have been obligated to step into that spot when my dad retired or if he died. It was so important that the fact that something might happen to Ravi was also seriously considered, and to cover that eventuality my parents asked Ravi to have sperm samples banked."

She paused, letting that sink in, then continued quickly before Andrea could interrupt.

"I wish I could bring my big brother back for you but I can't. However, if you really wanted to have Ravi's babies...that just may be very possible. In fact, as long as you are physically able to do your part, it could be guaranteed."

Andrea's jaw dropped and she spluttered a protest but Ana cut her off.

"No...don't say anything yet, hear me out please."

Andrea closed her mouth and nodded.

"The three of us discussed the idea for several hours last night, and although I know that there will be questions and conditions on both sides if you agree to this, all of us are very much interested in seeing it come to pass. We would be prepared for you to take your time reaching a final decision; in fact, we would expect that of you. With that in mind, and once I've given you a more complete understanding of what a 'yes' from you would mean for both you and any children that you might have, I'm prepared to answer any questions that you might want to ask now."

Ana managed a small smile.

"If you find the whole idea completely unacceptable already or if it's too early to consider yet, I'm willing to put it off until later or drop it altogether and never raise it again if that's what you want. If you still have an open mind about it at this point, I'm prepared to tell you more, exactly what it could mean to you and your future children. And, if you are comfortable with that, then I'd like to invite you to get together with my mom and dad who are very anxious to meet the woman who could melt my big brother's heart so thoroughly in such a short period of time. I should also tell you that they are going to be swept away by you and will warm to you as quickly as I have, welcoming you into their lives no matter what decision you reach."

Her eyes never left Andrea's as she waited for a response. Andrea played with her drink for some time before she answered.

"No. I won't dismiss it out of hand...and I'll listen to what you have to tell me, but it's not something that I can answer now. My whole world is upside down at the moment and it will take me time to sort things out in my mind. It's not the kind of decision I'd even consider making until I'm functioning normally again and very, very sure of how I feel."

Ana nodded, then lifted her hand from Andrea's and gave it a little pat as she leaned back into the well padded booth.

"Fair enough."

Andrea glanced at her watch.

"I think I'd better head home after we finish eating; my parents must be getting anxious and it's been an exhausting day."

Ana knew exactly how she felt and nodded her understanding.

"Okay, I can fill in some of the details for you and answer any questions while we eat, then I'll drive you back to your office, or if you don't feel up to driving I could drop you off at home. You can sleep on the idea and maybe we could have lunch tomorrow and discuss it further."

Andrea shook her head.

"No need to take me all the way home, I'm feeling much better now and can drive myself. I know that Inspector Chambers said that I could take as much time off as I needed, but I'm going to go back to work in the morning. They need me there, and I think that it would be best it I kept myself as busy as I can for the next while. As far a lunch with you tomorrow goes, I'd like that."

CHAPTER THIRTY-FIVE

Andrea was pleased that her parents were so happy to see her when she arrived home the night before that they had not argued when she said she wanted to just climb in to bed and get some rest.

Her mind had been spinning when she got into bed, and it had taken her quite awhile to get to sleep, but she awoke to her alarm feeling surprisingly well rested. Although her mind was still filled with conflicting images, she realized that she was beginning to sort things out.

She was glad that Tim refrained from any discussion of Ravi when he picked her up and drove them to work.

Sensing that she wouldn't be up to a lot of conversation, he had rambled on about a zillion inconsequential topics and she had been safely able to tune his banter out periodically and do some serious thinking of her own.

* * * * *

The conversation over breakfast at Chris's house had been dominated by a discussion of Kevin's second article which had, once again, made it on to the front page of the paper.

Janet finished it first and encouraged Chris to read it in its entirety once he had finished with the sports section of the paper.

The story, hard-hitting and filled with an impressive array of statistics, pulled no punches.

It portrayed the police as professional and highly successful at their job despite having their hands legally bound, and took aim at how the legal system handled cases after they passed into their hands, at both the judicial and corrections levels.

He was not surprised to find that the story was also the main topic around the water cooler at work when he arrived.

From Chris's perspective this was a good thing as it seemed to be helping his staff deal with the general lethargy that was a normal reaction to Ravi's death.

The morning meeting worked its way through the progress updates for each of the outstanding cases the unit was working on. Chris, on being informed that the gang members involved in the GTF incident which had resulted in Ravi's death had all been on parole for violent offences at the time of the incident in addition to currently being out on bail for pending weapons offences, immediately understood why Kevin's article on the consequences of the current 'revolving door' system being utilized by Canada's legal system had hit such a popular chord among his staff.

He realized that his people had locked on to the story because, although it was more related to sexual predators than gang members, it had provided them with a convenient target that allowed them to vent their frustration and anger over Ravi's death in an acceptable manner.

There had also been a direct tie in with IHIT as a result of the incident, in that the three gang members killed had been responsible for four of the gang-related murders that IHIT was currently working on. Lack of evidence meant they couldn't prove it, but regardless of that it allowed them to close the files on those four cases.

This cheered them all a little, and the atmosphere in the room seemed to ease somewhat. Everyone around the table had had the same thought, but it was Staff Sergeant Williams who vocalized what they had all been thinking.

"At least Ravi didn't die in vain... he managed to help take three murderers off the street and personally buried a fourth."

As in all killings committed by competing gangs against each other, police were normally not particularly displeased when they occurred, as long as they were directed at other gang members and did not involve the injury or death of any innocent bystanders.

They didn't investigate them with any less enthusiasm than they would a non-gang related murder. What made this type different was that the police knew that during the investigation they would not have to deal with any of the pain they all felt for the victims of a non-gang related murder. That coupled with the fact that a successful conclusion to any gang to gang murder investigation also served to lock up one or more additional dangerous gang members made them very satisfying.

It was one of the reasons why although they would never admit it to anyone other than another cop - most cops saw a gang war as a 'win-win' situation.

Winters updated them on the successful forensic results on prints, blood, and fiber that had been secured from the inside of the van that Fraser had used in the rape-murder. There was general agreement around the table that the case they would be turning over to Crown Council would be so overwhelming that Fraser's only defense could be one of insanity. In this case there wasn't a snowball's chance in hell of that tactic being argued successfully in court.

When the repeat offender hit court this time, with a little luck the bastard might actually be kept locked up for the rest of his life and prevented from killing any more kids.

As the meeting wound up, Chris touched base briefly with LaRue and Bernier to get up to speed, and then asked Winters to join him in his office.

Once there he inquired as to how Andrea was holding up and was pleasantly surprised when the Staff Sergeant advised that although that she definitely wasn't her usually upbeat self, she seemed to be burying herself in her work and appeared to be doing fine, all things considered

As he was in the process of leaving Chris's office he turned back and spoke.

"She's not very talkative, but I gather from what she did say that she and Ravi's sister hit it off well...in fact they are meeting again for lunch today."

Chris nodded and smiled.

"Good...I'm glad to hear it. Hopefully they can help each other get through this. When you get back to the lab, tell her that when she leaves for lunch she is to take the remainder of the day off. If necessary, make it an order."

* * * * *

Ana picked Andrea up in front of the IHIT building right on time. She was driving her bright red convertible Cadillac XLR roadster and Andrea thought that the car was a very good match for the woman behind the wheel.

They chatted amiably as they drove. No topic seemed taboo or unapproachable for them. It was Andrea who finally put it into words.

"You know, I can't believe how much we think alike. I feel like I've known you since grade one or something. It's as though you're the sister I never had."

Ana laughed and gave her a thumbs-up.

"And I thought it was only me who felt that way!"

Thirty-five minutes later they were comfortably ensconced in the private dining area of the family restaurant in North Vancouver; Ana was a little surprised but pleased to find out that Andrea had been there before.

The mutual grief each felt in relation to Ravi's death was something they could share easily when it presented itself, secure in the knowledge that it would be received with compassion and understanding by the other.

That made it easy for them to deal with the emotional

rollercoaster they were experiencing. They drew understanding and warmth from the other as it was needed.

Spending time together helped to make the suddenly surreal world they found themselves thrust into by Ravi's death somehow more bearable and safer for each of them.

As Andrea had the remainder of the day off, they felt no need to rush. They had plenty of time to enjoy their lunch and each other's company

* * * * *

Kevin, dressed only in his underwear, was sitting at his small desk working at his laptop.

He was tweaking the story scheduled to hit the paper in the morning, primarily to reflect the new numbers that he brought up to date from the material that Marshall had given him the night before.

He was working from the figures on the spread sheet that he had created to reflect the changing totals of the at-risk offenders across Canada, as well as a second spreadsheet that broke down the numbers of at risk ex-cons that were supposedly residing in the lower mainland area of British Columbia.

Now that his series of stories had featured nationally he took less interest in the second screen, although he did take the time to update it as well.

As he did, he noticed that the overall national total had remained fairly static, only a small increase, but that the number in the lower mainland had conversely dropped by a larger margin.

Concentrating on replacing the old numbers from his roughed out story with the new ones, he paid little attention to the significant difference in the changes in totals between the two areas.

* * * * *

Once the dishes had been removed and fresh coffee served, Ana reached into her purse and pulled out two neatly stapled packages of documents and placed them in front of her on the table.

"Have you had a chance to consider my parents' offer, and if so how do you feel about it?"

Andrea nodded.

"Yes, I have...and while I'm not ready to commit myself to anything just yet, I have come to the conclusion that I don't want to dismiss it out of hand. It's a very big commitment to make, and I find the whole idea a little scary, but I've decided to keep an open mind about it for now."

Ana smiled broadly.

"Yes, I tried to put myself in your position last night when I was talking to my parents about it and to be honest with you, even though I'm a part of that culture and know where such concepts come from, I found the whole idea a little hard to deal with too."

Ana handed one of the documents to Andrea.

"My dad asked me to draw these up yesterday. I think I should also tell you that he has begun the process of vetting your background. While that is only partially completed, both he and my mom were very pleased at what the process had produced so far."

She let their eyes meet.

"This is a draft agreement prepared for discussion purposes only, and is in no way written in stone, but my parents felt that it wouldn't be fair to ask you for a decision on something as important as this without giving you as much information as possible to assist you in making the right choice. It sets down what my parents are prepared to guarantee you and what they would like in return. As I said, my dad wanted to make sure that you understood that it was only a first step and fully expects that you may want changes, which he is prepared to entertain."

Andrea set the package down in front of her.

"You said your father asked you to draw these up?"

Ana flushed slightly.

"Yes, I'm the company lawyer."

She paused and noted Andrea's appreciative nod then continued.

"You can read it later, but, if you'd like, I can give you an idea of what it contains."

Andrea lifted her eyes from the document and nodded.

"Yes, please."

Ana took a sip of coffee before she continued.

"Upon your agreement to sign a contract based on this document, and whatever changes are mutually agreed upon by the parties before that time, you would receive for life an immediate monthly income of ten thousand dollars. In addition, you would be provided with a further ten thousand dollars per month for each and every child you produced over your lifetime. Under the terms of the agreement, all of Ravi's property, including his apartment, his trust fund, and his percentage of the family business would also go to you for the period of your lifetime, with the understanding that upon your death, your estate would then be shared equally between whatever children you had produced over your lifetime…

an amount that is roughly estimated to be worth eighteen million dollars today and that is expected to increase considerably in value over time."

Ana paused for a moment, her eyes meeting and holding Andrea's, to let her digest what she'd said so far, then she went on.

"In return, they would ask that any children produced under the terms of the contract would utilize the Sharma surname, and that, while they would in no way challenge your right as a mother to determine the future of your children, they be allowed to participate in each child's life as normal grandparents would. Also their wishes with regard to helping each child seek out and attain the best future possible for them as they grow to adulthood, must be given reasonable and sincere consideration when offered. Do you understand?"

Andrea sucked in a deep breath and then nodded her head.

Ana returned the nod and then continued.

"In addition, while they understand that you are a young woman, and may in time wish to marry, you agree that you will not make that step without discussing it with them first, and if you so decide, any children produced prior to that time under the terms of the agreement, would, from that point on, be legally considered to be under joint custody between you and them .They have also asked that you reach a decision one way or another within the next thirty days and have asked me to tell you that they are very eager to get to know you better and answer any questions that you may have."

* * * * *

Pat, who had nagging doubts about his last conversation with Jim and the day off; decided to find out if the rest of their group felt the same way that Jim had about continuing despite the articles that had run in the paper.

Because the group had agreed to never discuss their extra-curricular work over the phone, he arranged to meet with several of them.

The first four concurred with the conclusion that Jim had reached previously. At that point, Pat's earlier doubts were quashed and he bowed to the majority.

He decided to stop dragging his feet and arranged to spend the afternoon with Jim so that they could put the final touches on the scenarios that they had been developing on three prospective targets.

The plans would be put into action without further delay.

CHAPTER THIRTY-SIX

The reaction to Ravi's death among the staff had become less invasive around the IHIT office, and by Wednesday things had begun to revert to a reasonable level of 'business as usual'.

A small religious family service for Ravi was being held that afternoon, but Andrea, who, like Ravi and Ana herself, held no serious religious affiliation, had declined to attend when she had been offered the chance to do so. Ana, who was a second generation Canadian had never embraced the family's religion, and was immediately sympathetic to Andrea's position.

She assured Andrea that her decision not to attend would be understood by the family.

She and Ana had been in contact often over the past few days and Andrea had begun to consider her as a close friend and confidant. At Ana's urging, she agreed to attend a dinner with the immediate family that night.

The idea of meeting Ravi's family was somewhat daunting for her, but the fact that Ana would be picking her up and taking her to the gathering would make the whole thing easier and it was something she wanted to do.

She was, however, becoming a little unnerved by the whole idea as the day went on. Was she dressed properly? Would they like her? Would she like them? She found it difficult to concentrate on her work as the day progressed, bringing the time for Ana to pick her up closer and closer.

* * * * *

Chris was thankful that no new cases had come up that

required IHIT's participation since Ravi's death, and that things had begun to get back to normal around the office.

The police memorial service was going to be an extensive affair; it had been scheduled for the next Saturday. It was to be held at the city's armory, which had been selected because of its size and the need for a large indoor area that would offer enough shelter for the large number of police, family and public that had indicated a desire to attend.

* * * * *

The public reaction to Kevin's ongoing daily coverage of the at-risk prison releases had been massive and his editor had extended the expected life of the series for at least one additional week, provided that Kevin had enough material to allow him to keep the onslaught up.

Kevin had thrown himself in to it with a vengeance.

He began to tie in the overall information in each article to specific cases of an individual who had reoffended, and had managed, with the help of Marshall, to ensure that each day's story was delivered in all its gory detail.

The people across the country were eating it up, and interest in the subject had been shown by some of the international media.

The concept had taken on a life of its own, and his editor had even assigned him a full time researcher to assist him. Kevin had every intention of taking it as far as he could.

There had even been a suggestion that there might be a book in it if he was interested.

* * * * *

It was nearly four-thirty by the time Pat, Jim and Phil put the final touches on the unfortunate demise of a thirty-four year old ex-con, Kenneth Spiegel

They had been in the dismal one room skid-road hotel room for the better part of an hour and were removing their white protective gear as they stood just inside the door that led out into the dimly lit hallway beyond.

Once they had removed and bagged their gear, they left one at a time in ten minute intervals, Jim letting his eyes rove over the scene to satisfy himself that all was as it should be before being the last man out the door.

Spiegel's lifeless form was draped half on and half off the bed, his feet resting on the dirty floor.

His left shirtsleeve had been rolled up and the rubber tubing was still tied in place above the elbow. The syringe that stuck out of his motionless arm still contained the remains of the cooked "hot" cap of pure Heroin that had been provided by Pat.

Jim had no doubt that the dead man's well-documented history of drug abuse, which made up a large part of Spiegel's early criminal record prior to his crowning criminal achievement – which was the rape and strangulation of a seven-year-old girl shortly after his nineteenth birthday - would make the scenario very easy to accept by any investigating officers.

Once the story of Spiegel's death had gotten out, Jim sincerely hoped that the poor parents of the now brain damaged and vegetable-like little girl would be able to get some closure and some satisfaction that her attacker would no longer be allowed to enjoy his freedom, and his clear victory over the justice system.

There was of course one fact that Spiegel's death would absolutely guarantee. No other little girl would ever have to suffer an attack at his hands.

* * * * *

The now familiar red Cadillac roadster slipped agilely

into the curb and Andrea, despite her lingering uneasiness about the upcoming dinner smiled at Ana who was waving at her from behind the wheel.

Dinner was at seven and that still gave her two hours to spend with Ana beforehand. She hoped that she would be able to use the time to settle her nerves a little.

Once they had merged into traffic, Ana spoke.

"I'd sort of planned for us to stop for a couple of drinks and some girl talk before we went to the restaurant, but I'm afraid that I'm going to have to go to the high rise and do a quick tidy up of Ravi's apartment instead. My cousin Gary is arriving in town for a short visit, primarily to attend the memorial, and I wanted him to stay at Ravi's place while he is here. They were born only months apart and were best buddies, spending a lot of time together as we were growing up, and although he's been at university in the states for the last couple of years, he and Ravi remained very close. He stayed with Ravi whenever he found time to visit us. Under the circumstances, I think that he will feel more at home there than anywhere else. This has shaken him up and I know that he will appreciate being able to spend his visit close to the rest of the family and in familiar surroundings."

She smiled and let her eyes meet Andrea's briefly as she continued.

"I haven't had the time or the inclination to go into Ravi's place since that first night, but I don't think that it would be a very good idea for Gary to find the bedroom in the condition that... well, you know what I mean."

A mental image of Ravi's bedroom as they had left it, the rumpled, sweat-soaked bed and the pile of used condoms on the bedside table formed in Andrea's mind. She flushed a little.

"Yes...I know what you mean"

Ana reached for her hand and gave it a squeeze.

"You don't have to come in. You can wait in my place

while I do a quick clean up"

Andrea shook her head.

"No...I think that I'd like to help. My memories of that night are something that I will cherish for a very long time. Seeing the bedroom in its present condition can only bring back good memories for me."

* * * * *

Jim turned the knob silently and opened the hotel room door just a crack.

He checked to make sure that there was no one in the hallway before he stepped out and pulled the door closed behind him. He paused for a second to remove his surgical gloves and put them into his jacket pocket before crossing the hall to the alcove that led to a rear stairway.

He took the stairs two floors down to the ground floor and left the building through the back door. To the best of his knowledge, he was unobserved as he closed the door behind him and entered the laneway.

Finding it empty, he walked swiftly down to the cross street then headed directly for Pat's big SUV and climbed into the back seat.

The first droplets of rain began to fall as Pat cranked the engine into life and pulled away from the curb.

* * * * *

Ana took Andrea directly to her apartment and poured them good stiff drinks.

On the drive over, Andrea had asked if she could have a copy of Ravi's letter to keep for herself. The two of them carried their drinks into Ana's bedroom and raised their glasses in a toast as Ana pulled open the top drawer of her night table and reached in to get the letter. As she did she spotted something else and realizing that Andrea had seen it too, reached for it instead of the letter and held it up with a flourish. She laughed without embarrassment.

"A not so little present from my big brother, when I was in the dumps over breaking up with my last boyfriend."

Andrea joined her with a burst of laughter of her own as Ana flipped the switch at the base of the impressively large and very realistic looking, black dildo. It came to life, giving off a soft buzzing sound and vibrating very strongly and efficiently.

"He said it 'would help me forget the stupid, ungrateful asshole and with regular recharging it would, unlike my boyfriend, cause me no pain but much pleasure'. As usual he was right! I feel sorry for any girl who isn't lucky enough to have a brother like Ravi."

She switched the dildo off and put it back into the drawer before picking up the letter and handing it to Andrea.

"You take this. Keep the original and give me a copy when you have a chance."

They finished their drinks and then left Ana's apartment and headed for the elevator. A few minutes later Ana opened the door to Ravi's apartment and they stepped inside.

They paused for a few seconds, each of them needing time to take in the reflection of Ravi's taste in lifestyle and the still lingering odor of his recent presence there. Then, Andrea followed Ana into the bedroom and they set to work removing the traces of that last blissful night that Andrea and Ravi had shared together.

Ana stripped the bed then, as she headed for the laundry chute in the bathroom, she nodded toward the stack of condoms on the bedside table and grinned.

"Why don't you look after those, while I dump these? Then you can help me remake the bed. When we finish here we can go into the office. There is a copier in there and we can make a copy of the letter before we head back to my place. We can freshen up there before we go to the restaurant."

Andrea flushed slightly, then laughed as she scooped up the condoms and followed Ana into the bathroom where she held them briefly in her hand before flushing them away.

Once they had shared the remaking of the bed, they went down the hall to what had been Ravi's office and Ana used the copier to make a copy of the letter.

As Ana busied herself at the machine, Andrea studied the photographs that covered the large bulletin board that took up a considerable part of the wall behind the big desk.

The entire surface was covered with photographs, mainly of Ravi, Ana and two people she took to be their parents.

She was a little surprised to note that the woman she thought was Ravi's mother was not of South Asian descent, but as she studied them she understood where the strikingly beautiful golden skin tone shared by both Ravi and Ana had originated.

Her eyes shifted away from the outer row of pictures to an area in the centre of the board that contained a group of pictures taken at various athletic events depicting Ravi and another man. The two of them could have, at first glance, been taken for twins.

Ana turned and held out the original copy of the letter to Andrea and saw what she was looking at. She smiled and moved up beside Andrea and the two of them stood silently for a few seconds as they viewed the photographs together.

"Ah, I see that you have noticed the striking resemblance between them. Like two peas in a pod and very much alike in character as well, except that Gary is a little more polished around the edges and definitely takes life more seriously than Ravi. My brother was more outgoing and kind of took things as they came, living from day to day."

CHAPTER THIRTY-SEVEN

Andrea was apprehensive as she followed Ana into the private dining room of the restaurant.

The fact that she had instantly become the centre of attention as they entered the room didn't help and she felt a flush come to her face as the three occupants of the room stood and made there way across toward she and Ana, who was beginning to introduce them.

"Andrea, this is my dad."

Andrea took the hand that was extended to her and despite the fact that she'd sensed she was receiving a cool assessment from him as the big man crossed to her, she also felt that there was warmth and strength in the way he shook her hand.

He shifted his hand, taking her upper arm gently.

"Well, I can certainly see why Ravi was so taken with you. You are a very beautiful woman indeed."

As he released her, and stepped aside, Ravi's mother took his place and without hesitation wrapped her arms around Andrea and hugged her briefly but warmly.

She then stepped back half a pace, letting her hands rest on Andrea's shoulders.

"I have to agree my dear, and from what I understand, you have a brain that is just as impressive as your physical beauty. I think Ravi was very lucky to have met you and I'm so pleased to finally meet you myself."

She then hugged her tightly again.

Andrea, feeling a little overwhelmed, felt her eyes begin to mist at the mention of Ravi's name, and gave herself to the security of the hug that filled her with a sense of belonging and acceptance.

She returned the woman's embrace and they remained holding each other for a few seconds, before stepping apart.

Ana had crossed to the other side of the dining room to give the only other person in the room a big kiss and hug and she now spun around.

"Andrea, this is my cousin Gary."

Andrea gasped softly as her attention centered on him and she realized just how strongly his physical appearance mirrored Ravi's.

It took her a few seconds to realize that she was staring blankly at him, and it wasn't until he began to move toward her and extended his hand that she managed to pull herself together.

Sensing an awkward moment that she needed to break, she forced herself to speak as she took his hand and shook it.

"I'm very pleased to meet you; Ana has told me how close you and Ravi were."

He smiled at her.

"Yes...we were more like brothers than cousins. I'm going to miss him very much, and I'm very pleased to meet you as well. For what its worth, even though I've only just met you, I too think that Ravi was a very lucky guy to have found you."

* * * * *

Kevin, having completed the task of going over the daily incident reports, headed down into the basement and knocked on the door of Marshall's office waiting briefly before opening it and walking inside.

The sergeant was seated behind his desk reading reports and working on this third coffee of the day.

Kevin felt comfortable enough in Marshall's company that he moved directly across the small room and dropped into the empty visitor's chair without waiting to be asked.

Jack finished what he was reading before he looked over at him.

"Back so soon?"

Kevin reached into his jacket pocket and pulled out the two copies that he had made earlier at home. He looked at them for a moment then placed them side by side on the desk between the two of them.

"These are my lists of those released and considered a danger to reoffend, broken down nationally, and specifically in the lower mainland. I've just finished updating them using the latest printout from corrections that you gave me. The one on the left is the original and the one on the right reflects the additions and deletions I've made based on the info that you provided me. Does anything strike you as strange about them?"

Marshall gave them a cursory look and shook his head.

"Nope...seems okay."

Kevin picked up a yellow highlighter from the mug that held writing paraphernalia that was perched on the edge of Marshall's desk.

He opened the marker and used it to highlight the total number of subjects listed for the two areas, before the changes, and repeated it for the same numbers after the changes, then looked up at Jack.

"How about now?"

Marshall gave the highlighted areas a closer look, and shook his head again.

Kevin picked up the two sheets and turned them around and placed them on the desk in front of him. He reached into his pocket and brought out his calculator and after making a few entries, noted and circled percentages that he had jotted down under the highlighted numbers on each of the two pages.

When he had finished he re-pocketed the calculator and spun the sheets around, pushing them back across toward

Marshall.

"Don't you think it's a little strange that the change in numbers overall have pretty much remained constant, as have the number for the rest of the country, while the lower mainland figure shows a drop of four and one half percent?"

Marshall looked at the highlighted areas again taking in the percentage figures below them then shrugged and sat back in his chair looking at Kevin.

"So? This is only a look at one week. I imagine that blips like this occur on a regular basis."

Kevin reached for the two papers, and looked at them briefly before folding them and returning them to his pocket.

"Maybe, but I find it strange that there would be such a big difference between the lower mainland and the rest of Canada. You might be right, and I may be reading something into this that isn't there. I've been known to do that kind of thing before. But, my curiosity had been piqued and I was wondering if I could get some of the previous updates from you…then I can have a look at what happened over a longer period of time."

Marshall frowned.

"I don't see the point."

Kevin cut him off.

"If I got enough of the backdated weekly updates and charted them, I could see if this sort of fluctuation in numbers is a regular thing or something that just occurred by chance."

Jack frown faded slowly and he shrugged.

"I think you're wasting your time, but if you want old updates, I'll see if I can get them for you. I shred mine as soon as I'm finished with them, so I'll have to request them from Ottawa. It may take some time, but I'm sure I can get you some copies."

* * * * *

Reminiscing about Ravi, with some questions about Andrea's history interspersed, dominated the meal.

There was no mention of the agreement that had been offered. Andrea was feeling completely relaxed and at ease with the others by the time they were sharing an after dinner drink.

Ana had dominated the conversation, serving as a pivot point, around which each of the others had been drawn into reliving their best recollected times with Ravi. Andrea found it very enjoyable and interesting. Many of the blanks about Ravi's past were filled for her.

The stories she enjoyed most came from Gary who, although reserved and clearly more comfortable being a listener than a talker, obviously cared deeply for his cousin and complied when Ana pushed him to join in.

When they had finished their drinks, Ana suggested that they go back to the high-rise to help Gary get settled into Ravi's apartment, then move on to her parent's place for a nightcap.

* * * * *

Jim was the last of the group Pat dropped off at home. After Pat had pulled it into the curb in front of Jim's White Rock apartment building he turned off the vehicle and the two of them remained seated; talking inside the big SUV.

The darkness and pounding rain blocked out the sights and sounds of the world around them as they talked, going over the final planning stages of the two targets that remained now that their latest endeavor had been completed.

Phil, now eager to take part in as much of the work as he could, had thrown a monkey wrench into the plans that had been settled earlier with his desire to be included in the execution of these projects, and some restructuring of the plans was now necessary.

Before Jim left the vehicle they wanted to reach agreement on how and when they would take out the next two targets.

Additionally, the conversation that had taken place in the SUV between all of them after they had completed the earlier task was still fresh in their minds and Pat wanted to discuss it further with Jim.

"I don't know about you but the circumstances around Ravi Sharma's death certainly served to make me even more determined to keep our little organization going. Any remaining doubts that I may have had went out the window when that happened. It sure brought it home to me. Did you notice how the other guys used it to shore up their determination as well?"

Jim, who was by this point, beginning to crave a smoke and therefore ready to call it a night, paused with his hand resting on the door handle. The topic Pat had raised caused him to briefly put the need for a smoke aside.

"You got that impression too? Yes, I have no doubt that all of us feel the same way about it. All three of those bastards were on parole and out on bail. They didn't kill Ravi, the fucking system did. I for one will have no trouble sleeping tonight. That's for sure."

He opened the door and stepped out into the downpour, and when the door closed Pat fired up his SUV and pulled out onto the road.

He was pleased that the day had gone as well as it had, and any concern that he'd had previously about the necessity to back off and lay low for a time, had dissipated.

As he drove home, he admitted to himself that he was completely satisfied that there really wasn't anything to worry about.

* * * * *

Andrea and Ana stood in the parking lot watching her parents and Gary as they climbed into the big black Hummer. When the vehicle moved out of the lot and into traffic, Ana turned to Andrea and gave her a big hug.

Andrea returned it and when they parted Ana grinned.

"Well girl, I'd say you made quite an impression. C'mon, let's see if we can beat them back and get a chance to freshen up quickly before they arrive and we have to tackle getting Gary settled in."

They piled into Ana's car and left the lot.

* * * * *

The conversation in the Hummer on the ride to Vancouver from North Vancouver had centered around Andrea. It had been going on for some time and they were almost home before they finished.

Gary, who they had brought up to date on the relationship and the offer that they had made to Andrea, was listening intently, but had taken no part in the discussion until Ana's mother had turned and asked him for his opinion, both of Andrea and the deal itself.

Gary took some time to consider the question before he answered her.

"Well, I've only just met her, but she seems sincere and honest to me and there is no denying that she's very beautiful and seems to have a good head on her shoulders. It seems to me, though, that you are asking a hell of a lot from her. She's a vibrant young woman, and no matter how you look at it doesn't seem likely that she will be willing to put the rest of her life on hold while she takes on the responsibility of bearing and raising Ravi's kids, on her own."

Ana's father, who had played a very small part in the conversation up to this point, replied.

"First of all she wouldn't be on her own, we would be there for her; and secondly, we realize that she is very much a woman, and as such, is naturally going to need and seek other relationships in her life. We also understand and have addressed the fact that she will in time, no doubt want to marry. We've made it clear to her that she wouldn't be restricted in any way from doing that."

Gary let the words sink in before he replied.

"Look, don't get me wrong, I loved Ravi a lot and I think that the idea itself is great, and I could be wrong, and she might very well be very receptive to it. After all, she hasn't said no and has agreed to consider it. It's an unusual situation, but I just think it would be a hell of a big commitment for her to make."

Ana's mother looked from her husband and back to Gary.

"Well there is also the financial side to consider...she would be secure for life and that has to be worth something."

Gary smiled.

"You know, although I barely know this girl, I have a feeling that particular part of the deal won't really have much to do with her decision. She's very confident and I don't think she really has much concern over her ability to make a secure future for herself. No, if she agrees, it will have little to do with the money. In fact, if you want her to accept this deal, I strongly suggest that you make no further mention of that part of it and concentrate on the fact that, by doing it, she would be able to share a future together with Ravi, even though he won't be alive to participate. I really get the impression that that's the only reason that she is even considering it at this point, although she probably doesn't realize it."

Ana's father smiled.

"You might want to listen to him dear; after all he is only months away from completing his PHD in Psychiatry."

She looked over at him and laughed.

"Yes, perhaps I should."

* * * * *

It was no surprise to Andrea that they had indeed managed to make it home first, the way Ana drove. They made their way to Ana's apartment and spent a fair amount of time in front of the big mirror at Ana's dressing table before going up to her parent's apartment. They ran into them in the hallway as they arrived, Gary effortlessly manhandling a large suitcase in his left hand as they got off the elevator.

Ana's mother greeted them with a smile.

"Ah, here you are. Why don't the three of you go and get Gary set up, while we get changed into something more comfortable and see about getting us all a nice drink to cap off what has been a very long day."

Ana agreed taking Gary's free hand in one of her own and Andrea's with the other.

"Sounds good to me, let's go guys"

Moments later they were inside Ravi's apartment and Gary, who had spent a good deal of time there in the past, had at Ana's instance taken possession of Ravi's bedroom rather than the spare room that he had normally called home when he was in town.

He tossed his suitcase onto the big bed then turned to face the two women who had been chatting back and forth continually like two school girls all the way up in the elevator and into the apartment.

He stood by the bed, his arms folded across his chest, enjoying the obvious camaraderie between them and smiling broadly over at them as he waited patiently for them to wind down enough to allow him a chance to interject.

It took awhile before they realized that they were lost in their own little world and had been ignoring him completely.

They stared at him then turned back to look at each other and broke into spirited laughter.

Gary waited until they had regained their composure before he spoke.

"If it's okay with you two, I'd kind of like to get out of this gear and grab a shower before getting into some casual clothes."

Ana nodded in agreement.

"No problem, I wanted to show Andrea some of the photo albums that Ravi had. We can go get them while you get ready, and take them down with us when we go back to Mom and Dad's...c'mon, Andrea, they are in one of the desk drawers in the office, I think."

Gary watched them leave the room, and then turned to open his suitcase and pull out a clean shirt and jeans which he laid out on the bed before crossing the room to enter the big bathroom, closing the door behind him.

When he came out twenty minutes later wrapped in a robe and toweling his damp hair, he found the two of them spread out on the bed on their stomachs, side by side and with several albums arrayed around them, one of which was lying open between them.

They looked over toward him at the door opening.

"I guess I dress in the bath room."

He bent to pick up his fresh clothes, which they had unceremoniously dumped at the bottom of the bed, then turned and walked back into the bathroom.

Neither Andrea nor Ana said anything but once the door had closed behind him they exchanged a knowing look.

"I know, I know. If he wasn't my cousin, I'd be after him in a minute. Someday, when I get to know you a lot better, I'll tell you some stories about the three of us when Ravi, Gary and I were much younger and very curious about members of the opposite sex. The only thing I will tell you now is
that although none of it ever went past the point of looking

and touching, I can attest to the fact that Gary is definitely as much of a man as my big brother was. The whole experience has brought me a degree of disappointment once I grew up and found out to my consternation that all men are very definitely not created equal."

They started to laugh and Gary clearly heard them from the bathroom. He shook his head and smiled.

Although he was surprised at how fast they had bonded so strongly, he recognized that their mutual grief had been a major contributor and he sincerely hoped that once that had faded they would still remain good friends.

He loved his cousin very much and he'd taken an immediate liking to Andrea. The warm affection that they had built between them was a good thing for both of them and he hoped it would stand the test of time.

When he came out of the bathroom the second time, dressed in his clean clothes and sporting freshly combed hair, neither of them could look at him directly for more than a split second without risking a renewed round of laughter. Both looked quickly back at the other and covered their mouths to stifle the mirth that threatened to break free.

It was apparent to Gary that he was the source of their merriment, so he stopped and raised his hands in the air.

"What? I forget to do up my zipper?"

He looked down at himself and then back toward the two of them, who were now starting at him.

They lost the battle then and commenced rolling around on the bed hugging and laughing until tears began to roll down their faces.

Gary watched them in feigned exasperation for a few seconds, and then with a grin, turned and started for the bed room door.

"When you two have quite finished, you'll find me downstairs. I definitely need a drink and a return to some semblance of decorum, something that I'm obviously not going to find here."

The two women looked at each other again and rolled off the bed in unison, scooped up the albums, and trotted off after him.

* * * * *

It was just before midnight when Ana and Gary, who was behind the wheel of the Hummer, dropped Andrea off at home.

Each of the women had agreed with him that they were in no condition to drive. He had quietly and patiently listened to their incessant babble with more than a little enjoyment as he accomplished his task.

Andrea was relieved that the agreement had not been mentioned in the conversation that had transpired during the consumption of the family nightcap. She had felt herself an intrinsic and welcome part of the family.

Once they reached Andrea's, Gary walked her to the door and saw her safely inside before he returned to the Hummer, and he and Ana made their way back to the high-rise.

CHAPTER THIRTY-EIGHT

As the weatherman had predicted, the rain stopped in the early morning hours of Saturday, October 19th, 2007.

The parking lot of the Armory was filled by shortly after ten, and cars arriving were being directed to an overflow parking area two blocks away.

Ravi's family, with Andrea under their wing, arrived at ten forty-five and was immediately directed to the reserved parking area at the front of the Armory.

When they entered the building, they where ushered to their reserved seats at the centre front, to the left of the dignitaries that were headed by the Solicitor General of Canada and the Attorney General of British Columbia.

The stage in front of them contained a centerpiece with a huge photograph of Ravi in dress uniform surrounded by flowers, smiling down at them.

The building was already filled very close to capacity. The turnout was impressive, and very much dominated by uniforms.

The red serge dress uniforms of the R.C.M.P. drew most of the attention, but a multicolored sea of other uniforms that reflected the numerous Municipal, Regional, out-of-province and U.S. Police agencies and the similar contingents of EMS and Fire Department personnel easily outnumbered them.

The IHIT unit had been designated a seating area to the right of the family. Chris took a seat next to Ravi's father, who recognized him.

They shook hands and Chris introduced the Sharma family to Janet before they sat down. Ravi's father, his voice filled with emotion, leaned across to speak to Chris.

"On behalf of the family, I want to thank you Inspector.

I understand that you had a great deal to do with arranging this and it is certainly an overwhelming tribute to my son and very much appreciated by all of us."

Chris paused to look around the big room before he responded.

"Yes, it's one of the biggest turnouts I've ever seen, but I can't take the credit for it. Ravi was one of our own, and a lot of people took part in setting it up, much like a snowball running down hill and turning into an avalanche. Ravi was very well-liked by his peers and as you can see by looking around this room, cops support their brothers-in- arms."

Ravi's father shifted slightly in his seat in order to survey the room.

"Yes...I can see now that we weren't Ravi's only family."

* * * * *

Chris was the last speaker, following the Delta Police Chief. He remained on the stage to shake hands and share a few words with the other speakers as the building began to empty. After a few minutes, they left the stage as a group and went over to speak with the family members.

Kevin, who had been standing to the right of the stage periodically instructing the photographer who had accompanied him with regard to the shots he wanted, watched the group surrounding the family. When it began to break up, he approached Chris.

"Any chances of letting me buy you a drink?"

Chris, who was not particularly surprised to find that Kevin was covering the event for the paper, was a little taken aback at the request for a drink together as it was the first of its kind to come from Kevin. He nodded.

"Sure. I've already arranged to have one with Pat Dunne though, but I'm sure he won't mind if you join us. I've got to see my wife safely on her way home first."

Kevin pointed in the direction of the west exit of the building.

"I'm parked out there. Have you guys picked a spot yet?"

Chris shook his head.

"No, Pat's driving. We'll meet you at your car; can't be more than one like it in the lot. You can follow us."

Kevin laughed and headed toward the door.

* * * * *

Gary pulled the Hummer to the curb a few blocks away from the armory and got out to hold the back door open for his aunt and uncle.

Hugs were exchanged and he watched them cross the sidewalk and enter the parking lot where they had left their car, before he closed the back door and got back into the driver's seat of the big vehicle beside Andrea, who had been allocated the centre position in the front seat, between him and Ana, when they left the ceremony.

As he slipped the vehicle into gear he glanced at his watch and gave them a broad grin.

"Okay ladies, next stop airport and possibly a drink or two before it's back to the sweat shop for me."

* * * * *

Kevin was sitting behind the wheel of the Volkswagen with the engine running when the big Caddy SUV driven by Pat pulled up in front of him and Chris, seated in the front passenger seat, motioned him to follow.

The two vehicles made their way out of the slowly emptying lot in tandem and then Kevin followed the SUV for a few blocks into the parking lot of a small neighborhood pub.

Once he had parked, Kevin grabbed his battered briefcase off the passenger seat and climbed out.

* * * * *

Phil was thinking about the memorial service and regretting his having to miss it as he stood on the Stanley Park seawall facing the marina and the Vancouver skyline behind the protected bay.

He'd just suffered a short coughing fit and once it had passed, he'd idly tossed a rock into the water in front of him and watched the ripple effect as it fanned out from the point of impact.

As he did so, he caught movement out of the corner of his eye. A small cabin-cruiser was beginning to move away from the floating fuel station anchored a few hundred feet away from the marina proper.

He could clearly hear the sound of the accelerating engine as the boat began to pick up speed.

And then, the craft exploded in a ball of flame.

Seconds later a mass of splintered debris began to shower down around what was left of the boat.

Only the base of the hull remained, everything above the waterline had disintegrated.

Included in the debris were the shredded remains of one Clarence Morrison a forty-six-year-old paroled serial rapist and child killer.

Within a few minutes, what little that was left of the smoldering wreck began to slowly slip under the water which engulfed and snuffed out the few remaining flames, leaving only the debris and gently moving ripples upon the surface of the water.

Phil smiled.

Another poor soul incinerated by one of those unfortunate marine explosions after a careless refueling.

A single thought filled his mind briefly.

'That one was for you Ravi.'

He felt very pleased with himself.

For however long it lasted, the rest of Phil's life was going to be good; very good indeed.

He turned to walk across the road to the parking lot where Roger Phillips sat behind the wheel of his silver Toyota Camry, waiting for him.

* * * * *

Gary, Andrea and Ana had managed to find a booth in the Airport bar and were discussing various parts of the memorial ceremony as they waited for his flight.

Andrea uncharacteristically, had been doing more listening that talking. She was blankly studying her glass as she moved it around in small circles on the coaster.

Noting her subdued mood, Ana asked.

"What's bugging you? Still feeling the after effects of last night?"

Andrea set her glass down and looked from Ana, who was seated beside her, to Gary before answering.

"No. Just doing a lot of thinking I guess. I'm trying to decide about my future."

Ana nodded and set her drink down on the table beside Andrea's.

"To have babies or not?"

"Not so much that...just wondering what chance I would have of ever finding a guy, assuming that I would eventually want to settle down with one, if I agree to go ahead with this idea...not much likelihood, I guess."

Ana let the words hang in the air for a few seconds before she spoke.

"Well, why don't we ask Gary? He's a guy! How about it cuz...think that Andrea, with a kid on each hip, would have a chance of finding a guy to settle down with?"

Gary, who both women knew was a man of few words, looked at Andrea as he considered the question carefully before he replied.

"Well, I don't presume to be spokesmen for men as a whole, but if you are asking me specifically what I think about that particular proposition... I think it's a no-brainer.   Of course she would."

Andrea smiled.

"Okay, I'll settle for that."

Ana looked from one of them and then to the other as she sensed that there was more to the conversation than she had previously picked up on. She had been about to interject her own two cents worth, but decided to keep her mouth shut. She let her eyes settle on Gary.

Although both women were both starting at him now, Gary seemed to be aware only of Andrea's inquiring eyes, which were still locked with his.

"You two vixens are kinda putting me in a spot here. But I will say that I'm going to be back here in a few months clutching my brand new PHD in my hand as I eagerly accept my teaching position at the University of British Columbia, and I'd be a damn liar if I said that it wouldn't be a privilege to get into the line up for a chance to get to know Andrea better, pregnant or not."

* * * * *

Chris lifted his eyes from the paper spread out on the table and took a deep breath before settling back into the comfortably padded seat.

"So, exactly what the hell are you getting at Kevin?"

Pat, had been listening quietly to the two men, as Kevin had placed each of the sheets of paper before Chris and explained what they demonstrated.

"I'm not sure exactly, but based on these past update

reports that Marshall gave me, it's plain to me that the lower mainland is an unhealthy place for likely-to-reoffend ex-cons to live; more than elsewhere in Canada anyway. There doesn't seem to be any reasonable explanation for that fact. Sure, some of them die in the other areas, but they seem to be dropping like flies here; I'm just wondering why."

Kevin reached for his glass and took a long pull on it. Chris sat quietly for a moment then spoke.

"Are you suggesting then some vigilante group is out there knocking off these ex-cons?"

Kevin shrugged in response.

"I don't know exactly what I'm suggesting, but that possibility did occur to me."

Chris shook his head.

"Very improbable. You say yourself that these guys aren't being murdered. They are dying like anyone else; suicide, disease, accidents. Vigilantes commit murder and sooner or later, usually sooner because they commit their acts in mob-like atmospheres and do a messy job of it, they get caught. Nope, I think that you've just got yourself buried so deep in this that you are reading into it something that just isn't there."

Chris glanced over at Pat.

"What do you think? Any comment?"

Pat took a sip from his Perrier, as he considered the question.

"I agree with you. There are probably a hundred other statistical factors coming into play here. For example, the west coast is the retirement capital of the country and it tends to follow that the cons choosing to settle here will be older and likely have advancing levels of disease as a result, being more likely to die in a shorter span of time. It may be a strange situation, but I'm sure that there is no reason for one to think that there is some sort of conspiracy afoot."

Kevin shrugged and began to scoop up the sheets of

paper and return them to his briefcase.

"Okay, you guys are the experts; it just seemed really strange to me when I spotted it."

Pat laughed and pointed to the briefcase.

"If I were you I'd shove that stuff through the shredder and concentrate on your current theme, letting the public know just how many of these assholes are being released back into the mainstream, and keep on giving examples of the horror that results."

Kevin nodded, as Pat continued.

"Yep, the idea of a group out there knowledgeable and organized enough to do what you've suggested is just pure fantasy, although an interesting one. Farfetched as it is, wouldn't it be wonderful if it were true? Hell, putting a stop to a group accomplishing something like that, would be detrimental to society as a whole, don't you think?"

Kevin closed the briefcase and drained his drink then put the glass down and looked over at Pat.

"Yes you hit the nail on the head there. Nobody mourns the loss of these sick pricks when they disappear, and that's for sure."

He stood and picked up the briefcase, extended his hand and shook hands with each of them.

"Well if you'll excuse me gentlemen, I have a piece on a Police Memorial that needs writing."

Chris and Pat watched him leave and then Chris fixed the other man with his eyes and studied his friend for a considerable length of time before carefully choosing his words.

"Funny thing about those statistics of Kevin's... not easy to dismiss out of hand, but then, there are a lot of funny things about life. For example there is something fundamentally wrong with a society who readily accepts the fact that a murderer is guaranteed by law not to face the death penalty, and yet expects a cop on the street doing his best to protect them from those very murderers, to unquestioningly run the risk of losing his life in the line of duty as an everyday part of the job they ask him to do."

Pat who had been looking down at his bottle of Perrier, glanced upward and met Chris's appraising stare.

He said nothing and it was Chris who broke the silence.

"By the way, I think that I'm going to pass on joining the 'Old Blue Farts Club' after I retire. Figure I've got a few more years left before I could fit in there comfortably."

Pat had no doubt as to why Chris was declining the offer to join the group. It was with no small measure of relief that he smiled and nodded.

"Probably a wise decision, all things considered; however, rest assured that you will be a welcome addition when, and if, that time comes. Let's drink to it shall we and have a couple more to toast Ravi's memory."

Chris raised his drink and Pat upped his Perrier and let it touch the proffered glass.

"To Ravi."

Chris locked eyes with Pat.

"To Ravi. May he rest in peace. And to the Alumni, who, I would strongly suggest, would do well to find themselves a new hobby....at least for the next few months."

<u>**Also by Patrick Laughy**</u>

The Little Black Book

The 4th Reich
Books1-7

'Atlantis' a fantasy series

Kenny-The Making of a Serial Killer